THE HUNT: BOOKS 1 & 2

PREDATOR & PREY

LIZ MELDON

Cover Design: Covers by Combs
Paperback ISBN: 9780993894381

ACKNOWLEDGMENTS

Thank you to my fantastic beta reader Amanda for all your love and support. I love that you are just as passionate about Moira and Severus as I am. Much love to my phenomenal proofreader Phoenix, for catching my errors with poise and tact, and going along with my crazy publishing schedule. As always, much love to my author besties group, my sun and stars, and my parents for being incredibly supportive of this journey. A huge shout-out to the amazing #bookstagram community for all your love and support! Last, and certainly not least, a great many thanks to my readers. Without you, there's nothing but me and my imagination.

READER WARNING

The Hunt has a rating of EXPLICIT. Readers uncomfortable with graphic violence may find certain scenes disturbing. Beyond that, the series also contains graphic sexual content and coarse language.

PREDATOR

PREDATOR (THE HUNT, #1)

Black and Blue.

BLACK SOUL, SUFFOCATING IN SILENCE

Severus: demon, incubus, escort—leech. After centuries of scorn from his own kind in the underworld, Severus went topside and settled amongst the secret demon community in Farrow's Hollow. Located near a hell-gate, the city allows him to exist on Earth without sacrificing much of his demon abilities, but as with all incubi, he must take the life essence of humans to maintain his strength.

Working as an escort, he has been able to keep himself satiated, juggling enough clients to ensure that he doesn't repeat the mistakes of past incubi—the murderers, the gluttons, the true demonic leeches.

In his line of work, Severus sees much of the same every night: human women searching for surrender, for a connection, for love. He caters to them, steals from them, not realizing that he's desperate for all the same things.

BLUE EYES, WATCHING HER WORLD FADE AWAY

Moira Aurelia: grad student, TV-marathoner, bar trivia champion—unable to look in a mirror. Not anymore. Because when she does, she no longer sees herself. The person, the creature, staring back isn't her. It can't be.

Hair, skin, eyes. Nothing is the same as it once was, and no one can tell her why. Despite her fears that she might be dying from the same mysterious illness that killed her mom two years ago, Moira finds herself getting stronger, too, her senses sharper. Terrified by the lack of control she has over her own body, she retreats, withdrawing from her once active university social life.

After unsuccessfully searching for answers, a frustrated Moira goes after the one thing she can control: her sex life. Twenty-three and still unable to experience a satisfying climax, she schedules a session with Russ Tanner, highly recommended male escort, and hopes for something to go right for once.

LIGHT AND DARK COLLIDE—DESPERATE TO CONNECT

But the night takes a turn from the moment they meet. Severus, expecting just another dull session with a new client, is thrown by the otherworldly creature seeking his services—this strange, beautiful woman who arouses his long dormant demon side like none other. Moira, meanwhile, finds herself face-to-face with a man who can handle her newfound strength—and wears a dark stare and sinful smile like a second skin.

Two lonely creatures grapple with the undeniable pull between them.

Moira flees. Severus pursues.

Desperate for answers, the demon seeks her out--unaware that he isn't the only predator to have caught her scent.

CHAPTER ONE

The night began as it always did—with a sharp, jerky knock on his hotel room's door. His gaze dropped to the electronic clock next to the bed, the red numerals blazing back. 9 PM. On the dot.

They were seldom ever more than a minute or two late, and if they were, Severus knew they weren't coming at all. Women tended to honour punctuality like it was a lost art, and he *appreciated* it. For Severus, these nightly visits were a necessity, a breath of life. He didn't need his time wasted, but since he'd been in the business for years, more than his ladies would ever know, he had a handy black book of backups to call on, to schmooze, if necessary.

Crossing the room, he adjusted his skinny black necktie for optimal knot rigidity: not so loose that he looked like any old uncultured schmuck, but not so tight he'd remind his date of her husband. Happy medium. A quick sweep of his hand across the bed smoothed out the creases he'd left when he tied his shoes earlier. Unless otherwise specified, Severus preferred to get to the pre-booked hotel room first. He wanted to set up, to scope for exits, and let his natural *charm* ooze into the walls, the carpet, the linens. Whenever clients had a hand in crafting their date night atmosphere, it was like walking smack into a wall of stress. No thanks. Not optimal.

Besides, most of the women who saw him wanted to surrender control, no matter how desperately they clung to it in their day-to-day routine. They were the ones who ordered his services. They chose the time, sometimes the place. Yet once they stepped into that hotel room, they belonged to him. Severus sold himself on the fantasy of surrender, the safety of giving oneself over to another and truly letting *go*.

Little did his clients ever realize just how much they were letting go every time he touched them—he, an incubus whose strength, his very *existence*, relied on their life essence.

But that was another matter for another time—and Severus had long stopped thinking about it. For him, what he did came as naturally as breathing. Their lives were his nourishment. It was as simple as that.

Running a hand over his coarse black hair, he squared his shoulders and caught one last look at himself in the closet door mirrors. Wearing his suit, his hair neat and his facial scruff tamed, he was the epitome of many a human fantasy. What they didn't see was the paleness in his cheeks, the lack of vibrancy in his usually black eyes, tonight merely a dark grey, getting duller by the hour. It had been four days without the touch of a human—and Severus was feeling the effects.

He had only himself to blame, of course. *He* had decided to go on a four-day gaming bender with Alaric while his friend and roommate had time off from the bar. Video games these days were just so well done, so addictive

—so *violent*. So enraptured were they in the wartime simulation, four days had blitzed by without either Severus or Alaric realizing, excluding the odd nap here and there, and he felt like shit.

So, tonight, Severus planned to take a little more from dear Pamela Prescott than he ordinarily would have.

Grasping the doorknob, he turned it gently and opened the door with all the composed elegance required of him. There she stood, a widow in her early fifties, prim and proper as ever. They had been doing this little song and dance twice a month for a year now. In that time, he'd almost grown fond of her.

"Pamela," he crooned, stepping aside and letting her in. "Ever the vision."

She tittered, a delicate hand over her mouth as she breezed by. "Oh, I'm sure you say that to all the girls."

Well, yes. "Never."

After he locked the door behind her, they exchanged a few pleasantries—which mostly included Severus asking about her day, her week, her garden. Sometimes she brought him fresh produce alongside her usual payment, especially if he'd looked a bit run-down when they last met. However, given it was only early spring yet, she'd just begun the replanting. Come August, he would have more giant fucking zucchinis than he would know what to do with.

Pamela Prescott stood at an impressive five foot seven, shorter without her heels, and dressed like every day was a fashion parade. She'd finally started to treat herself after cancer took her husband three years prior, and every article of clothing Severus would soon peel off her body came with a designer label. She never balked when handing over his nightly fee, though the envelope was lighter this evening; no sex, only oral foreplay and some pampering. He never questioned why a regular changed up their routine, but merely sought out ways to ensure that it would still work for *his* purpose instead.

Sex was, after all, the quickest, easiest way for an incubus to refuel. The idiots in eras gone by used to fuck their victims to death, and so their reputations as demonic leeches had been born. Severus preferred a different approach. Many clients, always changing, *time* between visits with regulars. He took just what he needed for a quick boost, and should he sense them too weak to continue, he'd sever all ties and send them on their merry way. Despite being a demon, he couldn't have humans *dying* on him. That would tank his online reviews. Website flooded with hate mail. *Police* interest—or worse. No thank you.

After all, as one of the few male escorts in Farrow's Hollow, he needed to maintain a stellar reputation to keep up this little game. What kind of modern incubus or succubus *wouldn't* take the escort route? Fools, that's who. Severus was paid handsomely to sustain himself, to feed his body and fuel his supernatural abilities. He couldn't ask for a better profession.

"Is there anything you would like to discuss first this evening?" Severus inquired once he had tucked the payment envelope away somewhere discreet. When Pamela shook her head, he offered what he knew was an unassuming smile—sweet, *caring*. Despite his towering figure, broad and firm with muscle, many of his clients came over and over again—literally—because he presented himself as someone who *cared*. He spoke softly but decisively, using the information he'd ascertained in phone exchanges, paired with years of experience reading human body language, to present precisely what these women paid for. So, hands threaded together behind him, he nodded. "Then let's begin."

Despite being a regular, Pamela was always a bit nervous at the beginning, her body stiff and her breath falling in uneven, rapid gasps. However, as soon as he situated himself behind her and trailed his hands down both of her arms, she quieted. Severus started with her jacket, a lightweight mauve garment with pearl buttons, which he carefully folded and set on the dresser. Next came her skirt, which he unzipped from the back and let pool at her feet. Then the blouse, silky soft and dripping with expense. He trailed his lips along the nape of her neck, his body tingling to life at the caress.

An incubus needed no more than a ghost of a touch to glean a human's life essence. In his line of work, Severus was afforded much more than that.

Pamela shivered under his hands, her head tipping back against his chest as he undid her bra next. Now that her skin was exposed, he wouldn't break contact, always touching, caressing, licking, biting, until he'd had his fill, recouped his waning strength—and his client was satisfied, of course.

Thankfully for him, it didn't take much to please humans. Just as some spiders secreted a venom to numb their prey, or vampires emitted a toxin that deluded their victims into thinking their bite was pleasurable, an incubus had a number of talents at his disposal. First and foremost, skin-to-skin contact was like a drug to humans. His clients derived immediate pleasure from it, their senses heightening, their cunts dampening, their minds succumbing to indulgence without realizing they were being tricked by a demon.

Succubi had the same gifts, though he'd always thought they had it easier; men, especially human men, were so *easy* to please. One stroke of a succubus's finger and they'd be hard as a rock.

Women required more fine-tuning—a little more *time.* It was why Severus always began his sessions with a massage if he could. Not only would it relax the client, but it allowed him to take almost all he needed in a matter of minutes.

Because she'd requested no sex this evening, Severus undressed her slowly, rubbing his hands across her body, grazing his nose along her throat, up to her ear—taking what he needed, the hum of *life* flooding his veins, sharpening his senses.

No one had ever explained what, precisely, he stole from humans. Life essence had been the best term he could concoct, for while he couldn't *see* it, he could feel it, and if he took too much, the human would die. Whether it was their soul he was sampling, or something else entirely, Severus didn't ask questions—not anymore. He just drank it in, inhaled it, stole it with every touch. He let it course through his body, reinvigorating what had dulled and weakened since his last caress.

By the time he walked her over to the bed, the pink had returned to his cheeks. His irises were nearly their full black once more. Strength pulsed through his limbs, the beast within stirring faintly, and he would only feel better as the session went on.

After arranging Pamela on the bed, he knelt at the foot of it, threw her legs over his shoulders, and tasted her. Drank of her. Took from her. Straight from the fucking source. She cried out, moaned, thrashed about as she always did. His lazy exploration of her naked body while undressing her would bring her to the brink, and in just over a minute Severus had her climaxing against his mouth.

A quick glance at the mirror as he sat back told him he had reached an acceptable fullness. He'd be at his usual strength for a day or two, and then diminish with each hour that followed until he touched another human. Before he'd started escorting, Severus had relied on drunken rendezvous and the odd "accidental" brush of physical contact in public. Now, however, he needn't worry when he'd get his next fix. Women were beating down the door to give it to him.

"Oh, goodness," Pamela gasped, her chest heaving as Severus turned his attention back to her. She propped herself up on bony elbows. "I don't know what's come over me... That was... I..."

"Your promptness is never a bad thing," he said with a dark chuckle, relishing the way her cheeks flushed a brilliant red. "Do you want me to do it again? We have plenty of time left."

Forty-five minutes of the full hour she'd bought, actually. After she stumbled through a rejection to his offer, Severus nodded.

"How about a bath then? I've all your favourite scents."

"Oh, *Russ*, you do spoil me."

"I try," Severus murmured. He ignored the usual roil of disgust at the sound of his escort name uttered aloud before helping Pamela to her feet and steering her toward the room's en suite bathroom. After settling her on the closed toilet, he drew her a bath, chatting with her more about the garden, her weekly book club meetings, and that *vile* neighbour of hers who let his yappy little dog piss all over her front lawn.

Within three minutes, Severus had her soaking in a hot bath. Together they watched the lavender bath bomb explode in a cloud of purple and gold beneath the water; his cousin Cordelia had told him they were all the rage with human women these days, so he'd added a few to his supplies. True to form, most clients had lost their collective *shit* over them.

He couldn't understand the appeal, but he was nothing if not a man who knew how to please.

When it suited him.

After the bomb had turned the bathwater purple with flecks of gold, Severus got to work on washing Pamela's long black hair, edged in a pale grey along the crown of her head and at her sideburns. He massaged her neck, her shoulders, still taking from her, topping up his reserves so that they overflowed, all the while listening to her ramble on about, well, *everything*.

In all honesty, a big part of his job was just listening to women talk. Sure, they hired him for sex, for pleasure, for *surrender*, but in the end, most of his clients just wanted to be heard. Had he not been harvesting their life essence to boost his own, he would have found the task quite tiring. As it were, Severus left each encounter energized and *alive*.

Jacket off, beige dress shirt sleeves rolled up to his elbows and tie loosened, he worked every inch of her once more, diverting a hand to the crest of her thighs when she climaxed again—if only to make it seem legitimate, like she had a reason to come with his hand caressing all the right parts.

At fifty minutes into their session, he helped her out of the bath, her skin wrinkly and her knees weak. She would be fine tomorrow, though perhaps, given her age, it would take until the evening to recover.

Human bodies, for all their frailties and weaknesses, were remarkably resilient. They were programmed to survive, designed to protect themselves from all the dangers of the world. Severus knew for a fact that the clients he touched bounced back. Recovery time varied, of course. He had age limits for a reason. Naturally, to avoid the law, he served no one under eighteen—teenagers wasted much of their essence on other pursuits anyway. He also set a cap at fifty-five. Sure, everyone was *different*. Some women older than his limit might be able to withstand the process, but he couldn't risk it. His refusal wasn't out of kindness or charity; Severus preferred repeat clients to new ones, and he couldn't very well have his regulars waste away on him.

Pamela Prescott scheduled an appointment for two weeks from that night—the same as always. Every other Thursday, nine o'clock sharp. He needed to help her dress more than he usually did, and Severus didn't trust her to stumble to the lobby by herself, so he walked her down with an arm around her waist. She wore a dreamy smile the whole way, as they all did, their bodies inundated with pleasure. Still, perhaps he ought to have eased off toward the end. Her ankles wobbled in her heels and her speech slurred somewhat.

Maybe he should have had her sip something from the minibar. She certainly looked and sounded drunk as he led her through the enormous hotel lobby. Severus caught the eye of the woman working the front desk, nodding as he passed. As if on cue, her cheeks blushed a charming poppy-red. They had a little arrangement—or so she thought.

Claire worked the night shift and had fallen for his easy smile on her first day three years ago. Sometimes he'd stop by for a chat, touching her wrist innocently, fueling her with desire for him. In time, she had responded to him like they were lovers, when, in actuality, he'd never once bedded her. The arrangement was most beneficial; she felt the simple pleasure of his touch, and Severus carried out his business without anyone knowing what sordid things happened in room 212 three to five nights a week.

Outside, the air cool and crisp, he gently lowered Pamela into an awaiting town car, ignoring the concerned looks from the doorman. Careful not to touch her directly, he gave her arm a squeeze and smiled. "We'll see each other soon."

"Yes *please*," she said, words elongated by a moan as she arched toward him. Severus skirted her outstretched hands easily enough, giving her home address to the driver, and then closed the door before she tried to climb on top of him. As the car sped away, Pamela stared at him through the rear window—tinted, but not enough to shield her from his enhanced sight.

He waited until the car disappeared around the corner at the end of the street, the nighttime atmosphere slowly heightening around him. Located near a hell-gate, Farrow's Hollow boasted an impressive population of demons who blended seamlessly with the local humans. Their steady influx over the years had turned what could have been a mid-sized, slow-going city into a party hub. You couldn't walk ten feet without bumping into a demon these days. In fact, he passed one on the way back inside the hotel, but the demon refused to so much as flick his soulless gaze in Severus's direction.

Incubi weren't exactly high on the demonic food chain, and the rest of them just *loved* to remind him of it. Rolling his eyes, he hurried up to his rented room as discretely as possible. With no other clients scheduled, Severus tidied up, rubbed down all the surfaces to remove fingerprints, and then left a tip for the housekeeper on his pillow. He never stayed the night, but he always tipped. Just another way to ensure he was a welcome face around the hotel.

Then, with five hundred dollars burning a hole in his pocket, he left, energized and refreshed, to see where the night might take him.

"I can't believe I'm doing this."

Sinking deeper into her roomy twin bed, Moira Aurelia dragged her finger across her tablet's screen, whizzing through the services page of Russ Tanner's website for the umpteenth time tonight. She had gotten the link from the one "high-end" escort agency that promoted itself around town; when they didn't have a male escort available the night she requested, they had recommended him.

As far as she could tell, nothing about his website suggested he even did anything sexual. There was a lot of talk about massage and reflexology, but the prices were *beyond* outrageous for those kinds of services. She nibbled her lower lip, brow furrowed. He was her only hope—her only *option*, more like.

On his About page, he stressed that he preferred to work with referrals, but would consider taking on new "clients"—yuck—on a case-by-case basis. Moira wasn't looking for a forever sort of arrangement. She had spent the last year building herself up to this, and this *thing* was happening next Friday night, a week from tonight, or not at all.

She just couldn't bring herself to do more research into the sex industry of Farrow's Hollow—nothing ruined childhood memories of an idyllic hometown like learning prostitution ran rampant in certain areas of it. Although it had taken her *way* longer than necessary to find its official website, the one legitimate local escorting company had been very professional about the whole affair. Their website had been clean, upfront, yet it too claimed this wasn't about sex. It was about *companionship*. Right. Why hire an escort unless you wanted to pay for sex?

The careful, precise language on both websites was likely there to avoid any legal ramifications. She tapped back to the About page, wishing Russ had posted a picture of himself. Not that that would be a selling feature, but it would be nice to know what she was getting herself into. Moira had already tried Facebook-stalking him, but when nothing became of it, she figured Russ "Tanner" wasn't his actual name. Which made sense—given that what he did for a living wasn't exactly legal.

Well, more of a grey area, if she understood the law correctly. One *could* hire an escort as a dinner date. You could bring them to a high school reunion, use them as a beard to hide your sexuality from judgmental relatives. But Moira wasn't interested in any of that. Her request, her *purpose* for hiring Russ Tanner should she go through with it, was decidedly *not* a grey area.

Moira wanted sex.

Good sex. Sex to an orgasm, which, at twenty-three, she still hadn't had—either with a partner or on her own.

And if she *was* actually dying, she wanted to go out with a bang, you know? See what all the fuss was about.

"Moira?" True to form, Ella barged into her room without knocking, throwing the door open like she owned the place. Moira's tablet went flying, and she slammed the thing facedown on her bed, startled, cheeks red and eyes wide. Her housemate and best friend arched a thin black eyebrow, tawny brunette curls especially enormous tonight, and leaned against Moira's bedroom doorframe, hip cocked and arms crossed. "Well, hi there. Why do you look like I just caught you watching porn?"

"You didn't," Moira said tersely, sitting up and rearranging her squishy purple duvet cover, then reaching back to fluff her pillows. "And I wasn't."

Ella snorted, shifting her weight to her other foot as she pushed off the doorframe. "Right. So that guilty look on your face is for what, exactly?"

"You know, most people knock," Moira told her with a grin. Ella, of course, wasn't most people. They'd been best friends since the first grade, after a tumultuous kindergarten rivalry turned into something completely unexpected when they'd been forced to be desk buddies at the start of the following school year. They had done elementary school, high school, and undergrad together, and were now a semester and half into their respective Master's degrees together. Ella had even lived with Moira and her mom for their last two years of high school, back when her parents proved to be less than up to the task of caring for their kids. Never in their history had Ella knocked before breezing into Moira's room—and that wasn't about to change anytime soon.

"You coming?" Ella asked, skirting the issue entirely. She blew a bubble with her neon-green gum, snapping it noisily as she waited for a response.

The whole house was going to a movie tonight; on top of Ella, Moira had three other roommates living in their old two-storey Victorian home in the student suburbs surrounding the Farrow's Hollow University campus.

"No. I'm not really in the mood."

"Moira—"

"It's just a movie," she said with a shrug, knowing her

forced nonchalance was wasted on Ella. "Seriously. I have work to do."

They all did. On top of a full course load, all five housemates were teaching assistants in various university departments as they worked toward completing their graduate degrees. However, tonight was the premiere of some new slasher flick at the campus duplex, and Simone, genetics PhD candidate, had bought tickets for everyone. When she'd told them about it over breakfast yesterday, Moira had been quick to find an excuse not to go, even going so far as to insist that Simone bring her boyfriend instead so the ticket wouldn't go to waste.

"He's the biggest baby with horror movies. He'll be hiding inside his hoodie the whole time," Simone had said with a giggle as she slathered her pancakes with syrup, "but I guess I'll drag him into it. Just let me know if you change your mind, okay?"

At the time Moira had smiled and nodded, but she'd already known she wouldn't change her mind—still hadn't.

And from the look on her best friend's face, Ella was *not* pleased with the final decision.

"Just...leave it be," she said softly, shooting Ella a pleading look as the woman glared at her from the doorway. They'd discussed Moira's slow but steady withdrawal from their social circles many times over. At this point, the conversation was just going around in circles.

She appreciated Ella's concern, but at the end of the day, it was Moira's decision. With everything that had happened to her, that was *still* happening to her, she *chose* to step back. She chose to be introspective. She chose to focus on *herself*, forgoing the ultimate frisbee team they'd all played on, the pub bingo nights every Tuesday, and Sunday hangover brunches. All of it. A movie was innocent, just two hours of her time, but she had a game plan for tonight: she'd either book a session with this Russ Tanner, highly recommended male escort, or she'd chicken out for good.

"You look cute," she offered, hoping her tone sounded friendlier, more their usual style as her gaze swept over Ella. Clad in a pair of dark skinny jeans, her luscious thighs looked *ah-mazing*—her obsession with squats probably helped. Up top, she was wearing the good ol' FU sweater, which usually made Moira smile no matter what kind of mood she was in.

For a brief time in the eighties, Farrow's Hollow University had rebranded to just Farrow's University, until the geniuses in charge realized that the name change meant all their gear suddenly had FU blazed across it. Moira's mom had held onto one of the few pieces of old memorabilia from her days at the university, and after she'd died, this sweater was the only thing Ella had chosen to keep from her possessions.

She hadn't wanted to take anything at all, but Moira knew Ella loved her mom almost as much as Moira did. At the time, it hadn't seemed right for her to help Moira sort through the woman's possessions, choosing what to donate, toss, and keep, without allowing her to take something to honour her mom's memory—to remember the woman who had been more of a mother to Ella than her own.

Ella had fought it at first, arguing it wasn't right, but, at Moira's insistence, she'd chosen the sweater. Sometimes, fresh out of the dryer, when it still smelled like Mom, Ella would crawl into Moira's bed, the sweater between them, and they'd just breathe her in, reminiscing.

It had been two years since her death in the winter of Moira's third year of undergrad. Two years since the illness without a name struck. Two years since Moira had sat by her side in the intensive care unit, watching her wither away, listening to her rant on about Moira's twenty-second birthday and *onions*. Over and over again, twenty-two and onions.

Two years since her world had fallen apart.

Two years to try and rebuild herself, only to have her body fritz out without an explanation. But she had endured. Grieved. Tried to move on. Two years later, Moira was finally able to look at that sweater without her eyes watering and her chest tightening—now, she was finally able to smile again.

Because Ella looked good in it. Navy blue, FU in gold. It suited her, attitude and everything. Just a plain crew-neck sweater, no bells and whistles for someone so fashion conscious, but Ella wore it at least once a week.

"Thanks," Ella murmured, tugging it down over her hips with a sigh. Her caramel gaze drifted listlessly around Moira's bedroom for a moment before landing on her cluttered desk by the door. Moira knew right away what had caught her attention, and she braced herself when Ella snatched the recently purchased box of hair dye off the desk, eyebrows crinkled as she read the side. When she was done, she shot Moira one of those *girl, please* looks before tossing the box back onto the mess. "You need to buy better-quality dye. That shit will ruin your hair."

"My hair's already ruined." Without thinking, Moira reached for the wool cap on top of her head, then forced her hand back to her tablet. She'd been wearing it, or some variety of hat, ever since her naturally warm, thick, *beautiful* chestnut-brown hair had fallen out last summer, just before she'd started her grad studies, and grown back in white, coarse, and straight. Ella kept insisting that she could get away with it, that white and pastel and even grey were on trend, but Moira couldn't stand the thought of seeing it in every reflective surface throughout the day.

"I can stay," Ella said softly. "We can just watch TV or something."

"Oh my god, *go*," Moira told her, laughing and hurling one of her smaller pillows at her friend. It nose-dived about a foot from the end of the bed, and Ella snorted.

"You sure?" She sauntered in and picked it up, then chucked it right back, hitting Moira square in the face before she could block it.

"It's a fucking movie. Of course I'm sure." Moira hugged the pillow to her chest. "Seriously. I actually have stuff to grade and pictures from the art show my first-years did to upload to the class website. I won't even notice you're gone."

No, she most *definitely* would. Living in a creaky old house with thin walls and four other women, her home was seldom quiet.

"Fine, I'll just spoil everything for you when I get home," Ella teased, skipping back to the hallway at the sound of the others getting ready downstairs.

"Bring me some popcorn!" Moira called as Ella shut her bedroom door. Then, grinning, she added a long, drawn out, "Love you!"

Three sharp knocks on the wall outside her bedroom, which sat at the top of the stairs, was Ella's response. Shaking her head, Moira flipped her tablet over and found that, in the kerfuffle, she had somehow navigated away from Russ's website and was now four pages deep in her university inbox.

So, she sorted through that for a little while, half listening to the chaos downstairs as four women got ready for the movies—one searching for her phone, another the snacks she wanted to sneak in, a third complaining that her boots leaked and it might rain, then Ella, over everything, ordering the lot of them to hurry the hell up. It was like a whirling tornado anytime they all went out together, and when the front door finally slammed shut, the telltale sound of the lock clicking into place following shortly after, Moira let out a soft sigh of relief.

Unable to drag herself back to the escort's website just yet, her stomach knotted with anxiety, she locked the screen and clambered out of bed. She'd been in there since after dinner, leaving Ella and Hannah in front of the living room TV for the sanctuary of her bedroom upstairs—to research escorting services. She stood there for a moment, picking her wedgie and adjusting her hiked-up FHU track pants, then padded out of her bedroom and downstairs to the kitchen.

When they'd moved into the house last fall, Moira and Ella's first time living outside the two-bedroom campus dorm apartments, it had been eerie being in there alone. The whole place creaked and groaned at all hours of the day, three hundred and sixty-five days a year. She'd heard things that she knew weren't there. She'd seen things in the shadows, her mind playing tricks on her. Now, a semester and a half into living there, the house and its habits were old news.

After making a mug of hot chocolate, noting that her section of the shared fridge was looking a little sparse, Moira trudged back up to her room. Along the way, she fed Steve, the house betta fish, and turned off the TV, which the girls had left on mute. Both Simone and Hannah's bedroom doors were closed as she passed them on the way back to the stairs, and she knew Lee's and Ella's would be the same upstairs, but she caught a flash of her reflection in the dark bathroom mirror down the main floor hallway just before she started up the stairs.

Clutching the railing, she stared, her skin paler than it had ever been, her eyes a vibrant blue when they'd once been a muddy green. Unlike the hair, which she hid under her vast collection of wool hats, Moira couldn't pretend the change in her eye colour was due to the latest trends.

One morning five months ago, she had woken up and her eyes were a different colour. Poof. Just like that. Blue. And not just any blue—the most fucking intense shade of blue she had ever seen, and she had a bachelor's degree in *art*. She had seen a lot of blue in her time.

Her hand went to her cheek and she pushed at the skin, hating the sight of her reflection doing the same. It was like staring at a different person.

All her life, she'd had a cluster of freckles across her nose that matched her hair colour. Now, her skin was freckle-free. She always thought she looked sickly now, too pale compared to the natural tan she'd always sported, but Ella argued that her skin had an oddly exuberant glow to it —like a star.

Whatever it was, it was *different*. She was changing. No longer did she look like her mom, who'd had the same chestnut-brown hair and muddy green eyes. Even her eyelashes and eyebrow hairs had fallen out, at different times, which had been *great*, and then grown back in white.

She bit the insides of her cheeks. Gaunt. Strange. Different.

She had stopped looking in mirrors entirely these days.

Hand gripping the old dark wooden bannister, Moira flung herself back up the stairs, hissing when some of her steaming hot chocolate sloshed over the side of her FHU mug—and ignoring the fact that the scalding liquid didn't burn as much as it should. She cleaned the spilled droplets with her socked feet, then barricaded herself in her bedroom as the house continued to settle around her. Hot chocolate on her bedside table, she tugged the blankets up, sank into the pillows, and logged back in to her tablet.

Russ Tanner. Premiere male escort of Farrow's Hollow. If anyone was going to solve her little climaxing problem, it was probably him. And if she was going to pay some obscenely high fee for the services anyway, she may as well splurge on the *best*.

Still, she couldn't help but balk at the prices on his services page. Moira was frugal by nature. She had been all her life, even after inheriting a cool *million* from her mom after she'd died. When the lawyer had explained the situation, Moira had thought she was having a stroke. Her mom couldn't have had that much money. They had lived in the same two-bedroom bungalow all her life. Moira had worked part-time during the school years, full-time in the summers, since she was fourteen, and her mom's job as a nurse had never paid as well as it should have. But there it had been—1.2 million dollars, all passed on to Moira. Out of nowhere. As if things couldn't get any stranger.

So far, she had invested half, then tucked the rest aside for a rainy day in various accounts that let her grow interest. She could have afforded to rent this entire house on her own, but she'd always wanted to live with other people, with Ella.

And then everything had started to change. Her eyes. Her skin. Her figure. Then her hair fell out. In the last six months, she had morphed into a completely different person—literally. Nowadays, Moira couldn't help but wonder if she ought to use that huge chunk of cash and just buy a place all to herself. She spent enough time hiding herself away these days...

But if she was going to die from the same unknown illness that had taken her mom, what was the point?

Because what else could this be? Her body was losing its pigmentation just about everywhere. Only in her early twenties, she wasn't supposed to still be *changing* this much, and none of the doctors she'd seen could make heads or tails of it. They'd just concluded she wasn't contagious, that her immune system was stellar, and then offered to refer her to specialists with year-long waitlists.

Shaking her head, she realized she'd been staring a hole into her bedroom door for at least a few minutes, lost in thoughts of money and houses and her bright white hair.

"Okay, okay," she muttered, tapping around the screen again with renewed interest. "Contact page..."

No address. No phone number. Just a button that said Schedule Your Phone Consultation Now. She pursed her lips—which had also turned from a naturally burnt red to pale, dusky pink.

Phone consultation.

"That's not so scary." At least she could hear his voice before she met him. A consultation. She could ask all her questions in advance. That would certainly help her nerves. Maybe he would be more forthcoming about what he actually offered over the phone, too, where there was no written record of the conversation.

Moira just wanted to experience good, possibly *great*, sex that ended in a cataclysmic orgasm—was that too much to ask for? No guy had ever helped her achieve it, nor had any of the vibrators and various other toys she'd tried. School was crazy busy lately. TA work was at its worst toward the end of the second semester with all the projects and papers she needed to help grade. Everything was ramping up again as spring hurtled toward summer. And her physical appearance, her own body, continued to give her a giant middle finger on the best of days.

Why not treat herself?

Why not let a professional handle this one little thing she might kind of, sort of, maybe, be able to control?

So, hesitantly, she clicked the button to schedule her consultation, all the while hoping that she hadn't just started down the path toward the biggest mistake of her life.

CHAPTER TWO

The night began with a knock at the door—firmer than usual. Severus glanced at the clock next to the bed, noting that she was about five minutes early. Clearing his throat, he stood and smoothed his hands down the silky soft T-shirt he had opted for tonight instead of the usual suit. Moira was a college girl, if she'd been telling the truth during their phone interview last weekend, and didn't strike him as the kind who wanted refinement. So, he had chosen a less upscale hotel for tonight's session, and dressed down in a pair of dark jeans and a deep grey tee. The belt and shoes were still fine leather—he hadn't lost his sense of style completely—but her voice had sounded *young*, and he didn't want to send her running by dressing like her dad.

She knocked again, the sharp rap of her knuckles making Severus grin as he crossed the small hotel room. While missing the luxurious bathroom and generously stocked minibar, the establishment boasted near-soundproof walls. He had a similar arrangement with one of the night shift front desk clerks as he did with clerks across the city, and tended to bring his screamers here. From what he'd gathered of this college student, she didn't strike him as a screamer, but the hotel was on the south side of town, far from the sanctuary of her north-side campus, which meant she wouldn't run into anyone familiar in the parking lot.

He'd left his facial hair scruffier today. All the twenty-somethings swooned over dark, brooding, and dangerous—didn't they? No matter how he dressed, suit or no suit, he had a feeling he would still tickle her fancy, among other things. Most women found him irresistible, and not just because he was an incubus.

Unbolting the door, he opened it with one of his unassuming smiles—one that disappeared the moment he saw her. She stood about a foot away, a willowy, ethereal creature whose chin came up to his shoulders. Dark, mahogany hair, long and straight, hung around her sharp, angular face in curtains, and she swept it behind her ears with trembling hands. Slim, long fingers. Neatly trimmed nails. White. She was so very *white* that it threw him. And those *eyes*—an otherworldly blue—flickered up to him briefly before fixing themselves to the floor.

She was undeniably beautiful, and Severus found himself questioning why on earth she would even *need* his services.

"Russ?" she asked softly, her voice curiously melodic. It snapped him out of his staring, his admiring, and he opened the door with a nod.

"Moira. My apologies for keeping you waiting."

"It's fine," she muttered as she darted in. Dressed in a pair of slim-fit jeans, ankle-high brown boots with just a hint of wedged heel, and a black spring peacoat that nipped around the waist, she looked as though she belonged in the glossy pages of some fashion magazine—not here with him in a soundproofed room at the Kingsview Inn and Suites.

His dark brows crinkled as he gently closed the door, making sure that all his movements were obvious as he locked them in. New clients could be jumpy, and seeing him lock the door never helped.

"Now, we—"

"Here," she said, thrusting an envelope at him, presumably full of cash, as soon as he turned around. The woman still struggled to meet and hold his gaze; she had sounded so much more confident over the phone. Clearly she wasn't in the business of paying for sex regularly. His eyes narrowed somewhat as he assessed her, before gripping the envelope—holding but not taking, waiting for her to drop her arm back to her side.

She did, sliding that elegant hand into her pocket and finally lifting her stare to him, fixing it just over his shoulder. Severus smiled again, though the expression was far less modest than the one he'd used to greet her.

"Yes, thank you," he muttered. The white envelope was thin, and as he turned to set it on the dresser, he realized there were only two bills inside. Now, how was little Miss Moira withdrawing two crisp five-hundred-dollar notes from her bank? Did she come from money? Most who paid for his services did. Yet she was just a wisp of a thing—beautiful, puzzling, but still only a girl.

His jaw clenched when he faced her again. This was the first time a client had thrown him by mere appearance alone. Some of the women he catered to were physically attractive in their own way, but Moira was...something else entirely.

And he couldn't decide if that sat well with him or not.

"Now, tell me, is this your first time with an escort?" he asked, hands clasped behind his back as he strolled toward her—around her.

"Like I said on the phone, *yes*," she replied curtly. "My first and only time."

"I just wanted to clarify again." He strolled in a slow, easy circle around her, only then realizing he was even doing it. Demons were predatory by nature. With most clients, Severus had no problem suppressing his baser instincts, shifting his persona to whatever the woman desired, and yet with this Moira, he went straight to it—the predator within. He slowed his pace until he finally stopped in front of her. "You seem nervous."

"I don't mean to."

"No, I suspect not." He smirked, peering down at her with a steadily intensifying interest. "I don't mean to make you uncomfortable. It's perfectly natural to be a little uneasy with the arrangement." Severus went for her hand, but she slid that one into her pocket too—holding her ground and continuing to look over his shoulder. Curious. "If you'd prefer, we can just talk. I'm a good listener, you know."

During their phone interview, she had told him what she wanted: sex to completion, no oral, *definitely* no anal, kissing was fine. Many of his clients preferred not to kiss, and Severus didn't hold it against them. The act was so *intimate*, perhaps even more so than the sex itself. Studying her lips, pale pink like an aged ballet slipper, he realized he certainly wouldn't mind kissing her. In fact, if his slowly hardening cock had anything to say about it, it appeared Severus *wanted* to kiss her.

Strange.

And not entirely unwelcome.

"No." Her steadfast refusal startled him out of his musings, and he found her hastily unbuttoning her jacket and yanking it off her shoulders. "No, I'm fine. I want to do this. We... It's fine."

Severus continued to watch her in a contemplative silence as she crossed the small room and set her folded coat on the chair by the window. While she was an unearthly pale creature, her hair was so *stark*—and it didn't match her eyebrows. Sure, both were brown, but not the same brown. In fact, as she stalked back to him, fiddling with her nails, he noted that the eyebrows appeared drawn on. While faded, Severus also made note of dark brown smudges along her hairline, as though she'd recently used dye. Had she done it to disguise herself tonight? She hadn't given her last name on the phone—and Severus hadn't asked for it—but it would probably be easy enough to find her online, bad dye job or not.

"I don't want you to feel pressured," he told her when the silence dragged on longer than it should. He suddenly felt the urge to trail the backs of his knuckles across her cheek. Schooling his features, Severus curled his hand into a tight fist, recently clipped nails biting into his palm. Don't touch her yet. Don't send her running. Be a fucking *professional*. "Or we can do other things if you—"

"No, sex is fine." Her cheeks flamed at the statement, and he found himself trying not to chuckle. She wasn't a virgin, supposedly, yet her blushes suggested otherwise. "I'm just a little off-balance here with everything. I'll be fine. Seriously. Let's...do this."

She bit her lower lip, grimacing slightly, and this time Severus *did* chuckle. He couldn't help it.

"We have the full two hours," he mused, dropping his voice as he reached out and pushed her hair over her shoulder. It had fallen free from behind her ear when she'd taken her coat off. "There's no rush."

Moira took a deep breath, then slowly let it out as she murmured, "Okay. Thanks."

The air stood still between them, a weighted silence only made heavier by the soundproofed walls. He could always hear *something* everywhere else; people laughing, a TV blaring, water running. Here, there was nothing but thick air and the sound of her shaky, uneven breaths.

And the pounding of his own blood, headed southbound without delay, the demon within awakening.

For the first time in, well, *ever*, he found himself wanting to initiate—and not for the pleasure of her life essence. He'd had a client on Wednesday night. Sex. Oral—for both of them. Then a shower together. She'd stayed the night in the room he'd rented, so wiped out that he didn't trust her to get home at all. He'd been selfish, taking too much, and he'd had to remind himself to be cautious before tonight's session.

Yet he didn't want to be cautious. As Moira took two tentative steps toward him, the third closing the gap between their bodies, he found he wanted to touch, to take, to *consume*.

Instead, Severus forced himself to be still, to be patient. This was just a job. A necessity of existence.

Why was he so riled up? The beast within seldom blinked at his clients, yet now his entire being hummed with interest.

Finally, those hauntingly bright blue eyes studied his face in its entirety, and he felt the blaze of their path as though they'd burned him. In the end, they settled on his lips, and he tilted his face down just enough that if she stood up on her tiptoes, she could kiss him of her own free will.

And she did. Softly. Sweetly. Those blush-pink lips

brushed across his as he watched her beneath a hooded stare. Her eyelashes, black with several coats of mascara, fluttered somewhat before settling, her eyes closed as she leaned into him. When her hand came to rest on his chest, her touch like a whisper, faint, barely there—Severus was forced to lock his hands in fists again, if only to still them before they reacted.

For they were *desperate* to respond. Her sweet, innocent touches. Her diminutive grace. Her beauty. Her *smell*—heady and intense, like a lotus in full bloom. On their own, nothing. Together, the combination was deadly, for it stirred something within him, something animalistic, something *dangerous*, something he had suppressed ever since he left Hell, hoping to survive better among the humans than he had with his own kind.

His throat burned, the great cavern of his chest on *fire*. Desire. He hadn't felt it in an age. Desperation. Eagerness. The urge to take and to *defile*.

He knew he ought to send her away. Cut the session short. Make an excuse. Give Moira her money back. Spare her.

Yet as her tongue tentatively swept along the tight seam of his mouth, he couldn't. Severus succumbed instead, surrendering to a controlled fall as her long, willowy fingers crept to his cheeks, cupping his face. His lips parted, his arm curling around her narrow waist, and he smiled against her mouth when he realized that bold tongue was not quite so; in fact, it was rather shy. It hedged along the outskirts, unwilling to leave her mouth for his.

So, Severus gave her a reason not to be shy, thrusting his tongue, a tongue he could elongate for *optimal* pleasure should he desire it, into her mouth. Her little squeal of surprise emboldened him, his hand threading through her hair. It yearned to tighten, to wrench her head back so that he might graze his teeth along her neck.

Learn what sort of sounds she'd make then.

For now, however, he could content himself with her little moans, the racing of her breath as their kiss became frantic—dangerously so.

And then her hands fell to his chest again and *shoved.* He staggered back, startled by her strength, and held his hands out when he found his breath ragged. Jaw clenched, he forced his heart to slow, the damn thing slamming against its cage. If he'd thought her blushes prominent before, they were *nothing* compared to what he saw now. As if sensing it, she pressed her hands to her cheeks and turned away.

"I'm sorry," he offered, knowing he needed to say something, and that seemed like the most socially acceptable phrase to utter to a distressed human. "Did I...?"

"You didn't do anything," she told him over her shoulder. "It's me. I'm sorry. I swear I'm not normally this...stiff."

Well, that was one way to describe it. He ran a hand through his hair, sensing that if he asked her if she wanted to *talk* again, she might force herself to do something that would distress her further.

"I could give you a massage," he said, vocalizing the idea as soon as it came to mind. It would give him ample opportunity to take what he needed from her, skin-to-skin, and she could hopefully find some peace. His stamina was exceptional; he could massage her for the next—a quick glance at the bedside clock—hour and forty minutes, ten minutes for sex to what would likely be an easy climax if she hadn't fallen asleep, and then it would be over. This vexing woman would be gone, and Severus could forget what she did to him, how she roused his inner darkness. Pretend it hadn't ever happened.

Slowly, Moira faced him again, some of the redness in her cheeks dissipated. "A massage?"

"I find it, er," he gestured toward the bed, suddenly tongue-tied under the weight of her full, wide-eyed stare, "can be quite relaxing. Many ordinary couples use it for foreplay. I'm sure you carry a lot of stress with school."

Moira gathered her hair in her hands, tossing it to one side as she nodded. "Okay. A massage sounds," she swallowed noticeably, "nice."

"Why don't I wait in the bathroom?" he offered, needing a few moments of peace to collect himself anyway—yet another first. "You can undress and wait under the sheets, as you would at an actual massage appointment. If you find that's all you want, we can just do that."

"No, I want to—"

"Decide on it when the time comes," he insisted before striding into the bathroom and barricading himself inside. He leaned back against the door with a scowl, then quietly hit his head against the solid wood frame.

What the devil was *wrong* with him?

Shaking his head, Severus pushed off the door and found himself standing there with a raging erection—all from a bit of *kissing*. Something must have been seriously wrong. Was he ill? If she hadn't appeared so innocent, he might have thought her a witch, but he didn't get a whiff of demon from her. Not in the slightest. No magic. No tricks. It was just her—Moira without a last name. College student. Intriguing beauty. A threat to Severus's carefully cultivated control if he had ever seen one.

He pinched the bridge of his nose, taking long, deep, even breaths in an attempt to calm himself. However, by the time he'd finished, he was still rock hard, the inner beast demanding he march back into that room and simply *take* her. Even the slightest adjustment of his jeans was fucking torture. He needed release. He needed *her*, apparently.

No. This is absurd. Scowling, he stalked to the sink and turned on the cold water, waiting for it to get extra icy before splashing his face. Even the chilly blast did nothing to lessen his ridiculous state of arousal, and as he glared at himself in the mirror, he wondered if she'd drugged him—some hell-born elixir painted across those pale lips. Was he five seconds away from passing out with a massive hard-on? He leaned in to check his lips, his teeth, and his tongue. All looked normal. No lingering residue. His eyes were clear, not the least bit dazed, bloodshot, or out of focus.

Wait.

He leaned closer. His eye colour should have been darker. He'd had a generous dose of skin-to-skin contact. His body had responded *eagerly* to Moira's touch, and yet he didn't feel as he always did courtesy of a little heavy petting. Not stronger. Not sharper. Not energized or refreshed. The same as before. Horny as fuck, sure, but otherwise... Nothing.

He tugged at his cheeks, checked his eyes again, and then took a step back, scowling. He didn't feel *worse* by any means. In fact, Severus felt oddly *alive* for the first time in a dreadfully long time.

It was as though her kiss had awoken the long-dormant demon inside, kept quiet, pliant, and restrained around all these humans.

"Moira, Moira, Moira," he murmured, looking back to the bathroom door. "What have you done to me?"

And why?

After splashing his face with a bit of cold water again,

he patted his skin down and composed himself in front of the mirror. Whether she was aware of it or not, Moira affected him, but he couldn't let it show. Severus had to be in control here—and his cock, the inner darkness gathering within, suggested otherwise. No one could know, certainly not the temptress waiting for him to return.

Although he didn't have a watch on him tonight, he knew he'd given her ample time to situate herself under the bedsheets, and after rumpling his hair and checking his eyes one last time, he opened the door.

And found her precisely where he thought she'd be: facedown in the middle of the bed, the white duvet cover folded in half and the thin white sheets drawn up to her mid-back.

"Are you ready?" he asked, fighting the surge of arousal shooting through him at all that exposed skin. Odd, that his first instinct wasn't what he could take *from* her, but rather what he wanted to do *to* her. "Moira?"

"Yes." To her credit, she sounded more confident this time, her voice steady. As he approached, he found her head resting on her folded hands, and she slowly turned it to the side so she could glance up at him. "I'm sorry about before. I don't know why I'm so flustered."

"It's very normal for your first time," he told her, fighting the urge to run his gaze down the length of her body—what the sheets left exposed. Even if she was there for the explicit purpose of sex, he didn't want to openly leer. Not very professional—or, given the strange new circumstances, not in his best interests. Instead, he cleared his throat and nodded toward his bag, which he'd left on the floor by the dresser. "Would you like me to use massage oils?"

"Oh, uh..." She bit her lower lip for a moment as she

considered it, and Severus clenched his jaw, suppressing the image of him nibbling that tempting lower lip from his mind. Moira shuffled about beneath the covers somewhat as she said, "Massage oils sometimes give me a rash. Or they used to, anyway."

"Moisturizing lotion?" He lifted his eyebrows. "Scent-free. All natural. I use it for clients with sensitive skin."

Her cheeks flushed again as she nodded, then faced the bed—perhaps to hide the recent flood of colour. Severus marched across the room to grab the bottle from his bag, but found his legs mildly uncooperative, as though they had no desire to leave her side. Stranger still.

Once he had the appropriate lotion in hand, he dragged off his T-shirt, not wanting to stain it, and tossed it on the dresser. Returning to the bed, he noted that she had taken the time to fold all her clothes before piling them neatly on the armchair. For some reason, the very idea tugged at his lips and threatened to make him *smile.*

He took a deep breath.

Just get this over with. She'll be a puddle of wet, dripping desire soon enough, just like all the rest of them.

As he clambered onto the bed, he realized he had no idea where to position himself. Instinct told him to settle over the delicate curve of her behind, but the second he did she'd feel his still very present, *very* hard cock through his jeans, and Severus didn't want to startle her.

So, he knelt at her side, gently lowering the sheet to her hips. Silently, Moira gathered her splayed brown hair, which still didn't look quite right, and dragged it over to one side, exposing two highly sensitive areas—her spine and her neck. Severus stared down at her as a vision of running his tongue from the small of her back to the nape of her neck danced across his mind's eye.

Fuck.

Shaking his head, he squeezed the lotion onto his hands, rubbed it in a bit, and then got to work. The second his hands smoothed up her back, applying just the right amount of pressure, Moira tensed briefly, then let out a long, luxurious exhale. Severus smirked. *Just like all the rest.*

Only she wasn't. The longer he massaged her, lingering on some knots in her upper back, Severus realized he just wasn't getting *anything* from her. No matter how he touched her, no matter *where* he touched her, all Severus became was more and more aroused. Not stronger. Not sharper. Just hornier, until finally he yanked the sheets down, exposing her completely, and dragged his tongue along the hollow of her lower back. She shuddered, and, over the round, pert globes of her ass, Severus caught her toes curl.

A sinful grin crossed his lips, and his hands wandered lower, smoothing over her backside and gripping her thighs firmly. She gasped, feet digging into the bed now, and all Severus wanted to do was bury his face between her legs. He could smell her arousal. He could *feel* the heat radiating off her, the tension in her limbs when he scraped his teeth along the delicate skin of one cheek. Her legs twitched, as though startled by the flash of pain paired with what he knew was a sensuous rubdown. Severus clasped her thighs tighter, one large, firm hand on each, and used his thumbs to circle the tender flesh along her inner thighs. Goosebumps erupted—a job well done.

Severus crawled down the bed, running his tongue along the inside of her right thigh, using both hands on her left, and she *moaned*—the sweetest, most tempting sound he'd ever heard. Although she had requested no oral, he could easily imagine parting her legs and burying his face between them, spearing her wet heat with his tongue, tormenting her clit until she came with a scream. Bless those soundproof walls.

"Russ?" Moira's soft voice broke through the fog of lust. He blinked rapidly and found his mouth at the curve of her ass, his thumbs hiked up on either side of her swollen sex; he'd ventured in without even realizing it, so lost in the fantasy of what she'd look like when she came that he hadn't been conscious of his actions. Jaw clenched, he sat up quickly, about to apologize—when he found her studying him over her shoulder with a heat in her eyes that made his cock *sing*.

Something akin to a growl rattled around in his chest as he crawled up her, finally clambering over her and grinding his now-throbbing, yet still horribly confined erection against her backside. She arched below, head thrown back and lips parted, and whimpered softly when his teeth nipped at her neck.

Still he wasn't getting anything.

And Severus didn't give two flying fucks anymore.

All he could think about was her, this mystery woman who wasn't like all the rest, and driving himself into her over and over until he collapsed.

She turned somewhat frantically beneath him, hands sliding up to cup his face as it descended upon her, mouth claiming hers again. Last time, he had let her steer. He had let her tentative touches guide them, set the pace—but now it was time for her to taste the fire, the fury, of his kiss. Severus caught her with her lips slightly parted and took full advantage, thrusting his tongue into her mouth as she moaned, exploring every crevice, marking her in ways known only to the two of them. Her hands dropped down to his shoulders while he repositioned themselves so her legs wrapped around his waist, not the other way around.

Moira tasted divine—and all he'd sampled was her mouth. He pressed harder, driving her into the bed as her heels dug into his back. Her hands, with those willowy fingers and burning caresses, wrapped around the back of his neck, and it took every ounce of his restraint not to snatch them and pin them next to her head. Lash them to the bedposts with silk. Leather. *Rope* that would leave her marked for days to follow.

He tore his mouth from hers and dragged it down her neck instead, fearing what the kiss was doing to him—what it was truly awakening. As he sucked at the nape of her neck, trailed his tongue along her collarbone, he found her kiss like a drug, like a *weapon*, severing the tether of his control. His sanity, perhaps, if he let it drag on long enough.

What sort of creature could do that to an incubus?

He glanced up at her when she keened his stage name, her hips bucking against his, before nuzzling about to find her pulse. His tongue swirled around it, sucked at it, bruising the delicate skin of her neck. Her heart beat hurriedly, but not as dangerously fast as Severus knew he could drive it. With but the simplest touch of an incubus, human hearts danced. Not Moira's. He growled again, this time raking his teeth across her skin, and her nails bit into his neck.

"*Russ...*" Suddenly those hands jumped lower, skimming over his muscular figure, not stopping until they reached the brown leather belt around his hips. At the feel of her unbuckling it, he forced himself to straighten, chest rising and falling harder and faster than it should. She fumbled over the belt only briefly before wrenching it open. Next came the button of his dark jeans, the zipper sliding dangerously down his rigid shaft. He hissed when she cupped him through the remarkably thin fabric of his briefs, that damn lower lip caught between her teeth again.

With a hint of uncertainty playing across her features, Moira stroked him over his briefs, then gripped the waistline and tugged it down. His hands fisted when his cock tumbled free, falling like a lead weight between them. Her eyes widened, only for a moment, before she wrapped her hand around its head and swept her thumb over the glistening tip. His hips jolted on their own accord, and he clamped down on the insides of his cheeks.

Normally he had all the control. His clients had no sway over his body, no way to dictate his excitement. Most of all, they never took from *him*. Severus should have been brimming with energy, overflowing from all that skin-to-skin contact. Instead, he felt like putty in her hands, easily manipulated, suddenly pliable.

And that simply wouldn't do.

So, he nudged her hands away and bore down on her again. He meant to pin her, smother her with his weight, but once more she wrapped her legs around him, drawing his now-freed cock ever closer to her heat.

"You are *dangerous*, Moira," he growled, slipping a hand under the back of her head and grasping her hair. "Do you know that? More dangerous than I could ever be..."

"I'm ready," she whispered, eyes wide and wild when they met his, those ethereal blues forcing him to inhale sharply. She spoke as though she hadn't heard him, and he clenched his eyes shut when she eased her hips, her heat, along the full length of his cock. Gone were the tremors in her words, the blushes across her cheeks. Beneath him was a goddess—only Severus couldn't choke out her name even if he wanted to.

"Ready, are you?" he managed instead, battling to contain the beast within—the beast who lived, thrived, and *died* for lust. This goddess had revived him, brought him back from the abyss—and she had the *gall* to just *nod* up at him.

"Russ, I want you to—"

Moira squealed, the sound muffled by his lips crashing over hers. The moment they touched again, the firestorm resumed, and Severus was lost. In her. In the now. In the lust pounding through his veins. He reached between them and steered his cock to her slick entrance. With one sharp thrust of his hips, Severus filled her. She arched up against him, moaning as her hand clasped the headboard.

Certainly no virgin, but tight and hot all the same. He found himself momentarily stricken dumb, succumbing to the sensation. He'd had a *lot* of sex. Severus did it for a living these days. But he'd never felt a cunt like hers. Gone were the cares, the precautions, the measures he had in place for all his regular clients. He simply had to have her, utterly. He saw nothing beyond that.

He bucked against her before easing out and pounding back in, taking her harshly. Any other woman would have broken by now, but she clung to him with one arm around his neck, rocking her hips to meet each rough thrust. Soundproofed walls contained her cries, her moans, but he wanted more. Severus wanted her *screams*. He wanted her skin flush and slick with sweat. He wanted to see her become the same as he, two creatures of unbridled passion.

A thousand dollars sat on the dresser by the door—a thousand dollars to make her come. Severus grinned against her lips; she wasn't just going to *come*. Not once. He had another hour and a half to make her weep with such exquisite ecstasy—

"Your eyes!" She jolted suddenly, as though poked with the end of a cattle prod, then shoved him off. Severus toppled to the side, heart hammering and cock throbbing, desperate to return to its new favourite place, and quickly propped himself up on his elbow.

"What?"

"Your eyes..." She scrambled to the side of the bed, swinging her legs over the edge and pressing a hand to her forehead.

My eyes?

He faced the mirrors on the closet doors quickly. In his true form, his entire eye appeared black. Perhaps he had let his earthly disguise slip for a moment, so wrapped up in this delicious creature that he forgot himself entirely. Now, however, he looked like any ordinary human.

Well, close enough.

"I don't know what you saw," he started, forcing himself to calm, to settle, to regain control, "but if it frightened you, I'm sorry." When she said nothing, keeping her back to him, Severus reached across the bed. "Moira? Did I hurt you? Are you—"

She flinched out of reach the moment his fingertips grazed her shoulder, scampering off the bed, still naked, and making a beeline for her clothes.

"I shouldn't have done this," he heard her muttering, and Severus made a half-hearted attempt to cover his still *very* prominent erection by throwing a sheet over it.

"Moira—"

"It's not going to work," she said, the sentiment followed by a cackle as she shimmied into her panties. Her jeans came next, and it was only then Severus realized she was crying. His skin prickled as if kissed by a morning chill. When she looked up at him, she swiped a hand across each cheek, seemingly torn between hysteria and mania. "It never works. I'm just not destined to...to... It's *never* going to happen. I'm sorry."

"Moira, why don't you sit down and tell me what's going on?" Clearly there was an underlying issue she hadn't thought to share with him during the phone consultation. With her wearing more clothes, dragging her shirt over her head, bra shoved in her purse, he found it easier to restrain the beast within. Sort of. And probably not for very long. "If you need someone to listen to—"

"I don't need you to be my therapist," she said sharply as she grabbed her coat and purse.

"And I'm not offering to be. If you're having problems sexually, I just happen to know a thing or two about—"

"I made a mistake doing this," she insisted, boots crammed back on. When she faced him again, her eyebrows seemed—disheveled. As he'd suspected earlier, she had used some sort of pencil to colour them, because there was a patch of bright white peering back at him in the middle of her right brow. Curiosity at an all-time high, he stood, keeping the sheet around himself and extending a hand to her.

"You're upset—"

"And that's none of your concern. Keep the money." Tears streaking down her face in thick glossy tracks, she raced for the door and tried to open it. The lock gave him a few precious seconds to get his briefs and pants tugged back up, but by then she had everything unlocked and was gone. Severus called her name, hurrying after her—only to find an empty hallway on either side of him. The elevator at the far end of the hall was in use, but it was going up, not down. Logically, he could assume she'd taken the nearby stairwell, but he opted not to follow her.

She was right, of course. It *wasn't* his concern. She wasn't his to pick apart and put back together at his leisure. None of his clients were.

But Moira *was* a mystery. As he went back into the hotel room and closed the door soundly behind him, Severus found he couldn't make heads or tails of what had just happened. None of it. Not the fake hair colour. Not her strength. Not the way she affected him—the *real* him. And certainly not the way he couldn't *take* from her as he did with every other human.

Clearly, she wasn't a human. There was no other explanation.

Yet she was no demon either, no enchantress or witch. Not a creature of Hell, period.

So, what, exactly, was she?

And why did she make him feel alive for the first time in centuries?

Tonight, he had no answers—just a stubborn hard-on and disconcerting sense of powerlessness over his own body—but Severus was determined to find them.

And soon.

CHAPTER THREE

One moment Moira was staring down at the essay that she needed to mark, the words blurring in and out of focus, and the next she was shooting upright, heart racing, as her phone's alarm shrieked. Blinking rapidly, it took her a few beats longer than it should have to clue in to where she was —her professor's TA office, which all four of the grad students assigned to the first-year Introduction to Art History class used for office hours. Sighing, she slumped in the high-backed chair, its armrests peeling and seat cushion woefully understuffed after years of teaching assistants' butts crushing it.

She must have fallen asleep, because she was still on page one of the six-page essay, and hadn't done more than scribble a note in red pen about the title formatting being incorrect.

"Ugh."

Moira rubbed at her face, then leaned forward and tapped her phone screen. 9 PM. Office hours were officially over for the day. Somehow she had drawn the short straw this semester; every Tuesday and Wednesday night, she was *here*, in a cramped office, making herself available for freshman undergrads who never visited anyway. Sure, at the beginning of the year a few of the keeners would make use of TA office hours. However, given that the last term of the year was hurtling toward finals at lightning speed, Moira's seven-to-nine-PM time slot tended to be underused and under-appreciated.

Tonight had been no different. At least she hadn't drooled on the essay she was supposed to be grading when she fell asleep, head propped up on her hand.

Huffing, she grabbed the neatly stapled pages and set them on the stack of unread ones, then added the five papers she'd gotten through in the last two hours to the *read* folder that all the TAs used. With eight hundred students in the lecture, most of them thinking art history was an easy humanities credit to breeze through for their program's requirements, she'd had two *hundred* essays assigned at random to her last week after the due date.

Thus far, she'd made it through about twenty. The rest were due next month just before the undergrads took their final exams, and given that she would have her *own* final assignments to contend with then, Moira really wanted to get them out of the way. At this pace, it seemed more likely that she'd be done next *year*, not next month.

"Kill me," she muttered, then started packing up her things. The office was one in a row of a dozen along the east wall of McKinnon's Library, FHU's lone arts and humanities research center. When she stood up, Moira's outstretched elbows could touch either side of the walled-in cubicle. A little diamond-shaped window overlooked the courtyard below, usually brimming with students eating their lunches or tossing a ball around in the daylight hours. Old wooden desk from the fifties—check. Chair that should have been replaced ten years ago—check. Wall organizers that ate into the already-cramped space—double check. Four hours a week, she felt like she was in solitary confinement. No wonder students never came to visit; they had to stand in the hall if they wanted to talk, with a TA sitting in that shitty chair and the door open.

Before she left, she fired off a response to her best friend's recent text about her ETA; after Ella's hot mess of a date last Friday, they had plans to watch a movie tonight before bed with a tub of ice cream each to help her get over it.

Moira had insisted that she wanted her *own* tub of ice cream, which, given her love of the stuff, had gone unquestioned when they'd made their plans. However, she too needed to drown her sorrows in a bucket of cookies and cream—because *her* Friday night hadn't exactly been all roses either.

She clenched her eyes shut and slapped a hand to her forehead. Just the *memory* of her, what, forty minutes with Russ the Scrumptious Escort made her want to dissolve into a puddle of goo on the floor. Not only had she been a nervous wreck about paying for sex, acting like she'd never seen a member of the male species before, but she hadn't enjoyed an earth-shattering, heart-pounding orgasm either. Instead, she could have *sworn* she saw his eyes change, both orbs completely black as he pounded into her—and *that* particular memory made her shiver for more reasons than one.

Later, when she'd had time to think, she decided the whole eye-changing incident was probably just her imagination giving her an excuse to get the hell out of there.

Because, as intense as it had been, as amazing as the sex had felt when it finally started, she shouldn't have been there. She shouldn't have hired an escort—hello, *illegal*—and she shouldn't have gotten her hopes up that she would finally experience what pretty much every other woman her age raved about. It had all been a huge mistake, one she couldn't stop dreaming about days later. As sexy as her dreams about Russ had been, with his smoldering stare and sinful smile, the rumbling vibrations of his voice always getting dream-Moira off, they left her feeling restless. Distracted. Exhausted, honestly.

In short, the whole evening had been downright *mortifying*, and as much as she had wanted to spill it all immediately to a pissed-off, post-date Ella when she'd stormed into the house that night, she couldn't. It was too embarrassing, even to share with her best friend.

Instead, Moira planned to eat an entire tub of ice cream tonight, the first free night she and Ella could justify taking off together, and pretend it had never happened.

If only her subconscious could just get onboard with that, because she could really use a decent night's sleep. If she kept passing out trying to grade all these admittedly boring-as-hell essays, she'd never get them done—and being stuck with them for longer than necessary was almost worse than having to grade them in the first place.

As she loaded her things into her messenger bag, Moira caught her reflection in the small window facing the courtyard. Frowning, she tugged her wool cap down, then tucked the wisps of white hair underneath. She had dyed her hair for her night with Russ, hoping that might give her more confidence, and just as it had many times before, the dye washed out of her hair the following day. Permanent dye, at that.

So, not only had her hair *fallen out* last year and grown back in the exact opposite of what it had been her whole life, but it couldn't hold dye worth a damn anymore either—and it *grew* like nobody's business. She had to trim it weekly now just to keep it manageable.

And it was getting a little too warm to wear her wool caps every day. She shot her reflection a scowl, then grabbed her bag and shuffled out of the TA broom closet—"office". Thick, unrelenting silence blanketed the library this time of night, with just a few students here and there working at the individual study cubes, headphones on and the world tuned out. She waved at a cluster of softly murmuring English lit TAs in passing, but didn't stop to chat—mostly because they only knew her as Ella's weird roommate who never went out anymore.

Rather than taking the rickety elevator down to the main floor, she took the winding cement stairwell. Here, the air was even more oppressive, cold too, the silence thicker and more disconcerting. Gripping her pleather bag strap, she picked up the pace, all but throwing herself through the thick, heavy doors that led to the main floor.

Breathing in the scents from the coffee stand, she found her unease dissipating at the quiet, constant chatter of the first floor; upper floors had noise restrictions, leaving the sprawling main level, with its archival rooms and long tables with bench seating on either side, the one place study groups could meet and talk as loud as they wanted.

She almost stopped to grab a coffee, knowing she'd need one to stay awake through tonight's movie, but decided against it when Ella sent a string of texts telling her to hurry up or she'd start without her. The weekend would have been a better time to do this, but Ella had been reluctantly visiting family, then had TA work of her own to tackle over the last couple days—so a midweek movie night featuring what Moira suspected would be a lot of date bashing was the best they could swing.

Pausing between the two doorways at the entrance of the library, she texted Ella back, insisting that she was *coming* and to not take her ice cream out of the freezer just yet. When she was through, she tucked her phone away and pushed through the exterior door, marching out into the night.

Only to stop when she felt it again. Arms crossed, Moira scanned the empty courtyard before her, the looming shapes of the social sciences building on one side and the arts building on the other casting long shadows that engulfed the entire yard. She paused at the top of the steps, nibbling her lower lip.

For the last few days, every time she had stepped outside, a chill had skittered down her spine—because she felt like someone was watching her. Thus far, Moira couldn't validate her feelings. Couldn't confirm or deny. Couldn't decide if her overactive imagination from her night with Russ just hadn't settled yet. But it was there, the sensation of a stranger's gaze creeping across her body, and it hadn't let up yet.

Slowly, she descended the cement stairs one at a time, pausing again at the bottom. Beyond the lamps on either side of the courtyard, one flickering, and the arrangement of benches and trash cans, she was totally alone. The path from the library steps carried on across the courtyard, between the two buildings, and into the huge grassy area in the middle of campus. Its informal name was the Hills, and even it looked empty this time on a Wednesday night.

FHU campus was shaped like a giant rectangle, with buildings making up the four exterior walls, and grassy, gentle, rolling greenery and gardens in the middle. Frosh orientation week was held on the Hills, along with other big outdoor events, but most of the time students sprawled across it when the weather was good, enjoying the much-needed green space amidst the oppressive gothic architecture that made up most of Farrow's Hollow.

She glanced at the narrow windows of all the buildings around her, momentarily searching for the source of that *feeling*. It followed her even after she gave up and headed for the bike rack, the hairs on the back of her neck standing upright. The pumping adrenaline made her a bit uncoordinated as she dug her keys out of her bag, searching for the one to open her bike lock, but when she turned her attention to her trusty bike, Moira realized it didn't matter that it had taken her a few seconds to fumble with her keys. She wouldn't be using her bike tonight anyway.

Because some asshole had stolen her seat.

Last September had been *the* month for bike seats to mysteriously disappear. The cold, snowy winter had put a dampener on that, and now apparently the culprit was right back at it. Jaw clenched to the point of pain, hands balled to fists, Moira stared down at the six other bikes also locked to the metal rack, all of them with their seats. Why hers and not theirs?

Sure, she lived on the outskirts of campus—it was a twenty-minute walk, fifteen given how fast she hoofed it at night, but it *could* have been an easy three-minute bike ride instead.

"Fuck!" Not knowing what else to take out her sudden blinding rage on, she kicked at her back wheel—and clamped a hand over her mouth when the entire thing bent in half. Spokes, metal, wheel—everything bent, like a folded piece of cardboard, and she hadn't even kicked it that hard.

It was moments like these that made her think she

wasn't, in fact, dying—that her physical transformation into this walking white corpse had to be something else entirely. She'd never been a weakling, but Moira had chosen choir over sports growing up. She was a *sprinter*, not a fighter. Cardio was her friend.

And now, apparently, she had enough strength to kick the back wheel of her bike in half.

Breathing shakily, she forced her hand to her side, turned, and power-walked out of the courtyard.

All the while ignoring the way those unseen eyes continued to follow her—straight to her front door.

~

"My, my, my..." Severus crouched before the warped bicycle wheel, his fingers ghosting across it. "Someone has a *temper*."

From his position in the shadows across the courtyard, he hadn't been able to see what had caused Moira's outburst. Now, however, he could deduce it was likely to do with the fact that her seat was missing. Not exactly conducive for comfortable cycling anymore, was it?

Not unless you wanted a bit of kink with your ride.

He cocked his head to the side, eyes roving the bent wheel. An ordinary human couldn't have done that. In a burst of anger, she'd folded metal and plastic like they were nothing. Each day that he watched her had steadily confirmed his suspicions that she wasn't entirely human, which, for Farrow's Hallow, wasn't out of the ordinary.

At the sound of students leaving the library, chatting animatedly as they went, he stood and started off down the path next to the social sciences building. He needn't have tracked Moira to know that she'd gone home, as she did every night, afternoon—anytime she wasn't in class or working, really. He grabbed the cigarette he'd tucked behind his ear earlier and stuck it between his lips, then fished out his silver lighter from the pocket of his black trench coat. Normally he wasn't one for dressing so *obviously* demonic, but he lacked the ability to warp the shadows to his liking as others did. So, he'd opted for all black on his nighttime prowls, and typical college garb when he followed Moira between lectures during the day.

A flicker of flame in the darkness. He held the fire to the end of his cigarette, breathing in the burning bitterness of the initial puff for a few moments before returning the lighter to his pocket. He really ought to let it go. He ought to let *her* go. Logically, Severus knew that. But he couldn't. Not after the way he had responded to her on Friday night —and especially not after she'd coaxed the demon to the surface, igniting the fires of his true self as no one ever had before.

He just needed to *know*, damn it.

"You're just annoyed because you didn't get her off," Alaric had teased over breakfast Saturday morning, bleary-eyed and grouchy after working the night shift at his father's bar downtown. Severus had ignored his roommate's blatant attempts at goading him into an argument, opting instead to continue with his digital stalking before commencing the physical.

It hadn't been difficult to locate Moira, a graduate student at the local university. Unfortunately for him, most of her social media channels were set to private, and she hadn't accepted the friend request he'd sent from his alter ego nice-guy profile, which he sometimes put to good use in this digital age.

She did, however, have a brief profile on the university's

art history department website. Moira Aurelia. Twenty-three, with a bachelor's degree in art and psychology. Her little biography professed an interest in pursuing a career in art therapy, and she supposedly planned to get her doctorate in social work after completing her master's in art history. Ambitious. Private. Social, to a degree, given the number of other pretty, albeit *loud*, women she lived with in that old Victorian on the edge of university limits.

None of that really mattered, of course. What mattered was her personhood—her *essence*. Why hadn't he been able to take anything from her? If she wasn't a demon, and he was about 99.9 percent certain she wasn't, then what on earth *was* she?

With tonight's surveillance complete, he lost himself in thought, mulling through all he'd read and seen of her. Her eyes were different in most of her photos—green, not that unearthly blue he'd been so taken with. Sometimes he still saw them when he closed his eyes, staring back, unblinking, burrowing straight to his core and picking him apart.

Distracted as he was, Severus trusted his feet to steer him right. Forty minutes later, he'd walked from the FHU campus to downtown, through the more family-oriented suburbs separating them and straight to Alaric's father's bar —The Inferno. Given it was owned by Verrier, a retired prince of hell, and located in a city on the cusp of an active hell-gate, the name wasn't exactly subtle.

Despite it being just before ten o'clock at night on a *Wednesday*, the line for the human side of the Inferno was already halfway down the block. Cigarette smoke pluming alongside him, Severus strolled by the row of humans standing about three deep between the wall of the enormous black-brick building and a thick velvet rope. A few of the women tried to catch his eye along the way, but he carried on with a grin, then took a sharp turn into the alley between the two-storey nightclub and Rose's Corner, the restaurant next door, both of which were owned by Alaric's father. He'd used a little more tact in naming the restaurant—after Alaric's human mother—than he had with the Inferno.

The bulk of the two-storey club catered to humans. Farrow's Hollow had a young, vibrant population, thanks in part to the thriving university campus. Although they didn't know it, humans felt a draw to the Inferno; there were lines out the door every night of the week, even in the winter. Demons always had a special pull with humanity. Their auras, their *beings*, were elusive and intriguing, and most demon business owners used that to their advantage. A human couldn't explain *why* they were drawn to demons of all kinds—they just were. Therefore, the Inferno's street-facing bar, rooftop patio, and second-floor dance club thrived in Farrow's Hollow, overflowing with young, adventurous humans enticed by its darkness.

The true heart of the Inferno, however, was strictly for demons and their guests. Off the street, halfway down the alley between the bar and restaurant, was a black steel door. No exterior handle. To a passerby, it looked like an emergency exit for the interior of the bar. Severus, and the entire demon population of Farrow's Hollow, knew better. With his fifth cigarette of the night hanging between his lips, he leaned against the brick and rapped his knuckles against the steel. Once, twice, three times in rapid succession, then once more. The code changed monthly. No code, no entry, demon or not.

He stepped back at the sound of clicking lock mechanisms, then slipped inside when the door popped open about two feet.

"Dartanious, always a pleasure," Severus said, flashing the doorman a smile. The seven-foot-tall demon ignored him, sliding all the locks back into place.

"Leeches should pay full price for what they drink," he growled when Severus finally turned away, intent on joining Alaric at the bar. He paused, jaw clenched, and glanced at the grey-haired giant. Generally not one for smiling in any capacity, Dartanious wore just a hint of a smirk. Sliding one hand into his coat pocket, Severus pursed his lips, flicked his cigarette butt at the demon's chest, then gave him a quick salute before sauntering into the bar.

Behind him, the doorman all but *snarled*, but he couldn't touch him. In fact, the Inferno was one of the few places Severus was untouchable, despite his lowly incubus status. As the best friend of Alaric Crowley, famed son of Hell's former prince Verrier, he had special privileges inside these four walls. Not that he ever pushed his luck more than necessary; all he needed to do was insult the wrong demon, stumble drunk into the alley, and find himself smeared across the concrete. It wasn't worth the risk, but he *did* enjoy pissing Dartanious off whenever he could, the prickly old bastard.

While the human side of the Inferno was likely wall-to-wall people by now, the inner sanctum offered more breathing room. Even so, the place was curiously busy for a Wednesday night. Just about every table across the main floor was full, succubus and witch waitresses expertly navigating the controlled chaos with full trays of every sort of alcoholic concoction available on Earth and below, and any empty booth along the walls to the left and right of him had a *reserved* placard on the table. As Severus made his way through, he spied Alaric waving him over to the back bar.

His friend usually worked the smaller of the two bars by himself, while a trio of pretty women managed the larger bar near the front door. The outer walls' exposed black brick flecked with red and gold carried on inside, paired with dark wood furniture throughout. Upstairs were Verrier's private rooms. Downstairs was the dance floor, along with additional sublevel chambers for more *salacious* activity.

Farrow's Hollow boasted an impressive bar scene, but the Inferno had long been one of Severus's favourites.

As he neared the back bar, he spied his usual seat at the end of the row empty, one of the black *reserved* signs resting on the padded leather barstool. He snatched it off and set it on the other side of the counter, then reached over and helped himself to the bottle of malt whiskey that Alaric always left out for him. Ignoring the miffed stares of the other demons seated at the counter, he treated himself to a healthy dose of the seventy-five-year vintage, filling the glass he'd also swiped from a row of clean ones, capped the bottle, then settled in for the night with a grin.

"Be with you in a minute, Sev," Alaric said, his coppery hair slicked back, wearing a white button-down with the sleeves rolled up to his elbows, a black apron, and a scowl for the demon sitting next to Severus. He spoke with the poshest of English accents, courtesy of a childhood in his mother's London high-society circles and an education at Eton, though it would be a mistake to think that had softened him any.

"Take your time," Severus insisted. The first sip of whiskey burned the whole way down, but it settled quite nicely, warming him from the inside out. "No hurry."

"Now look here, you dimwitted *fuck*," Alaric growled at the customer before him, arms crossed and scowl deepening. "Your card's been declined, so sort it out." When the perfectly round, alarmingly thick demon started to sputter back in protest, Alaric pointed a menacing finger at him. "Don't you deal with debts? Aren't you a fucking collector? Get it together and pay your bill."

Severus held back a chuckle, always a fan of his friend's crusty barman persona. The portly demon, so plump that it was a miracle the stool could even hold his body weight, didn't seem quite as enthused by the schtick. As soon as Alaric disappeared down the line to attend to the other patrons, Severus heard him grumble, "Fucking half-breed scum. Should've put him in the ground with his bitch human mother."

Protecting Alaric from the prejudices of the demon world came almost second nature to Severus at this point. Twelve years of unwavering friendship would do that to you.

So, glaring, he clamped a hand down on the back of the collector demon's bulbous head—then slammed it onto the bartop. The demon went down with a shriek; clearly he'd been so focused on staring daggers at Alaric that he hadn't seen Severus coming. His trio of shot glasses shattered into his face on impact. Severus got a full view of the gory aftermath when he dragged the demon back by the collar of his shirt, then, with some effort given his enormous size, wrenched him off the stool.

It was a wonder the whole building didn't quake when the creature landed in a heap at Severus's feet, dark red blood spilling down his puffy cheeks and bits of glass sticking out of his skin, eyes bloodshot.

"Why you—"

Severus was off his own stool in an instant, his movements practically *nimble* compared to the oaf on the floor, and as a hush descended over the rest of the bar, he planted a foot on the demon's chest.

"Don't you start," he growled. In his peripherals, he could already see Dartanious and his bouncer crew moving in. "Or would you like to repeat that little comment for everyone to hear? You know how Verrier *adores* when people reminisce about the greatest love of his life—and the son she bore him."

All the color drained from the demon's face, save for the blood still trickling down it. Hybrids may have been just as lowly as incubi and their ilk, but Alaric was the son of a prince of Hell. It didn't *matter* that Verrier had decided to spend his retirement on Earth, running a bar and a restaurant, his finger on the pulse of the city's various demon mob families—and their violent squabbles. Anyone with a lick of sense feared his wrath.

"Apologize to my friend," he ordered, gesturing to Alaric. The man needn't announce his presence for Severus to know he was there. He could feel him, hovering, brow furrowed and jaw clenched.

"Just leave it," his friend murmured, and Severus glanced back, surprised.

"Alaric—"

"Get him out of here," Alaric ordered, his voice stronger this time, firmer as he snapped down at the wounded demon. In an instant Dartanious and his boys swarmed, swathed in black leather and a cloud of malice. Once they had the stout demon upright, blood staining the white button-down that barely concealed his protruding midsection, he heard Alaric add, "You are henceforth banned from the Inferno. See that he never sets foot in here again."

Pleased, Severus settled back on his barstool as they

dragged the shrieking demon toward the door. A cluster of the witch waitresses followed, their eyes black and their hands pulsing red. Just before they tossed the guy out into the street, the witches pounced, and the demon's screams intensified. Everyone, Severus included, strained to get a better look, delighting in the torment, a few cheering when the bouncers and waitresses stepped back to reveal the ugly branding across that sweaty, bloody forehead. The mark would fade from sight in a day or two, but it would always be visible in the underworld—and it would bar the demon entrance to any of Verrier's establishments.

"You didn't have to do that," Alaric muttered. Severus smirked as Dartanious booted the demon out the main door.

"Why not? He deserved it for what he said about your mother, about *you*."

"Half the demons in this bar share his opinion," Alaric said as conversations resumed, the unobtrusive music tinkling from the overhead speakers getting a little louder once more. Severus downed his glass of whiskey in a single shot, then refilled it.

"Well, they've got the brains to keep their ridiculous opinions to themselves, I suppose." He'd do the same to anyone who bad-mouthed Alaric, whether they were an easy target or not. While he lacked physical strength, given his was dependent on how often he stole from humans, Severus always had the element of surprise on his side. No one ever thought to keep an eye on the leech.

"Lucky Father wasn't here. He detests brawling in his bar."

"Unless it's for a worthy cause," Severus countered, then raised his glass and toasted Alaric. "Cheers, mate."

"Yeah, yeah. Cheers." Alaric grabbed the bottle before Severus had a chance to cap it, taking a quick swig and setting it down heavily. "Now, try not to make any of the other customers bleed. We're swamped tonight."

Severus held up his hands innocently. "I'm just here to drink."

"Only because Moira's gone home, right?"

His eyes narrowed when Alaric shot a knowing grin over his shoulder. In no mood to argue about her again, Severus contented himself with his drink, and for the next hour watched in a contemplative silence as his friend served patrons and managed the bar. Although the crowd swelled around midnight, most demons preferred the trio of gorgeous ladies manning the main bar to Alaric. Severus couldn't blame them—one was wearing nothing but nipple pasties and a barely-there miniskirt—and he was pleased that after twelve he could finally have his friend to himself for a bit.

"So, how was your hunt tonight?" Alaric asked as he poured himself another glass of whiskey and clinked it against Severus's. "Any news to report?"

"She's strong. Bent her bike wheel in half when she kicked it."

"But you knew that already."

He nodded. She'd been able to shove him away more than once the first night they met. It was as if she didn't know her own strength, which struck him as odd.

"I still think you're just bitter," Alaric mused after a sip of whiskey, face momentarily puckered before he set his glass aside. "You couldn't get her off, and it's a blow to your escort ego. Makes perfect sense to me."

"You weren't there. You don't know what she..." Severus huffed, glaring at the bartop. "It's not that."

When it came to his job, Severus didn't really *have* an ego. As an incubus, he cared very deeply about his sexual prowess, as it was a part of him—ingrained in his spirit. However, human women were easy to charm, even easier to make come. It wasn't about ego—it was about using the skills he was born with, skills that he had all but mastered by now.

"Then what is it? Why are you so obsessive?"

"I'm not *obsessive.*"

"You haven't seen a client in days because you've been following *her,*" Alaric said, sounding rather pleased with himself. "You know it's true. You're becoming obsessed. It isn't healthy."

"She made me..." He exhaled sharply, then downed the rest of his whiskey. Rather than going for a ninth refill, he flipped the glass upside down and nudged it aside. "She could influence me, whether she was aware of it or not. I'm curious. I'd also like to know *what* she is, and I suspect you would too if someone could control your inner demon."

Alaric snorted. "If I've got an inner demon, the bastard isn't exactly one for making himself known. I doubt even a pretty girl could change that."

"Either way, I can't read her energy and I don't like it. I need to know." While Alaric's father had infinite connections in the demon underbelly of Farrow's Hollow, Severus wasn't quite so fortunate. No one would be willing to help an incubus—not for free, anyway. He had more than enough money to pay for intel, but it was the *principle* of the matter; Severus had no intention of giving any thieving, overcharging demons a *penny*. This was a mystery he could solve on his own; it would just take time.

"Maybe she's a hybrid," Alaric offered before shooting back the rest of his drink. He shuddered, his tolerance for large quantities of straight alcohol pathetically low for working at a bar, and Severus ignored the temptation to poke fun at him—just this once.

"I couldn't get a whiff of demon off her—"

"But you always say you can't really read my energy either," his friend said with a shrug, fussing about behind the bar. "What is it you once told me? I'm like a, er, *void* of nothingness?"

Severus bit back a smile. Demons, angels, witches, vampires, shifters, elves, fae—they all gave off a certain vibration specific to their species. Humans gave next to no vibration, no pulse of supernatural energy surrounding them. Hybrids tended to be the same.

Hmm. He'd discounted the theory back at the hotel because he couldn't sense a demon side to her, but perhaps *that* had been his error.

"Perhaps she *is* a hybrid."

"You could always ask her," Alaric mused, his gaze drifting down the bar as a few new arrivals took their seats. "Or just carry on with your little game of admiring from afar."

"I'm not *admiring*."

"Right. Of course not. This is all very clinical. Scientific, even." He strolled away with a dramatic nod and a thumbs-up, leaving an annoyed Severus behind to see to the new drink orders.

Rather than sitting there to stew about it, Severus slid off the stool, then dug a fifty out of his wallet and set it behind the bar. Although he would never tip his roommate, as per Alaric's request, he knew all the staff pooled and split tips at the end of the night. Since he didn't, in fact, pay for all the booze he drank at the Inferno, he usually left something behind. Considering the trouble he'd caused, despite defending Alaric's honour, he added a second fifty to the first. He caught Alaric's eye briefly, pointing down to the cash, and then drifted into the crowd. Despite the place being jam-packed with demons, not a single one was worth his conversational prowess—nor would any stoop so low as to engage in conversation with an incubus, anyway.

So, he sent Alaric a text that he was headed for home, and slipped out the main door. This time, Dartanious had nothing to say, and he wondered if he'd earned himself a modicum of respect by knocking that demon flat on his ass.

Out in the breezy night air, just as he paused to light another cigarette, a sob washed over him. He lifted his gaze curiously. Down the alley, by the edge of the sidewalk, stood Diriel, a demon of no real significance in Hell who had somehow built a reputation for himself in Farrow's Hollow. The woman cowering before him, distinctly human, appeared more than a little drunk, needing his support to stand upright. Sensing an opportunity, Severus strolled toward them, tucking the unlit cigarette behind his ear and feigning concern.

"Miss, are you all right?"

"Fuck off, leech—"

"I wasn't speaking to *you*, Diriel," he crooned, swooping in on the redheaded woman, her teal dress hiked up to the tops of her thighs, her ankles wobbling in her high heels. "You seem distressed."

Diriel puffed his chest out, the dozens of silver chains with pearl-laden crosses hanging from his neck rustling about over his Armani suit. "She's *fine*. Fuck. Off."

"I just want to go home," the woman wailed, and it was then that Severus noticed how deeply Diriel's nails dug into the soft flesh of her arm. He tsked, shooting the demon a chastising look.

"Verrier prefers you keep your human drama inside the bar, Diriel."

The raven-haired demon scowled, the whites of his eyes overtaken by black. "If I have to tell you one more time—"

"Fortunately for you, I'm here to ensure no one tells him you were harassing a human on his property, in public," he said, smiling as he grasped Diriel's thin, bony wrist and wrenched his hand off the woman. "You ought to *thank* me."

Before the demon could get another word in, threat or otherwise, Severus steered the wobbly woman to the sidewalk. With a huge line still waiting to get into the human side of the Inferno to the right and patrons leaving Rose's Corner to the left, Diriel had no choice but to remain in the shadows of the alley, fuming.

The handling of humans varied from demon to demon. Most saw them as a lesser species and treated them as such. Severus preferred *using* them to having any sort of opinion about them, though he had many regular clients he genuinely enjoyed spending time with. While the former prince of Hell appeared neutral toward humanity, Verrier's dislike for drama of any kind on his property was notorious. No brawls. No squabbling. No murder. *Especially* where humans could see. Keep it civil. Take it somewhere else.

"Now, let's put you in a taxi, shall we?" Severus touched as much as of the woman's skin as he could. Alaric had been right: he'd been so wrapped up in Moira these last few days that he hadn't even bothered scheduling any clients, and he could certainly use a boost. His hands rubbed up and down her arms under the guise of warming her. His thumb brushed away her tears, as if to comfort her. And he held onto her hand and elbow when he lowered her into a cab, smiling kindly at her garbled thanks.

After slamming the door shut, he stepped back onto the sidewalk, hands in his pockets, suddenly a bit buzzed himself. That was always the way with drunk humans.

Poor thing was in for a hell of a hangover tomorrow. Grinning, he retrieved the cigarette from behind his ear and lit it. A quick glance over his shoulder told him Diriel had fucked off—likely back inside the bar to find a new victim for the night. As renowned as Verrier was for his policies on public order and demon civility, Diriel had an equally well-known reputation for carnage and torture. Not that most demons *didn't*, but if the rumors were true, Diriel could win awards for his creativity, and he had a penchant for pretty, young humans. Women, mostly, but Severus had heard the demon became less picky as the evening dragged on.

Still, the fact that he'd made the night just a touch more annoying for a prick like Diriel—well, that just made him warm and fuzzy all over. Smirking, Severus took a long drag from his cigarette, then headed for his and Alaric's home up the street, humming as he went.

CHAPTER FOUR

As Moira glanced at the heavily tinted exterior of the natural science building, the only piece of non-gothic architecture on campus, she was certain she could finally put a name to the face.

Russ Tanner—dreamy escort and stalker extraordinaire —had been following her, on and off, for the last week. She was sure of it. Although she had never seen his face straight on, she had caught enough glimpses by now to finally make a positive identification.

After all, he had an impossible face to forget. Those shadowy eyes and kissable lips, that royal nose and gritty facial hair. Cheekbones models lusted after. He'd towered over her on that night, and the man she had pinned as Russ was pretty tall too. Well-built. The kind of man who made her stomach lurch and her heart race—and her sex tingle with interest.

He wore some variation of hat during the day, and always kept his distance, but she was *sure* of it. As she stared at him in the reflection of the nat-sci building's dark grey windows, Moira was *certain*. Dressed in a pair of fitted light-wash jeans, a faded purple tee, a grey hoodie, unzipped, and a red hat, he had been following her between classes this morning. Not only that, but he had sat in on her thirty-person Issues in Postcolonial Gendered Art seminar; not exactly subtle, given he had never attended a session before and half the class had been absent anyway—which also wasn't surprising, given the grad club hosted booze-filled ragers every Thursday night, and this was an eight AM seminar on a Friday morning.

From there, he had been a permanent fixture in her usual routine, always in the corner of her eye, always following, tracking, *prowling* at a safe distance. She couldn't imagine why; in her hurry to get the hell out of that eerily quiet hotel room, she'd left the money behind. As if she'd had the nerve to stand there and argue—or ask for change, given he hadn't met the requirements she'd set out before their appointment. That night had been intense—more so than she'd expected—but it had eventually dissolved into a puddle of suck, just like all her sexual encounters had in the past, when she got too deep inside her own head.

It couldn't have been the first time a client left unsatisfied. Sex was personal. Intimate. Unique to the individual. He might have been stunning, but there was no way Russ could please everyone. It just wasn't possible.

So, why the *fuck* was he following her?

She lingered in front of the reflective building, ignoring the throng of first-year science kids chattering noisily as they swarmed around her and up the steps, then pretended to check her phone. Moira stood there as innocently as possible, tapping at the screen—all the while studying his lurking figure under her heavily mascara'd eyelashes. As soon as she'd stopped strolling around the FHU campus, so had he, and she rolled her eyes when he too dug out his phone, mirroring her almost exactly.

"Fucker," she muttered, then tucked her phone inside her bag and took off toward the Hills. Sure enough, a casual glance over her shoulder confirmed that he had resumed tracking her. Sometimes she lost him in the crowd; noon at FHU meant most classes had paused for lunch. The food court was about to get swamped. Given the warm*ish* spring weather and relatively dry week Farrow's Hollow had experienced, most would be taking their midday meal on the grass or at a picnic bench within the university's very own Central Park.

She wasn't under the impression she could lose him. That sensation of being closely watched had plagued her since last week, and now that she'd identified the source, Moira had a feeling Russ wasn't someone you could shake. More likely—he needed to be confronted. She couldn't go to the police because that would shed light on their shady beginnings, but as Moira darted down the three steps separating the Hills from concrete and glass buildings behind her, she assumed he wouldn't want much attention brought on him either.

Maybe it was time to use that to her advantage.

When she was sure he had followed her onto the main pathway of the Hills, the wide-set unpaved one that branched off in every direction, Moira picked up the pace and power-walked along one of the offshoots, leading him into a more heavily treed area. Another quick glance over her shoulder, and, yup, there he was—prowling. Given the crowd had thinned and most people were sitting on the grass, he was obvious as sin behind her. Couldn't he see that?

Moira put him to the test, taking less traveled paths,

darting across the lawn and around trees. At one point she thought she'd lost him, but then he'd turned up in her peripherals again. Finally, she slowed to a near stop, then whirled around. About fifteen feet stood between the pair, and Russ turned sharply under the guise of tying his shoe, foot propped up on a bench.

Right. No one was buying *that*. Biting the insides of her cheeks, Moira grabbed her phone again.

"Ella!" she cried. "Oh my god, girl, how is your day going?"

She pretended to listen, nothing but dead air greeting her, and then laughed as she started a slow march down the path away from him. This time, Russ followed almost right away, as if giving up on the whole lurking-at-a-distance thing. Her heartbeat quickened the nearer he drew, his pace unrelenting, his footsteps growing louder. When she peeked over her shoulder, smiling but not talking, phone pressed to her ear, he looked like he meant to brush by her and keep going, his dark gaze lifted to something in the distance.

No. This ends now.

Moira waited, her entire body tense, until he was in the exact right position...

Her fist slammed into his gut as soon as he was *right* beside her, their bodies too close for comfort, and she leapt back when he exhaled noisily and collapsed to his knees.

"Stop following me!" she shrieked, her voice carrying through the trees around them, and then shoved his shoulders as hard as she could. He went down fast, catching himself in the nick of time so he didn't faceplant. Instead, he rolled himself onto his back, baseball cap tilted and face exposed. Russ Tanner. In the flesh. Staring up at her with that dusky, unflinching stare, his brow furrowed.

Moira stared right back, refusing to be bullied by that look, her hands clenched to tight fists. A hurricane of *feeling* roiled about inside her. Revulsion, her suspicions now confirmed. Betrayal, that this man who had appeared so professional had decided to stalk her. Humiliation, blended with desire, at the memory of what had happened that night.

And curiosity. That was the one that surprised her the most. Intrigue. A strange, unwelcome sense of *attraction*. Interest in *him*, in what went on behind his onyx stare.

She could feel that familiar, unwelcome blush charging across her skin, and she tugged at her wool cap—fern-green today, to match her leggings—like that would hide it.

Moira knew her strength had been growing—changing, intensifying. She'd broken more things lately than just her bike wheel, but Russ appeared unfazed by the attack. Surprised, yes. Startled, maybe a little. But as he stared up at her, she saw the same curiosity she felt deep within herself, the same unsettling sense of intrigue that made her stay fixed where she was—rather than running like she should have.

"What *are* you?" he asked. Murmured so low, so softly, it seemed more a question for him than Moira. When he sat up on his elbows, his eyebrows lifted slightly, those sensual lips quirked. "You're not human. Not entirely, anyway."

She blinked, a flash of cold unease taking root. "W-what did you just say?"

Moira had wondered it herself sometimes, usually as she stared in the mirror after a shower, hating what she had become. Hating the changes. Hating that she didn't see herself staring back anymore. Was she dying—or was this just a new stage of living?

Her mom had warned her before she'd died that

twenty-two would be a banner year in her life, that nothing would be the same. At the time, Moira had chalked the premonitions and warnings up to the insane dosage of painkillers the hospital had her on. People say the craziest things when they're high as a kite.

Yet her words rang true. Moira wasn't the same, not even close, and it had all started after her twenty-second birthday. Glaring at her reflection, she thought herself reptilian, artificial, corpse-like—inhuman.

And now someone else had said it, aloud, for all the world to hear.

Russ drew a breath, as if to speak again, but the booming footsteps of a newcomer had his lips pressed right back together, his intense curiosity shifting to exasperation.

"Hey, are you okay?" Moira looked the new arrival over: tall, blond, athletic build, already wearing shorts despite the fact it was still sweater weather. Behind him, a group of wide-eyed undergrads looked on. His words, however, were muffled by the combination of a high-pitched whining and what felt like thick, unyielding cotton between her ears. The hand he placed on her shoulder—Moira hardly felt it, his touch nothing more than a ghostly caress. Just like all physical contact in her life lately—all except for Russ.

"I—"

"Is this guy bothering you?" he asked again, jabbing a finger at Russ as he stood. "Do I need to call campus security?"

"What?" She shook her head, forcing herself to tuck the shock, the *fear*, over what Russ had just said away for later. The brain fog dissipated, the world suddenly too loud. She fidgeted with her cap. "Him? No, no. I'm fine."

"Are you sure?"

"She said she was *fine*," Russ growled, his voice

sharpening from the velvety purr she had become accustomed to, his glare positively withering. Her white knight rounded on the spot to face at him, but suddenly the color drained from his cheeks, and he shuffled back to his friends without another word.

"Thanks anyway," Moira called after him, but he didn't look back. Odd. Russ, meanwhile, looked as though the interruption hadn't even happened, dusting himself off as his gaze swept up and down her body. She crossed her arms, scowling. Hadn't he gotten a good enough look spying on her from across the courtyard all week?

Or, you know, when he'd fucked her, almost fully clothed while she wore nothing at all?

Moira bit her lower lip, cheeks colouring at the thought —and darkening further when he grinned somewhat smugly down at her.

"What did you mean when you said I wasn't...human?" she demanded, lowering her voice and stepping closer—mostly to show he didn't affect her, that his roguish good looks and penetrating stare did nothing to rattle her. However, just as she'd felt that first night, Moira found herself inexplicably *eager* to be close to him, too. It had frightened her then, and it should have frightened her now.

"I think you know exactly what I meant," Russ told her. He waited for a moment, lips still twisted in that sinful smirk, until the silence dragged on long enough to make her shift about uncomfortably. With a soft clearing of his throat, he slid his hands into his pockets, then leaned closer. "Don't you?"

"*Obviously* not," she hissed back, her stomach looping and her head thick with fog again. "I don't understand *any* of this, but clearly you seem to have some inkling of—"

"Can we speak somewhere less public?" he asked,

scanning the area and once again towering over her. "Somewhere with fewer idiots watching."

While there weren't many lunching students around, the few that were, seated under shady trees or on top of picnic tables, feet on the benches, openly stared like she and Russ were performing an impromptu skit. Flustered, Moira readjusted her cap again, tugging it down as far as it would go, and shook her head.

"I don't—"

"I know you know I've been following you," he stated, far too frank for her liking, "and you've no reason to trust me. But I know you aren't...all that you appear. After the other night, I'd like to talk."

The last thing Moira knew she should do was take him somewhere private to "talk," but for the first time in a long time, alarm bells weren't shrieking inside her head. Sure, her stomach continued to loop over and over itself, and her sweaty palms had to mean something, and the head fog, and the way little tendrils of pleasure licked up her body the longer they held eye contact...

She ought to run.

But she didn't.

"Fine, we can talk somewhere," she agreed, then cleared her throat and hardened her tone. "But if you touch me, I will *literally* put you through a wall."

"Oh, little Moira..." Russ smiled his most dangerous smile yet. "I bet you will."

CHAPTER FIVE

Severus hadn't been in a college girl's room since the seventies. Back then, everything had stunk of drugs and sex, and no one locked their doors. As he stood in the middle of Moira's bedroom, surrounded by purple and photos, he realized the times had changed.

Or, at the very least, Moira wasn't as much fun as the college girls he used to know.

In the old Victorian home, he could hear just about every step she made. Her long but quick strides echoed as she checked each of her roommates' doors downstairs, just to ensure no one was home—no one could overhear. They wouldn't be home, of course. Severus knew most of their schedules by now, all five of them. He had been a keen observer of the house for over a week now. He knew where the paint chipped, which boards on the porch squeaked, and that the drain pipe needed a good cleaning.

While he didn't know *all* the female inhabitants, he'd been able to match names to Ella and Simone. The other roommates eluded him—frequent partiers, if their drunken antics five of the last seven nights suggested anything.

Moira, meanwhile, had been home and sequestered in her room by 10 PM most evenings, unless she was watching television with Ella—which he had been able to see perfectly from his shadowy hiding spot between their house and the noisy bungalow beside it. Four men lived there who seemed to think every day was garbage day, given the mountain of bags at the end of their driveway, the grass overgrown and one window covered with a wooden board, lines of empty liquor bottles on the ledges of the others.

Ahh, college.

Hands in his pockets, Severus took these few moments of solitude to study her room. They hadn't said more than five words to each other on the walk back to Moira's house from campus. It had surprised him, at first, that she would bring him here. However, her threat about putting him through a wall, literally, sprang to mind as they climbed the porch steps together and Moira jammed her key into a fussy lock. She had confidence in her strength—something he hadn't suspected, given her reaction to damaging her bike wheel the other night. Still, she had let her guard down and invited the monster inside, thinking her physicality could overpower his.

Unlikely, but should the conversation be civil enough, Severus hoped he wouldn't need to show her the error of her ways. After all, he had meant what he said: he wanted to talk. He had let her catch him following her these last three days, making himself more and more obvious until she finally snapped. Moira, with her unearthly blue eyes and svelte little figure, thought she had the upper hand. She thought *she* had initiated contact. Yet if he looked hard enough, he'd find strings on her wrists and ankles, ever his little puppet.

Severus smirked at the thought, his gaze drifting along

her haphazardly made bed. She could think her strength intimidated him. If it opened her up, if it beguiled her into divulging her secrets, let her think whatever she wanted.

Purple pillowcases. Purple sheets. Purple bedspread. All varying shades, but a sickening amount. The blinds over the one window overlooking the two-storey colonial next door were in serious need of a dusting. Her desk was cluttered, her garbage can full of empty printer ink cartridges and hair dye boxes. While she appeared quite social in all the photos pinned to the tackboard over her desk, a few patterned around her bedside table, she looked *different*. Not so different that he couldn't tell it was her; the basic building blocks remained, but much of the rest had changed. Slimmer, gaunter, leaner, her high cheekbones apparent now. Her eyes. Her hair. The hue of her skin—all different.

Severus squinted, plucking one photo of her and Ella off the wall. Ella looked nearly the same, so it must have been recent. Arms locked around each other, lips peeled back in laughter, they looked ordinary enough—*human* ordinary at that. Half-finished pints of beer sat in front of them. Only Moira's hair was brown—a deep, lush chestnut. Nothing like her hair the other night, clearly the product of one of the many dye boxes in her trash can. And certainly not like the whites of her eyebrows now, a shade he assumed carried up to the rest of her head.

Strange. He tossed the picture onto her messy desk, then busied himself with a bit of snooping at the sound of her still marching about downstairs. Closet only half full of clothing, a handful of dresses hanging neatly while boxes filled the rest of the space. The four-drawer dresser caught his attention next. On a whim, he opened the second drawer—and found a treasure trove of panties. All kinds, too. Silk. Cotton. Thongs. Bikini-cut. Every colour of the rainbow...

His eyebrows shot up when he plucked a lacey red one from the pile. "Crotchless? Moira, Moira, *Moira*—"

"What are you *doing*?"

He whirled around, the undergarment still hanging off his index finger, and grinned at her scandalized expression, her hands clutching the door and frame so tight her knuckles had gone white.

Well. Whit*er*.

"Where were *these* the other night?" he drawled, holding them out to her when she stomped into the room. Red-faced, jaw noticeably clenched, Moira snatched them off his finger, a whiff of her floral scent wafting over him as she shouldered her way to the dresser and shoved the bit of cloth back in its drawer. After she slammed it shut, she glared up at him.

"We're not here to talk about my underwear."

"I'm game if you are," he mused. Elbow propped up on the dresser, his grin widened at her bristly exhale. "My afternoon is *wide* open."

"No thank you," she muttered, stalking across the small rectangular room and closing the door. She stood there for a moment, clutching the doorknob, the silence thickening around them, until the leering sort of smile Severus had produced fell away too.

Then, with practiced caution, her hand edged up, up, up to her wool cap—a garment far too warm for the time of year—and gripped it. Lower lip caught between her teeth, she finally tugged it off. White, staticky hair fell free, tumbling down her back, stick-straight as he remembered and nothing like her photos. Shyly, Moira smoothed her hand over it, catching the flyaways, and then gripped the cap tight in front of her.

His gaze swept over her quickly, astutely, and while Severus found her shyness oddly endearing and the white hair strangely suited to her pallor, it was the inner demon that roared to life at the sight. A tremor rippled through his right hand, and his heart thundered against its constraints. Even his cock stirred, and in that moment, all he, the demon within, wanted to do was march across the room, slam her up against that flimsy door, and mark her with his teeth as she screamed—in agony, in pleasure, it didn't matter.

And that pissed him off. Royally.

Who's the puppet now?

He strode toward her, only to force himself to stop and ignore the need pounding through his veins. Instead, he grabbed the picture he'd tossed aside earlier and held it between them.

"What happened to you?"

"I don't know," she told him, all the earlier fight and indignation gone. Her cheek twitched as she reached for the photo, and Severus closed the distance between them with an additional step. Carefully, she took it, studying it with a furrowed brow, then pressed it to her chest. "Something no one can explain. No doctors, no specialists."

He snorted. Of course the medical community had no say in the matter; the change was likely supernatural in nature. Her face blanched, seeming startled by his reaction.

"Before my mom died, she told me that once I turned twenty-two, everything would change," Moira offered, both arms dropping to her side. "I thought maybe she meant... personally. Emotionally. Professionally. I don't know. She didn't elaborate, but she was also on a *lot* of painkillers. She kept talking about onions too. Like. All the time. I chalked all the twenty-two stuff up mostly to, uh, her being high."

"But you now suspect she meant," Severus gestured to her body, his gaze fixed on her stark white hair, "*this*."

"Maybe." Closing her eyes, she took a deep breath, then slowly let it out. When she was through, Moira tossed the cap and the photo on her desk, then skirted around him to the closet. He watched, curious, as her reaching fingers went for the box on the top shelf, highest of the lot. Curiosity sparked to desire when her shirt lifted to reveal a patch of creamy white skin along her lower back. No blemishes. No marks. His eyes dropped lower to her firm little ass, cupped in thick green leggings that matched her cap.

Annoyed, Severus rolled his shoulders back and bit the insides of his cheeks. This was getting ridiculous. He was a fucking *sex* demon. A flash of skin and a cute figure shouldn't be so distracting.

When she finally had the box she needed, grappling with it a bit as she brought it down, Moira shuffled over to her bed and perched on the end of it.

"After I turned twenty-two, things started to happen. Freckles disappearing. The weight loss. Last summer all my hair fell out." She looked up at him, cheeks pink. "*All* of it. Everywhere. And then it grew back like this."

All of her hair, eh? His eyes dropped down to her thighs, trying to recall if the hair down there matched that on her head. Hmm. If he remembered correctly, there hadn't *been* any hair down there, but much of their physical encounter seemed fuzzy in his memory—like he'd been drunk off her, off the scent of her skin and the sound of her cries.

"My eyes changed—"

"They are rather startling," he said, hands clasped behind his back as he frowned. "How did you explain it?"

She shrugged. "I said I'd always worn contacts. Now I just wore colored ones."

His lips thinned; what sort of idiots did she spend her time with? "And they *believed* you?"

"Some. Most, but not all."

"Not, er," Severus reached back for the photo again, holding it up and tapping at the woman he guessed was her closest friend, "*her*, eh? You two seem especially close... You and Ella."

"Exactly how long have you been following me?" she snapped, setting the box aside, her tone sharp.

"Since Sunday."

"*Why?*"

"Because you're a curiosity," he told her, sharpening the edge of his tone to match. "Continue your story."

"But—"

"That *is* what we've come here to discuss, after all. My prowling around the outskirts of your life this past week is insignificant by comparison."

Moira glowered up at him, unflinching the longer their staring contested waged, until she finally turned and lifted the lid off her box. "Fine. We'll put a pin in it. Don't forget that I can still *literally—*"

"Yes, yes, put me through a wall," he said with a dismissive wave. "I remember."

Any rational individual would demand to know more about his stalking habits—he couldn't fault her for that—but Severus was just more interested in her story. She ought to be too. Big-picture thinking, hers was the one that mattered.

Alaric's suggestion that she could be a hybrid was starting to ring truer and truer. Not all hybrids expressed both parts of themselves. Alaric was more human than demon, despite being lucky enough to have a former prince of Hell for a father. He had always been assured that the dark depths hiding within would surface, but it wasn't an exact science. Perhaps for Moira, her other side was finally making itself known.

But why now? Why had her mother cautioned her about her twenty-second birthday?

"My mom was kind of out of it toward the end," Moira admitted softly, staring into the box, the lid on her lap. "I didn't take half the stuff coming out of her mouth seriously, but she said my dad would be able to explain it all. He'd have answers, the kind she hadn't found yet."

"Have you ever met your father?" Very likely, if the hybrid theory was true, *he* was the supernatural one of the two.

"No. She never talked about him either. Not until the end." Moira leaned over, rooting through the stacks of papers, envelopes and frames inside. When she straightened, she had an off-white business card in hand, its embossed lettering gold. "No matter how much I pried growing up, she never said a word about him...until she handed me this the day before she died. Apparently, he works here. Which," she laughed weakly as she offered the card to him, "makes me sick to think about. I've walked by that building a thousand times. It's near the movie theater Ella and I worked at when we were in high school."

She prattled on about it, but Severus was only half listening. He plucked the card from her hand—and once he caught sight of the name emblazoned across it, he stopped listening entirely.

Seraphim Securities. The gold letters stared up at him mockingly, and he nearly dropped the thick, unbendable card at the first prickle of fear. Moira trailed off, slowly searching out his gaze when he stared down at her—looking, but only truly *seeing* for the first time.

The white hair. The colourless features. Those *eyes*.

How could he have been so stupid?

"What?" she asked, standing, and Severus took two large steps back with a shake of his head.

"Don't—"

"You asked me what I was," she said, as if finally finding her voice in the face of his fear. "You said I wasn't human. You said things I've only ever dared *think* this last year, too afraid to say out loud. You *know* something."

As she went back to the box, he tossed the business card onto her bed. His inner demon should have recoiled at the very idea of her—yet there it was, still prowling about within Severus's chest, still desperate to push her over the side of her bed and *fuck* her into sweet oblivion.

The saner part of him insisted he get the hell out of the house—immediately—and Severus was inclined to agree.

"There's no information online about the employees who work there, but last summer I tried taking pictures of all the people who come and go," Moira told him, hurriedly darting in front of him when he attempted to stalk toward the door. She thrust a series of polaroids at him, her cheeks flushed and her eyes bright. "I thought it was an issue with my phone, so I did it the old-fashioned way. Every single time I tried, the faces were obscured."

He clenched his jaw, stiffly accepting the photographs. Sure enough, a brilliant circle of fiery light engulfed the face of every suited figure, no matter how close, no matter the natural lighting. In action. Standing still. She'd never get a good picture. Never.

"It's because you can't photograph angels," he said

simply, handing the photos back. Only she didn't take them. Moira stood before him, her chest noticeably rising and falling now, and slowly looked down at the polaroids.

"W-what?"

"I know you heard me." He went for the door, but she continued to block him, backing herself up against it, a vise-grip on the doorknob.

"What do you mean...angels?"

"I mean precisely what I said," Severus remarked. "I mean, *angels*. Warrior angels, to be exact. Servants of *the* archangels. None of us exactly know their caste, but those men," he tapped a finger on the stack of photos, then shoved them into her free hand, "are not to be trifled with."

Seraphim Securities. It was about as subtle a name as the Inferno. Vicious creatures charged with protecting the cities, towns, villages, *whatever* located on the cusps of hell-gates, the angels employed at every branch were a nightmare to the demon community. While demon mob families might run the dirty underbelly of Farrow's Hollow, the fuckers at Seraphim Securities were there to ensure that the darkness didn't seep into the light—that the precious humans going about their days, oblivious, remained unharmed.

Though, from what Severus had heard, the boys at this particular branch weren't opposed to making examples of humans who dared cross the proverbial line either.

He frowned at Moira, at her heaving chest and her watery eyes and her pouty lower lip, begging for him to sink his teeth into it. If she wasn't careful, this infuriating creature was going to get herself killed.

"Move."

"What? No." She buckled down, throwing her very likely newfound strength around as if that would intimidate him. After a bit of awkward scuffling at the door, with Severus trying to slip around her and Moira throwing herself in his path, he finally grabbed her arm and shoved her aside. She shoved right back, her cheeks bright red.

After stumbling a few paces, he grasped her outstretched forearms with a snarl and *pushed.* Her back and shoulders slammed into the door first, followed by her head, and Severus let out a long, annoyed sigh as she sank to the floor with a whimper.

"Get out of the way," he ordered thickly, the demon raring to go—thinking their physicality some sort of twisted, lovely foreplay. Severus, meanwhile, kept his tone as polite as possible, glaring down at her. "Now."

"*No.*"

"I have my answers," he told her. "Now, move out of the—"

"*No!*" The window rattled and her eyes flashed, each wide, round orb glistening with unshed tears. There it was —that electric blue. He'd thought it ethereal at first, not paying much attention to the adjective. But that was what it was, that color. Ethereal—like her father's, no doubt.

"Moira, I really don't—"

"I..." She opened and closed her mouth, fat, heavy tears finally falling when she blinked. "I thought I was dying."

"Just the opposite, I suspect." With another sigh, he dragged her upright, clutching at her slim, delicate forearms again. Delicate. *Ha.* There was nothing delicate about her. "You're changing, Moira. Your other side is coming out. It happens. It's frightening, I imagine, if you don't know it's happening, but now it's happened. So. There you are."

"But I don't understand—"

"Look," he growled, plopping her down at the end of her bed and ignoring the way her cheeks warmed when she glanced up at him, "your mother was just an ordinary human, right? Nothing strange or special about her?"

"She was a nurse. She dedicated her life to helping—"

"All right, all right, save the indignation." Severus rolled his eyes—and only then realized he was still holding her. He retreated quickly, no more than a few steps, and she stood to follow, looking a little unstable on her own two feet. A part of him yearned to reach out and touch her again. Nudge back the sleeves of her white long-sleeved shirt and caress her skin. Instead, he said, "I meant she was nothing supernatural. Just...human."

"As far as I knew, yes, but—"

"If what she says is true, and your father is a member of Seraphim Securities, then he's very likely an angel. A poorly behaved angel, sure, but an angel all the same." He nodded to her hair, his dark stare roving her body. "You've got the characteristics. Not all of them are quite as pale, but the white hair. The eyes... You might lose that pigmentation too. I've only ever seen one up close, but his were nearly grey, verging on white. Something to look forward to, I suppose."

"You... You've met an angel?" She still sounded like she didn't completely believe him—but that wasn't Severus's problem. As far as he was concerned, he had done his civic duty in enlightening her, broadening her once-small mind without fucking her in the process.

Not a bad day's work—for a demon.

"Yes, I saw one. Once." He wouldn't exactly classify the encounter as a meeting—more of a stare-down from afar as the creature took out an ill-behaved demon. Severus, thinking he was about to die too, jostled himself out of his stupor and ran for his life. You didn't fuck with angels. Demons called them nancy boys and do-gooders and every other name under the sun, but when it came down to it, you just didn't fuck with them. Not unless you had powerful friends to help you with the fallout.

And Severus didn't really have any powerful friends.

In fact, he didn't have *friends*, period. *Friend*, singular—Alaric, whose father had washed his hands clean of angelic affairs after he fell from Heaven.

"Can you... Can you help me find him?"

He lifted his brow at her. "What makes you think he wants to be found?"

She stood there, silent and still, nothing but a lost child braving the storm as her whole world fell to pieces. He ought to delight in her turmoil, her devastation, but Severus found he wanted to draw her in and press her cheek to his chest, over his pounding heart, and nuzzle his nose in her hair.

He had to get out of here.

"You just seem to know so much," she murmured. "I don't know if he... I don't know *anything*. And you do. Please, can you—"

"No," he said, hoping he sounded more resolute than he felt. When she started to sway, threatening to pitch forward, he braced her by the shoulders, then walked her back and sat her on the edge of the bed again. Those wide, imploring eyes peered up at him, lips slightly parted. Inhaling shakily, Severus found himself trailing his thumb along the seam, plucking at the lower one just enough to make him hard.

Get. Out. *Now*.

He moved for the door with a shake of his head. The knob came off in his hand when he wrenched it open, and he held it up for her to see, then set it on her messy desk. He hadn't meant to break it—he hadn't meant for any of this—but it didn't feel as though that was the first time the thing had come loose. Moira simply stared, eyes still imploring and lips begging to be touched. He scowled back briefly before all but hurling himself down the nearby staircase, each step creaking and groaning underfoot.

At the base of the stairs, his hand ghosting over the chipped railing, he heard her crying. Not soft, mewling whimpers, but hard, desperate sobbing. He stopped, hand clamping down on the wood, eyes closed.

Severus understood that feeling—to suddenly realize you were alone in the world. It was a bitter, hardening sensation that crept across your body, seeped into every pore, until eventually you stopped feeling the cruel sting. Abandonment. Loneliness. Two of his oldest, dearest companions. A chuckle breached his lips at the thought; apparently he *did* have more than one friend.

Moira's sobs filled the whole house, the air, once silent and still, now drenched in sorrow. He wrenched his hand from the bannister when the wood started to cool, the change palpable, and his gaze darted around. No wind. No open window. Yet a cool breeze whispered across his skin. He glanced up the dark stairwell, at the horrible floral wallpaper that carried on throughout the upper level, save for Moira's bedroom. That had been an off-white.

His stare hardened. So her world was falling apart. So what? Severus had survived it, and she would too. Severus had endured the disdain of his own kind for *centuries*, always reliant on humans to maintain his strength. Moira only seemed to grow stronger with time, not dependent on anything or anyone. She was a phoenix. This was her rebirth.

Everyone wept after drawing their first breath.

He moved for the front door, yet how quickly his arm fell back to his side when he reached for the handle. With a huff, he adjusted himself, tucking his rigid cock up and out of the way.

"You realize," he snarled, glaring down at his chest, "that you are lusting after an *angel*, do you not? Hybrid or otherwise, you can't possibly..."

Want her.

Desire her.

Need her.

Yet he did. At least, the inner demon did, and as much as Severus tried to disassociate from it while he was on Earth, that demon was his truest self.

And he wanted Moira.

"Fuck." He caught the glint of his reflection in the stained-glass window embedded in the door. How fuming he appeared, his mouth in a thin line and forehead crinkled —and his eyes completely black. She was a threat to him. A danger to his grasp on the carefully cultivated control he had built over the years.

So, why couldn't he just walk out the front door?

"*Fuck.*"

Severus jogged up the staircase, taking it three steps at a time, then flung himself around her doorway. Still seated at the end of her bed, Moira looked up sharply, her trembling hand pressed to her mouth. Tears streaked down her cheeks, her skin flushed and her eyes bloodshot.

"Listen to me," he growled, anger and arousal warring within him. "If you stick your nose where *they* don't want it, they'll kill you. That's their entire purpose on Earth—to punish and contain truant demons and the humans who associate with them."

"Demons?" she squeaked from behind her hand, her eyes wide. Severus's snort straddled the line between amusement and incredulousness.

"What, you think there're only angels? It's all real, Moira. Angels. Demons. Witches. Vampires. Everything that goes bump in the night." He pointed at her. "And you're one of us now, so I'm going to need you to drop this wide-eyed innocent thing and get with the program."

She sat up straight, her hand falling to her lap. "O-okay."

Okay. That was easier than he'd expected.

"Seraphim Securities is staffed by warrior angels, and they don't play around." He planted his hands on his hips, rather enjoying the way she hung on his every word, her lips parting again as she drew breath. How desperately he wanted to slip his tongue, his fingers, his cock, between them. Teeth gritted, Severus closed his eyes for a moment, pushing the inner demon down until he was sure he could stay focused. When he looked back to her, she was standing, holding herself in a solo hug.

"Okay."

"If your father is one of them, and he hasn't been recalled to Heaven for defiling a human, I doubt he'll want to know you." Angels weren't exactly encouraged to procreate with Daddy's creations.

"I've thought about it my whole life, that my dad doesn't want me," she told him, lifting her chin slightly. "That's not a deterrent."

"Well, it should be. You've spent your whole life thinking he was a human, not a creature who can set you on fire with just a look."

She gulped, shoulders slumping.

"But if you stick with me, I'll do my best not to let that happen." Because it would be a shame to lose her over something as frivolous as a paternity confirmation. He'd keep her alive and well—at least until he could fuck her properly.

Yes. That was it. That was what he'd tell himself when he tried to fall asleep tonight, his thoughts inundated with her, his senses still overwhelmed by her. Sure.

"So, you'll help me?" She seemed hopeful, innocent once more, her whole being elevated.

"Only because I think it'd be a pity to see you killed," he told her, adding a leer for good measure. She crossed her arms over her chest, deflated.

"Gee, thanks." Moira wiped at her cheeks. "Good to know where we stand, I guess."

"What did you expect to hear?" Severus hardened his features. "That I'd fallen in love with you our first night together? That I couldn't stand the thought of losing you?" He scoffed when her cheeks reddened. "I know what you're going up against. If I don't help, you'll be dead within the month."

"And you think that'd be a pity." She studied him, eyes narrowed in scrutiny. "Why?"

"I've never met a human-angel hybrid before," he said, spouting whatever nonsense first came to mind. "I find you fascinating. Who knows what you can truly do."

They stared at one another for a long moment, the air still and tense again, no longer cold and bitter. Finally, Severus looked away and cleared his throat.

"Russ?"

"It's *Severus*," he clarified. If they were going to be spending more time together, he refused to let her call him by his escort pseudonym.

"Oh. Severus what?"

"Just Severus." He held out his hand. "Incubus."

She retracted her own hand hastily at the word. "Incubus? Like a...a..."

"Demon. Yes. *Lust* demon, specifically." He grinned, head cocked to one side as his hand hung between them. "Still so keen on my help?"

She nibbled her lower lip for a moment, then flinched back when he blinked and revealed his true eyes. Practically tripping over her own two feet, Moira scrambled to the other side of her bed.

"Well?" He held his hands out, then rotated in a slow, gratuitous circle, reveling in her distress. When he faced her again, Severus fluttered his lashes and bit back a laugh. "Does this change anything for you?"

Slowly, Moira forced her arms to her sides, then cautiously shuffled back to him, not stopping until she was about two feet away.

"Are you going to hurt me?" she asked. The inner demon was positively beside himself at the thought.

"Not unless you ask me to."

He thought he'd seen her blush before—but the ruby-red flames licking their way across her face now were just *delightful.*

"I'll hold you to that," she said in a deliciously shy tone. He suspected she meant she would hold him to not hurting her—but Severus preferred to acknowledge the other implications.

"See that you do," he purred, offering his hand one last time. "So, that's it then? Partners?"

"Until we find my dad," she slipped her hand into his, grasping it firmly enough to make his inner demon sing, "partners."

He watched them leave the house with a clenched jaw and an air of rage boiling around him. Invisible to all eyes, he stood on the sidewalk corner, stiff as a statue, as they descended the rickety porch. At the bottom, his child, the mistake none of the others knew about—could ever know about—touched the demon's arm and held out her phone. The creature took it, then offered his in return. Swapping phone numbers. Humans did it all the time these days, didn't they? To the unobservant, the gesture was innocent, unimportant.

But he knew better.

He had been watching her for years. Watching her grow up to look like her mother, the wretch who had weakened his resolve just enough, that one time, that he took her to bed. He had watched the girl change in the wake of that woman's well-deserved death.

He had seen her start to show her true self, the other side, fearing that the others would detect *her*, a half-breed in a sea of this, that, and the other. An abomination sired from his own loins.

Accursed *Nephilim.*

The very word made his lips curl into a sneer.

They were handing back each other's phones now, his daughter eyeing the demon warily. With a curt nod, the beast strode down the front walk, then made a sharp turn to the left, carrying him away from the university campus. He watched, enjoying how the incubus shuddered when their paths crossed. He was invisible, yes, but the cockroach would *feel* his presence. The beast stopped briefly, taking a cigarette and a silver lighter from his pocket, before hurrying on up the street.

Attack a human. Feed from her before mine eyes. Give me a reason to slit your throat, beast.

Wishful thinking, of course.

He dragged his gaze back to the daughter, the child, the girl he should have smothered in her crib. She stood at the end of her walkway, her expression unreadable—until she lifted those eyes, the same eyes as his, and stared directly at him. Across the street, a few houses over, he held his breath. Invisible to the human eye, yet she wasn't exactly human, was she?

For a moment she continued to stare at him, perhaps into him, until those eyes lifted upward, then darted from side to side, her brow pinched. Good. She might sense him, the eyes that had watched her all her life, but she still couldn't *see* him.

And if he had it his way, she never would.

The demon complicated things. He had never seen the creature before, but the agency was aware that several incubi and succubi used the escorting profession as a means to steal essence from innocents. Thus far, no one had died from their little games, but give it time. Demons simply couldn't control themselves.

His nails bit into his palms. Control. Even angels lacked control under the right circumstances. He burned his gaze into the middle of her back, watching her go, another wool cap on her head, as she headed toward the university at a good clip.

Did she know?

Had the demon told her? They were rather good at that—telling humans things they shouldn't, whispering the sweet secrets of the universe in their ears, secrets humanity wasn't ready for, under the guise of liberation.

If she knew, she would seek him out.

And he couldn't have that.

Yet he couldn't kill her himself. The others would know—they'd see the blood on his hands, the darkness in his soul.

It was time to call in a favor. A favor from one who lived in the darkness, who relished the opportunity to spill and drink and bathe in blood.

He looked to her one last time, waiting on a street corner a hundred yards away, watching a car pass. A gentle breeze sent her loose hairs, the ones poking out from under the cap, tickling across her skin. Moira brushed at them absently, a curious sort of smile on her lips.

Yes, smile now, daughter of mine. For I promise your days of smiling are numbered.

He would see to that. One way or another—the darkness would have to take her.

PREY

PREY (THE HUNT, #2)

Pearls and Polaroids.

PEARLS AROUND HER NECK

Moira Aurelia has put her faith in a demon. She offered her hand and he took it. Partners. Just like that. Black eyes and sinful smiles, she trusts an incubus to lead her into the abyss if it means she'll finally find her dad on the other side. Her real dad. The creature who cursed her.

Or blessed her. Because from the way Severus—snarky, *seductive* Severus—watches her, touches her, ravishes her, Moira can't decide if this new body is a curse, or if she's finally growing into the woman she was always meant to be.

POLAROIDS AT HER FEET

Unable to fathom how this woman, this ethereal creature, has so much raw power over his inner demon, Severus tries to keep her at an arm's length while he helps her hunt down her father—but he can only abstain for so long.

Moira is the sweetest hell he's ever tasted, a woman who squares off with his truest self and doesn't even flinch. When he's with her, the loneliness disappears, the bitter ache in his heart—mended. How can he resist such a divine temptation?

Meanwhile, the Farrow's Hollow demon community is positively aquiver when news of Moira's heritage leaks—and suddenly Severus isn't the only demon in town who must have her...

CHAPTER ONE

"How could you keep this from me?"

Moira tried not to glare at the glossy photo of her mom, but she couldn't help it. Her fingers clamped down on the flimsy bit of memory, thumbs leaving fat prints at the edges. If Russ—*Severus*, she had to consciously remind herself—was correct and she *was* a hybrid, then all her recent changes would almost make sense. She was developing powers, not dying of some crazy illness that no one in the medical field could figure out. This was rebirth, not the end.

But why hadn't her mom *told* her?

Sure, she had been out of it toward the end—all that pain medication would do that to a person. But she'd had her entire life to tell Moira what she was, what the possibilities could be in the future, and she *hadn't*.

Moira's glare grew heated, burning into the face of her smiling mother. Those eyes, that hair—Moira had once shared both of those characteristics. Green eyes. Warm chestnut-brown curls. If her mom had still been alive today, she wouldn't have recognized her. Not really. She had issued a warning before she passed: everything would change after Moira turned twenty-two.

At the time, Moira hadn't put much thought into it. After all, her mom, the only living relative she had any connection with, had been on her deathbed—she was *raving* as the illness took her, raving about twenty-two and onions and Moira could hardly stand it.

Once she'd passed, there had been the mourning period. Then Moira had needed to deal with all her mom's remaining worldly possessions, which had ripped her grieving heart open *again*. And *then* she'd had to try to figure out how to move forward with her life, her career, her education—and the whirlwind of it all, preparing for this next stage with Ella by her side, had been exactly what Moira had needed to bounce back to being someone who resembled her old self. But then the changes had come, just as her mom had said they would.

And according to Severus, a fucking *demon* of all things, Moira's other side was finally making itself known.

Her *angelic* side.

How could her mom not have known she'd had sex with an *angel*?

Moira's glare lost a bit of its venom as she considered it. According to Severus, most of the supernatural beasties you heard about in stories were real, and humanity had no idea. Well, *most* of humanity. A few were privy to this secret society of supernatural monsters—and angels, apparently. If *she* hadn't known angels or demons or, or, *vampires* were real just by going about her day-to-day existence, then logically she couldn't fault her mom, especially if she hadn't known the guy she was taking to bed had a pair of feathery wings and a halo.

Moira had sort of had sex with Severus without realizing he was anything *but* human. Sort of.

His eyes should have been a dead giveaway, but Moira had summed her brief glimpse of them up to her mind providing a reason for her to get the hell out of that hotel room. But it had really happened. She'd seen a piece of his true self, of his *soul*, if demons even had souls, and she still couldn't decide how that made her feel.

Frightened? Not really.

Aroused? A little.

Concerned? Yup.

Her mind could have rebelled against all this—easily. It was only two days ago that Severus had stood at her underwear drawer, crotchless red lace panties in hand, and shattered her entire view of reality. She could have chosen not to believe him, called him insane—but that would have been a pointless waste of time. Moira couldn't deny that some of the changes she'd experienced, particularly her sudden and curious new strength, had a supernatural edge to them. She had just been too frightened to consider it.

Before he'd left her house, Severus had told her that he'd felt the air turn cold when she cried—yet another thing to add to the ever-expanding list of personal weirdness.

Moira had given the whole thing a lot of consideration, two long days of thought and reflection holed up in her room whenever she wasn't attending classes, and she had decided to just *go* with it. Severus's intentions had read as genuine, though she had promised herself to stay on her toes around him. He was still a demon; his offer to help didn't negate that.

If she tried to fight it, to reason her way through everything, to come up with another saner rationale, nothing would get done. Severus had offered to help her find her dad, who they both now assumed was an angel working for Seraphim Securities. The longer Moira spent in an existential crisis, the more it would delay meeting the man who had cursed her—or blessed her—with this side of herself. If she could find him and just *talk*, just get her questions answered, Moira would be happy. She didn't expect a tearful family reunion, although it would be nice to be on good terms with the only being who would truly understand what she was going through.

Still, for all his callousness, Severus had had a point. There were two possibilities when it came to dear old Dad. One: that he had known about her and what she would become her entire life, and just hadn't bothered to reach out. Shitty, but probable. Two: that he hadn't known of her existence at all. Maybe her mom had hidden her somehow, but Moira had lived in Farrow's Hollow all her life, and supposedly her dad *worked* at the local angel security office downtown. The chances of him having zero idea about her existence seemed slim, but they were odds Moira was willing to work with.

Before her mom died, Moira *had* been an optimist. It would be nice to finally get some of her old confidence back. Looking at the world through a grey haze, hating herself for what she had become, helped no one—least of all Moira. She had someone on her side now, demon or not, and she planned to make the most of it.

All the while trying to ignore what the breathtaking creature did to her. Good *grief* was he ever gorgeous, and learning that Severus was, in fact, a demon hadn't changed that by any means.

It certainly made him more dangerous—and Moira wouldn't, couldn't, forget that.

Not that she had any idea what to do should his demon

side rear its ugly head—or handsome head, depending on the circumstances. From digging around internet forums, archives, theological debates, she'd gained *some* additional information about demons and angels, but nothing that would make her an expert. No one could agree on anything, be it in books or online, and a lot of the intel she dug up, wrapped in her blankets and surrounded by pillows, sounded more pop culture, pop *fiction*, than reality.

She had always been adept at thinking on her feet—learning on her feet. Sure, the last couple years had been a little all over the place for her, but Moira was ready to throw herself into this new world, this new life, with everything she had. What did she have to lose? If Severus acted out, her threat of putting him through a wall still stood.

Her phone chirped softly at her side, coaxing her out of one of the many headspace dives she'd taken lately. The last one had gone on for hours; one moment she was staring at her laptop screen, the latest Wikipedia page on angel hierarchies blazing back, and the next it was midnight and her battery had died.

It was all just a lot to digest.

Lower lip caught between her teeth, she unlocked her screen and found a text from Severus awaiting her. It had been his idea to swap numbers, and she'd spent a long time staring at the photoless profile he'd crafted on her phone, wishing she could call at two in the morning and unload her thousands of questions on him, hoping he might have actual answers.

Instead, she kept it all inside. Talking about it, saying the words out loud, still made her feel a little crazy.

As crazy as one could feel reading a text message from a self-professed lust demon.

Are we still on for today?

They had plans to meet at the coffee shop across the street from Seraphim Securities. To anyone watching, they were just two friends sharing lunch, but Severus had wanted to do some reconnaissance work before they got into anything too serious. Even though Moira had staked out that damn building for all of last summer, its rigid lines and hard edges of slate grey and black openly mocking her, Severus wanted to make his own observations.

Leaving the house shortly, she texted back. *Will take the 11:50 bus.*

From her place on the other side of campus, it would take roughly half an hour to get to downtown Farrow's Hollow. Not ideal, but she didn't feel like trekking all the way to the university to grab an express bus—which, in the end, would only *maybe* shave ten minutes off her ride.

I'll be here when you arrive. Look for me at the front by the window. I've already taken two seats facing the building.

She rolled her eyes, resisting the urge to poke fun at his punctuality. They weren't meeting for another forty minutes, but apparently *someone* was eager to get started.

Grinning, Moira typed out a saucy reply, but then worried that that might come across as too friendly, too forward. Sure, he'd seen her naked, but after the other day, their relationship had basically started again from nothing. Moira wasn't the woman who'd blushed red as a fire truck and run off into the night, angry tears streaking down her face. And Severus wasn't the soft-spoken, understanding escort who'd stalked her for a week.

She was the daughter of an angel. She could bend metal like it was nothing and turn the air cold with her grief—and Severus was a lust demon who made her heart and her sex feel strange, unsettling, wonderful things. Their relationship had begun again as soon as he'd told her the sordid truths of this world, and that was that.

It had to be.

So, instead, she erased everything and fired back a succinct *Cool*, then started to get ready. Five minutes later, she had pinned her mom's photo back on the tackboard over her desk, shimmied into a pair of skinny-fit black jeans that were too loose on her these days, and added a black T-shirt and wool cap to complete the ensemble. In the shared bathroom down the hall, she brushed on a hint of makeup, if only to make her look like she belonged in the land of the living. With some color on her translucent cheeks, she snagged the jean jacket hanging on the back of her door in passing, then hurried down the stairs.

Only to nearly run smack into Ella as her bestie swung up the staircase, anchoring herself with a hand on the railing.

"Ah!"

"Oh my god!"

They giggled, separating from one another, and Moira breezed by her to slip on her poorly aged black flats, dug out from the pile of housemate shoes next to the front door.

"I didn't even know you were home," Ella remarked, looking quite cute in that short-sleeved yellow sundress. Moira stared at it for a moment, wondering why it looked so familiar, then realized it was *hers*; Ella had a penchant for raiding her closet, though she hadn't seen that little number in at least a year. Not that she cared. After all, Ella had the boobs for it, while Moira's had steadily deflated from an almost-D-cup to a handful of B. Just another bit of angel weirdness to wrap her head around.

"I was in my room," she said when she felt Ella staring back. "Just getting ready."

"Don't you usually have class right now?"

"Decided to skip." She'd been too anxious about her meeting with Severus to sit through a mind-numbingly boring seminar.

Ella gasped, half mocking, half serious. "*What*? You *skipped* a class?"

While rare, Moira didn't think it was a momentous enough occasion for her best friend's dramatics. "It's been known to happen."

"Does that mean you're free for lunch?" Ella asked as she swept her enormous mane into some semblance of a bun at the back of her head, her hair tie stretching to its limits to contain everything.

"Er, no." Moira went for her purse, one of two hanging on the coat hooks next to the door, all the while knowing Ella would need more than a stammered *no* to satisfy her. "I'm meeting with one of the other TAs for my class to go over some stuff. We're going to grab lunch downtown."

Ella's perfectly plucked eyebrows shot up. "You hate all the other TAs in your class."

"Well, I hate this one just a bit less," she said with a forced chuckle. Over her shoulder, she read Ella's skeptical look loud and clear, but she didn't need permission to go out —or to *not* go out with her. "I'll see you tonight?"

Ella hummed in agreement, arms crossed as she leaned against the coiled bannister at the bottom of the stairs. "You sure will. Have a fun lunch."

"Trust me, I won't," she announced as she hurried out the front door. Knowing she hadn't heard the last of *that* conversation, Moira jogged to the bus stop up the street, her heart pounding—and expectations high.

Moira had about two minutes to get here before he left. Jaw clenched, Severus tore his gaze from a looming Seraphim Securities across the street, a building marred by hard lines and bleak tones. A quick glance at his phone told him she wasn't late per se, but he didn't like the idea of loitering around a hub of angel activity longer than he needed to.

After Moira's breakdown and his subsequent offer of assistance, Severus had spent the last two days wondering if he'd had an aneurysm. Demons were impervious to such ailments, of course; they healed quickly from wounds on Earth, and were all but indestructible in Hell, although still vulnerable to pain.

Still, what other explanation was there for his decision to help her hunt down the angel who might be her father? Outside the brain injury angle, Severus blamed the demon inside and the appendage hanging between his legs. If he hadn't been so inexplicably attracted to Moira Aurelia, angel-human hybrid and walking beacon for curious onlookers the stronger her new powers became, then he wouldn't be risking his life.

Risking his *freedom*. No angel wanted a demon digging into their history, especially an angel who had fucked up royally enough to get a human pregnant. He exhaled sharply, staring down at his untouched coffee and scone. This could all go to pot—*fast*—if he didn't play the game carefully. He wasn't sure how determined Moira was, how *desperate* she was, to find her father, but family had a knack for making you do things you wouldn't ordinarily. Family had a knack for fucking you over, too. Severus knew that firsthand.

The coffee shop had seemed like a safe bet. Crawling with humans, the two-storey building afforded him the ability to study his enemy inconspicuously. Plus, you could smell the delectable baked goods all the way from the Inferno on a good day; Alaric never shut up about them. However, now that he *had* the baked goods in question before him, he found he didn't have an appetite.

Not because he was *worried* about being so close to the Farrow's Hollow angel HQ. No, it couldn't be that. He was just annoyed. Annoyed that she was almost late. Annoyed that Moira fucking Aurelia wasn't—

"Hi! I'm here!" A hand ghosted across his back as Moira's voice, jarring and ethereal as ever, carried from his right side to his left, and Severus tried not to flinch at the intrusion. Seconds later she was seated on the stool beside him, her purse on the thick oak counter that ran the length of the front window, her cheeks bright pink. "Sorry. The bus stopped for like ten minutes on campus for no reason, though I think the driver needed a bathroom break. I..."

She pressed her lips together, blush deepening when he slowly looked up at her. The two studied one another in a thick, measured silence, before Moira muttered something about getting a coffee and slunk away. He watched her join the short line by the counter, fidgeting with her cap. Beneath it lay a head of pure white hair. Severus both could and couldn't understand why she bothered to hide it. While it wouldn't have suited her before, judging by her pre-hybrid-transformation photos, it was just fine now. More than that. Attractive, even.

His dark eyes wandered her figure, noting the obscene amount of black she'd worn today. Severus snorted and faced the street again, finally picking up his coffee and taking a sip. The liquid had turned downright cold since he bought it almost an hour earlier, but he drank it all the same. Black clothing. Honestly, did she think they'd be sleuthing about today? Sneaking into Seraphim Securities through some exhaust vent so they could crawl through the ducts like spies?

Humans were so predictable sometimes—even hybrids. All the demon groupies he'd seen over the years dressed in either black or red when they knew they'd be in the company of hellspawn. Black, red, tight, sheer—provocative, and a *fuck you* to today's pastel and polyester fashions. From his experience of following her around, Moira tended toward warmer colors: greens, yellows, oranges, plus the occasional bit of purple leaking in from her bedroom color scheme. He almost preferred that—but, really, he needn't have an opinion on how she styled herself. Her appearance wasn't the point of this little endeavor; Severus had vowed to keep her safe and assist in the hunt for her father however he could. He planned to see that through, for he had given his word.

Never mind that his inner demon, currently caged deep within the recesses of his being, was *desperate* to touch her again. To trail his tongue across her bare skin, to sink his teeth into the swell of her backside and hear her *squeal*. The inner demon wanted to do all sorts of wonderful, horrific things to her, for her, and Severus had to exercise every ounce of restraint to maintain control. He could do it, restrain himself—but it'd be more fun to give the inner beast free reign. He'd been dormant for so long, fed off the essence of Severus's escort clients. He deserved a little hybrid treat—but Severus didn't trust himself not to go overboard.

He wanted to *take* her, yet he knew the risks of allowing that to happen.

What he couldn't understand was *why* he desired her so desperately—and it was driving him up the fucking wall.

So, for now, repression was his best bet. Repression,

control. Ignore his dark instincts, his deepest cravings, and wear a mask of indifference in order to get the job done.

It was rather Catholic of him.

Ten minutes later, Moira had returned not with a coffee, but a creamy soup that smelled strongly of canned mushrooms, which struck him as an odd choice for such a warm day, and a baguette. Condensation dribbled down the fruit smoothie she set next to his coffee, and his lips thinned as she got herself settled again.

"So," she started, running her large spoon through the top layer of her soup, the steam rising in angry swirls, "what's the plan for today? When are we going inside?"

At her nod toward the security building, he let out a snort and took another sip of his coffee.

"We're not going in there today."

"*What*?" She let her spoon slide into the soup, catching the end before it succumbed to the creamy mess completely. Her frown had a rather charming quality the longer Severus stared at it, and he tried not to grin back in return.

"You heard me."

"I did. My *what* was for clarification."

"Look, we don't know any of the beings who work there," he argued, and before she could get a word in edgewise, Severus leaned down to the laptop messenger bag sitting at the foot of his stool. From it, he dug out a sketchpad and a small leather case filled with charcoal drawing tools. "All of your pictures are worthless, and I'd like to start matching faces to names."

It would certainly take longer this way, but Severus wanted at least a basic idea of whom he was dealing with, and since he had no personal experience—thank fuck—with the angels working at Seraphim Securities, this was the best approach to start things off.

Her disbelief was palpable, eyebrows shooting up her forehead. "So, you're going to...draw them?"

"Sketch them, yes. From what I've heard, they all dress the same," Severus told her, flipping the sketchpad open to a blank page, then digging into the case for an appropriate tool. "A bit like your legends of the men in black. Suits. Neatly combed hair. Blank, listless expressions."

"You're joking."

"Not one bit," he said frankly, then set his supplies down and faced her. "Do you have a better idea? One that won't get me killed on sight? The stories are true, you know. We don't exactly get along, angels and demons. This is an extreme risk for me to take, so we're going to do it my way—which is the *right* way. Am I clear?"

"But—"

"It's a yes or no question."

Her glare sharpened. "Don't speak to me like I'm a child. I'm not."

"I'm perfectly aware you're not," Severus mused. His gaze wandered up and down her figure, slow and purposeful, and stopped back at her blushing face. "However, in this respect you are a *figurative* child. You know nothing about this world beyond what I've told you."

"I've been researching," she protested, and folded her arms across her chest when he snorted again.

"You think either of our kinds would let the *real* story be told on the *internet*?" he drawled. "In books? There's just enough of the truth out there to make it plausible, but there's so much more you *don't* know. Thus far, you've failed at locating your father. I'm taking point here. So, again... Am I clear?"

He waited, basking in the heat of her glare, before arching an eyebrow.

"*Yes*," she said tersely, then tucked into her soup with a huff. He let her stew for a few moments, preparing himself for the task ahead. Angels would be strolling in and out of the building throughout the day, in their black suits and gleaming cap-toe derbies, the same routine that happened at any of the other corporate mid-rise buildings around them. Severus might not have had personal dealings with any, but the demon community as a whole had a vague knowledge of their habits. They'd break for "lunch," despite not needing to eat. They'd flock in and out in the early morning and evening, mirroring the start and end times of the workday. In that time, Severus would catch them. They couldn't be photographed, but they could certainly be sketched.

Once he and Moira had a face, they would have a name. All he'd need was a demon willing to match the two, provided his sketches were as accurate as possible. No easy feat, given he'd be making them across the street, inside a different building, with Moira grumbling in his ear.

But Severus happened to be a rather adept artist, a talent honed through years of dreadful solitude—before the era of Alaric. He'd had much more free time back then.

He was midway through unraveling the paper wrapping of one of his favourite charcoal pencils when a light flashed brightly beside him. Blinking rapidly, he looked up to find Moira checking her phone with a little smirk on her lips.

"What was that?"

"A selfie," she said, running her finger over her phone screen. "You mentioned my pictures, and it got me thinking about how angels can't be photographed. I wanted to see if that was the case with demons."

"And?" he asked dryly, setting the pencil aside and

propping an elbow up on the counter. She studied her phone for a moment, then held it out to him.

"You look normal. I...have a bit of a glare." She didn't sound all that impressed with the idea. "Which is new."

Sure enough, there was a hint of light reflecting off her face, though not enough to obscure her features. Severus appeared to be looking away, focused on his pencil, while Moira wore an enormous grin—almost like they really *were* just two friends goofing around at a coffee shop. As he shifted on the stool, angling his body toward her, he did a quick sweep of his surroundings. Whether she realized it or not, she'd just added to their cover story.

"Take another one," he insisted. "This time I'll smile."

She hesitated, as if sensing a trap, but then did as he asked. With a soft clearing of her throat, she leaned into him and lifted her phone to the appropriate selfie angle, then flashed a quick smile as he did the same. They held the pose until she tapped the screen, light flashed, and a small *click* sounded over the dull roar of coffee shop conversations. When Moira checked the photo, her brow furrowed and her jaw dropped.

"Oh. Your eyes—"

"We don't exactly pose for pictures either," he noted with a glimpse at the screen. As always, his demon eyes shone through, not a hint of white in sight. "There's a guy in town we all see to get licenses and photo identification done. Well, most of us. Some don't really care for human law, which is why the angels are even here in the first place."

She nodded somewhat absently, still frowning at the screen.

"Do they frighten you?" He tapped the top of her phone, and Moira straightened sharply, momentarily startled, the poor little fawn. Severus retracted his hand, resting it on the counter and drumming his fingers. "My eyes. Do they scare you?"

Her shrug was a dangerous attitude to have. "Not really."

"Why? They're the inner demon." *And you should be frightened of him.*

"I don't know," she said, tucking her phone into her purse. "I guess demons just don't seem so bad. I mean... You're okay."

"Your compliment moves me," he crooned back wryly. "But you should be frightened, Moira. You should be frightened of all this."

"Why?"

"Because *they* are merciless to their enemies," Severus told her as he grabbed the charcoal pencil and stabbed it toward the stark building across the street, "and you've only met *one* demon." His mouth twisted into a sinful smile. "And I've been on my best behavior."

She didn't miss a beat. "*Stalking* me is your best behavior?"

"The stalking was a necessity, I'm afraid, and it turned out for the best." He went back to unravelling the pencil's outer layer, noting it needed a sharpening before he put it to use. "When it comes to my kind, you won't always be so fortunate."

She swallowed hard, and his gaze inadvertently dipped to the delicate bob of her throat before it returned to the pencil.

"So why then?"

"Why what?" He knew what she meant—he just wasn't in the mood to talk about it, especially with her.

"Why are you on your best behavior with me?"

He clenched his jaw as he rooted through the pencil case, not stopping until he found the bit of sandpaper sharpening pad he needed to shape the charcoal.

"Severus?"

Just hearing her say his name threatened the inner demon's constraints. It rattled the cage, desperate to respond, but he merely took a deep breath and pressed onward.

"Does it matter?"

"To me it does," she insisted, breaking her baguette in two and offering him half. He waved her off, almost annoyed at her charity. Didn't she see he had his own fucking scone?

"I thought," he started, choosing his words carefully, "that after a lifetime of ill deeds, I ought to do something decent for someone else for a change."

Quietly, almost hesitantly, she said, "I don't believe that."

"Believe what you'd like," he muttered. "It doesn't matter to me. In the end, I'm helping you. I'm keeping you alive—"

"Do you have a vendetta against the angels?"

"All demons do." He could feel her staring, those unearthly blue eyes piercing right through him. "But I don't have a *personal* vendetta against anyone in there, no."

"So why—"

"Oh, look," he said, jumping at the opportunity to quash the conversation once and for all. "There's one now."

Just as he'd suspected, that got her attention off him in a heartbeat. She faced the building across the street, her eyes wide and her lips slightly parted, and they both tracked the angel strolling out the main doors, a lit cigarette in hand. Not once did the creature bring it to his lips. He merely stood there for a moment, head tilted back and eyes closed, basking in the midday sunlight, before strolling down Gabriel Street amidst the rest of the lunch crowd.

"Did you get…?" She trailed off, no doubt realizing he was already deep in the sketch—outlining the face, rough estimates of the features. Severus felt her study him a few beats longer, the heat of her gaze unyielding, until she finally tucked in to her lunch in a merciful silence.

CHAPTER TWO

"Well, don't you look smart."

"Do you think so?" Moira tugged at the slightly too-tight waistline of her black knee-length skirt, one of the few articles of clothing she owned that still kind of fit after her physical changes—a piece she hadn't been able to wear since the tenth grade, back when it was part of her high school's uniform. It flared gently around the knees, but the belted area up top was digging into her already-smallish waist like it wanted to lock around her spine.

"Well, your butt looks good in the skirt," Severus said after giving her a slow once-over with that brooding black stare of his, and Moira felt her cheeks warm in an instant. Thankfully, they only went a little pink now; two weeks into this working partnership, Moira had *almost* gotten used to his flirty attempts at making her squirm.

"And the blouse? Not too frilly, is it?" She'd borrowed it from Ella, since she didn't have anything that fit the business wear aesthetic Severus had insisted upon as they texted before bed last night. With a plan to go straight into the belly of the beast, he'd wanted them both to look the part. While he was handsome as ever in a tailored grey suit and crisp white dress shirt, the checkered red tie surprisingly fashion forward, Moira felt like an imposter.

Which was accurate to the situation. In all the time that she and Severus had worked together, she'd never felt smaller than in that very moment, standing across the street from Seraphim Securities. She was a grad student—an *art history* grad student, at that. She had no business waltzing into any of the corporate buildings downtown like she belonged there.

But then again, Severus was an escort in his free time, so, really, neither of them had a place here.

"I think you need a bigger bust to fill it out properly," he remarked after another painfully long moment of study. He pinched the mustard chiffon between his fingers. The color was always a knock-out on Ella's darker skin. On Moira, something had seemed off, but she hadn't had time that morning to scrounge up something better.

"Cool," she snapped, swatting his hand away. "Thanks. Great confidence boost."

"Your bust is *fine*," the demon muttered, rolling his eyes. "The perfect size, if I remember correctly." Her blush darkened. "This just seems a bit big, that's all."

"Well, it's the best I can do."

"Come here."

She tried to shuffle away, but he was too quick, catching her wrist and tugging her toward him. Then, as one might with a child, he spun her around, tucked his fingers under that too-tight waistline, and started stuffing fabric into it. Moira bit the insides of her cheeks, stock-still and blushing *furiously*.

And here she'd thought she had kicked the habit. Moira had met Severus at the café for breakfast every day for the last two weeks. She would get their meal—whatever that morning's special was—and he'd reserve their seats at the front counter overlooking the street. For the most part they'd sit in silence, both eating and watching, Severus sketching up a storm. Although she didn't know much more about him now than she had at the beginning, she had gotten used to him—to the way he purposefully leered and snarked and made comments with the express purpose of making her squirm.

She should have hated it—his forwardness. She should have put him in his place immediately. But she let it happen. She blushed and sighed and rolled her eyes, all the while battling a burn deep inside her, one she only ever felt around him.

Moira liked him. She knew she shouldn't. He seemed to be trying hard to ensure she *didn't*, but she did, and there was no denying it any longer. Not only was the guy breathtaking, but he seemed genuinely intent on keeping her safe—despite all the grumbles about her *naivety* regarding the demon world, which were accurate—and he had proved to be a talented artist. As of today, they had ten near-perfect sketches of the different angels they had seen come and go from Seraphim Securities these last two weeks. The likenesses were uncanny, and Severus intended to approach his demon contacts in the community soon to start matching names to faces.

Today, however, he wanted a rough idea of the interior layout of Seraphim Securities. If they eventually did manage to find Moira's dad, Severus figured the best approach would be to confront him head-on at work when his guard was down. Severus wouldn't accompany Moira inside for that, but he'd expressed an interest in the building's floor plan just in case she needed help.

It was almost...sweet.

Of course, he could want that kind of info for his own purposes, but that wasn't Moira's business. If it made no impact on the search for her dad, let the guy do whatever he wanted.

When the Farrow's Hollow Building and Service Development Center insisted there were no floor plans on file for Seraphim Securities, Severus had suggested they press the woman who sat at the front desk in their ground-floor lobby. The whole thing seemed risky, and Moira had been a bundle of nerves ever since she'd woken up two hours before her alarm went off that morning. Yet as Severus fiddled with her outfit, a little handsier, a little *rougher*, than he needed to be, she had some confidence in the fact that he appeared cool and collected.

Moira might not know a thing about this world, about the *real* angels and demons walking amongst mankind, but she almost felt safe so long as he was with her. In recent months, she had felt her strength grow, and she was only *half* angel; Severus was a full-blooded demon—from Hell. Should something go wrong today, that ought to count for something.

"There," Severus said, taking longer than necessary to smooth the creases out over her hips. "All sorted—"

"Stop." She batted his hands away, then stepped to the side to study her reflection in the café's front window. He'd managed to turn a flouncy, slightly-too-puffy blouse into something that looked tailored to her figure—an hourglass figure at that. When was the last time she'd seen her body sport an hourglass figure? Months. Maybe even a year. Chin lifted, she appraised herself a moment longer, then gave a curt nod. "Nicely done."

"I think so." He slid his hands in his pockets as the sounds of early morning rush hour traffic pervaded the early morning quiet. "Your hair looks good too. I was worried it'd be too noticeable, the white."

She swallowed hard and ran her hand over each side, catching any flyaways. Normally Moira wasn't one for painfully tight French braids, but when she had told Ella she had a seminar presentation that morning and couldn't wear a wool cap, her bestie had taken pity on her.

Knowing Moira didn't want the whole world staring at her new hair, Ella had slicked it back with some styling product, then braided it in a rigid French plait. The tail end tickled the nape of Moira's neck whenever she looked down, but all the styling product had managed to make her hair look a bit darker than the usual blindingly bright white. All the other angels had the same insane shade of hair, and it was a wonder more people weren't curious about why everyone who worked in Seraphim Securities rocked the same styling.

Ella had been all too eager to help with her hair and outfit, and Moira had left the house with her stomach in knots. She hated lying to her, but the truth was still *way* too out there, even to share with Ella. So, Moira had told the most harmless lies possible, hoping that should she ever tell Ella the truth, her best friend would understand the need for secrecy.

Understand, sure, but Moira didn't expect her to forgive. Not right away, at least. Best friends don't keep secrets. They'd made a pact in elementary school.

But when it came to all this—

"Okay, okay, stop staring at yourself." Severus's voice cracked sharp as a whip through her musings, and she straightened up, her palms clammy, and faced him again.

"So, are you sure about this?" she asked, hoping to hide her nerves with a confident tone and moderately direct eye contact. "About, you know, *this*."

Severus's gaze followed her nod toward the depressingly masculine building across the street.

"Not really." He pursed his lips for a moment, then shook his head. "Look, we're here before they usually arrive. I estimate we've got about forty-five minutes to get the information we need and get out. If things go south, there's a fire exit just off the lobby that'll take us into the alley."

Her eyebrows shot up. "And then?"

"And then we hope that I know the side streets of this city better than they do," he told her with a cheeky grin. Severus thought he was *so* charming sometimes, so slick. A part of her knew it was an act—no one could draw like that, possess the attention to detail, take the time and care, all for something that had no obvious benefit for himself, *and* be a total arrogant horndog too. The act became more and more transparent with each passing day. The other half of her, however, didn't want him to stop.

"Come on," Severus muttered, moving toward the road. "We've wasted enough time already."

Moira hurried after him, her kitten heels clicking noisily on the sidewalk. They stood side by side on the curb, waiting for the sudden rush of cars to pass, then darted across the street. Severus's hand hovered over her lower back the whole way there, straight up to the tinted twin glass doors at the entrance. Moira glanced up as he held one open for her, catching *Seraphim Securities* scrawled in gold, antiquated font across the front of the building. Severus was right; the angels weren't trying to hide it. But then again, why should they? If their purpose on Earth was to corral wayward demons and discipline problematic humans, they had nothing to hide.

Taking a deep breath, she strode inside. Shoulders back, chin up. Confident, but not too showy, not like she was better than everyone in a ten-foot radius—which only consisted of Severus and the woman behind the enormous metallic front desk in the middle of the empty foyer, a woman who couldn't have been more than a few years older than Moira. As she marched forward, the clack of her damn heels thundering with every step, she tried to project that she *belonged* in a place like this. Because, from the receptionist's slow, unimpressed up-and-down appraisal, she would need to prove that.

Moira bit the insides of her cheeks, ruffled but less annoyed than she could have been, and stopped about a foot from the metallic monstrosity of an information desk. At no point did the receptionist mirror Moira's forced saccharine-sweet smile.

"Can I help you?" she droned, pushing her chair away from the computer and standing. The enormous wall hiding her actual workstation came up roughly to her waist; the woman was a giraffe. "The offices won't be open until eight."

"We're a little early, but I was actually hoping I could speak to you," Moira said as she offered her hand for the woman to shake. When the receptionist continued to stare back like Moira was the gum she'd just peeled off her shoe, she retracted it and forced it to her side. "My name is Rachel Clemmons, and this is..."

Shit, what was his cover name? They had both agreed to

use fake names during this initial run into Seraphim Securities; Severus had suggested it after he'd had a good ol' guffaw over the fact that Moira had used her real name when she'd booked him for that night. At the time of his less than gentle ribbing, Moira had just continued to eat her ham and cheese omelet in a stony silence, not responding until he changed the subject.

"Aaron Tanner," Severus said, sidling up and planting his hand on the desk. "We're architecture students from the university interested in acquiring some building blueprints for a research paper we're working on." When the receptionist's entire face seemed to pucker, a rejection nigh, he carried right along. "We won't need to take it out of the building. Photos will suffice."

"If you need a floor plan, you should ask the city—"

"We did," Moira told her, feeling only *slightly* smug when the woman pressed her lips together in a frown. "We were told your employers haven't registered one with the city."

"As I recall, my *employers* are not required to do so," the receptionist said snippily, "nor am I able to just *give* out private information—"

"Perhaps we could come to some sort of agreement." Quick as a striking viper, Severus snapped his hand around the woman's wrist. At first she appeared startled, but then, as if injected with a fast-acting tranquilizer, her entire body seemed to melt under his touch. Her eyelashes fluttered, and suddenly she was all smiles.

"Oh, an agreement, eh?" The brunette practically *purred*. "What did you have in mind?"

"What are you *doing*?" Moira whispered heatedly to Severus as she searched for surveillance cameras. Besides the golden-doored elevators just off to the left, the emergency exit to her right, and two bushy ferns on either side of the main doors, the lobby was the epitome of stark—and not a camera in sight, as far as she could tell.

"You're the one going on and on about how kosher we demons are," he murmured back. "Take a look, firsthand, at the effect of an incubus on a human."

Moira swallowed hard, staring wide-eyed at the receptionist—who had very likely heard Severus say he was a *demon*. However, it soon became apparent that the woman couldn't tell you what decade this was, let alone what Severus had admitted. She just gawked at him like he was some sort of god, and a twinge of unwelcome heat roiled inside Moira when Severus smiled right back—that handsome, endearing, *genuine* sort of smile she'd only seen him use on her.

"Come now—" his eyes darted down to the woman's breasts, which she'd thrust in his direction, her hips pressed up against the computer station below—"*Mary*. Honestly, is that your real name, or do they just make you wear the name tag?"

"It's my God-given name," she cooed back, rubbing her hand over his arm. "You feel like *ecstasy*."

Moira wrinkled her nose. "Yikes."

"Well, I'm taking more than I usually would," he said with a sigh, then glanced back to Moira. "She won't remember this encounter."

"That's a relief."

"For who, exactly?"

She bit her cheek, wanting to slap that *smile* right off his face. It was pathetic that this had such an effect on her. Just disgraceful. And weak-willed. And... And...

Ugh. Now she could see why women fell for assholes all the time. They really knew how to get under your skin.

"All right, Mary," Severus rumbled, his attention on the receptionist again. "We'd like the floor plans for this entire building. Every nook and cranny. Do you think you can do that for me?"

"They're upstairs," she said dreamily, now clutching at his sleeve. "In a locked room. Off-limits."

"How *scandalous*. Perhaps you could give me a tour—"

"Hey!" barked the deepest voice Moira had ever heard. Its rich, somber timbre reverberated off the walls, hitting her full force, rattling her *bones*, and both she and Severus whirled around at the sound of a briefcase slamming into the tile floor.

There, almost engulfing the main doorway, was Angel number seven, dressed to the nines in the standard well-fitted suit and tie getup. He must have been pushing seven feet—seven feet of rippling muscle, that is. Near-identical eyes to Moira's darted between her and Severus. Black-skinned, yet somehow still sallow like her, and robust; they'd giggled over the fact that while he had no hair—a glint of sunlight off his bald head could cause an accident on a good day—his eyebrows were just as white as hers.

They had also argued about his jaw; Moira always said Severus made it too sharp, that it was bulkier, more square. Now that they were up close and personal, Severus would be pleased to know he'd been right.

"Time to go," Severus muttered, immediately releasing the receptionist, who flopped back into her chair with a moan, and grabbing Moira's hand.

"*Out*, demon," the angel roared, striding toward them with a fury that made Moira's knees weak. Luckily for her, it didn't matter if she was weak-kneed or not—because Severus was doing all the running for her. With an arm hooked around her waist, he hoisted her up and bolted for the emergency exit, keeping her flailing body squarely between himself and the pursing angel. As soon as they all but fell through the steel door, an alarm blared overhead, its piercing shrillness like a drill buzzing into her skull.

They were off and running as soon as they stumbled into the alley, and Moira trailed after Severus, clutching at his hand, hoping she wouldn't roll her ankle in these damn heels.

When they reached the end of the narrow corridor, the alarm muffled by the now-firmly-shut door, she finally clued in to what Severus had done during their hasty retreat.

"Wait. Did you just use me as a *human shield*?!"

Severus wrenched his hand from hers with a yelp.

"Mind the rage, sweetheart," he shouted back, neither of them breaking their stride as they turned sharply to the right and raced down the alley behind the low-rises next to Seraphim Securities. Skirting garbage dumpsters and wayward trash bags, Severus made a big show of blowing on and shaking out his hand, and when he looked over his shoulder at her, his eyes were completely black. "You nearly burned my hand off."

"Well, maybe you deserved it." Not that she'd done it intentionally—or even noticed it had happened. But good. Moira hoped it hurt as much as his dramatics implied. "I'm not your human shield."

"No—technically you'd be a *half*-human shield," he said, throwing her a wink before grabbing at a rusted door, which was slowly opening as an employee in a grey chef's jacket sauntered out of it, phone and cigarettes in hand. The man leaped out of the way, and Moira muttered her apologies as they blitzed inside.

"If you ever do that again—"

"I'll consider myself *warned*," Severus called as they

hurtled through what looked like a high-end kitchen—one of the many obnoxiously expensive restaurants one block over from Gabriel Street. Italian, given the amount of pasta prep she caught in passing, a chorus of *fuck you* and *get the hell out of here* accompanying them all the way to the dining room. They made a pit-stop at the front, the room quiet and dark, the tabletop linens needing to be changed. Severus had the doors unlocked in a matter of seconds, and she followed him out, her heart pounding.

They pushed on until they had about four blocks between them and Seraphim Securities, darting across throughways and cutting off cars. By the time they finally stopped, Moira was winded—but not as winded as she should have been—and rightly terrified.

"He knew you were a—"

"Of course he did," Severus muttered, shooting her one of those *duh* looks he was so good at before peering around the corner of a building. "They'd know in a second."

"He *caught* us—"

"We just need to lay low for a couple hours," he insisted, taking her hand and hauling her across the intersection when the light changed. "Demons heckle angels all the time. *Stupid* demons, but those pompous fucks know the difference between hecklers and the big players. I'm a nobody. We'll be fine."

While he might have sounded confident, the twitch in his cheek and the clench of his jaw told a different story. Swallowing hard, Moira readjusted her grip on his hand and held a little tighter, her surge of human shield–rage ebbing—for now.

"Where can we go? They'll find us—"

"My place," he said curtly before another sharp turn took them down yet another alley. "My cousin spelled the place up tight as per my roommate's father's request. The entire building is hidden from demons, angels, and everything in between."

Severus stopped so abruptly that she ended up crashing straight into him—it was like colliding with a wall. Glaring, Moira pulled her hand free and rubbed at the faint sore spot on her arm.

"Look, I know that was a bit of a disaster, but we'll be fine," he told her, his tone soft—comforting, almost. "We'll regroup and try again. It's not our only option."

Too jumbled from what had just happened, the best Moira could offer in response was a nod. His gaze flickered down to her hand, but rather than reach for it again, he stuffed both of his in his pockets.

"Come on. We're not far from my place."

Moira would have preferred to sit in a dark, quiet room, preferably her bedroom, and decompress—but that hardly seemed like an option. So, she followed, an ear cocked for the sound of fluttering wings, all the while wondering if they were in deeper shit than Severus let on.

~

"Well, have we settled down yet, or are we still feeling prickly?"

Moira stared at the half-drunk tea in the oddly charming china Severus had rustled up from his cupboards. Green tea—nothing special. Given all that she'd seen in the last hour, she had expected some weird magical herb blend that was supposed to calm her down, but no. Just green tea—from the shop up the street, where Severus and his roommate Alaric got all their groceries.

"I don't know," she said, slowly lifting her gaze to where

he stood across the open space, leaning against the black metallic railing. Behind him, a thousand tiny, too-steep steps connected all four floors of his enormous, invisible house in downtown Farrow's Hollow. Moira was *still* trying to wrap her head around that, but she resented the accusation that she was the only one rattled by what had happened this morning. "*Are* we?"

She stared pointedly at the tumbler of whiskey in his hand—his fifth glass, if she had been counting correctly.

"I'm fine," he fired back. "It's you I've been worried about."

Something between a snort and a scoff leapt from her mouth, and she ignored his eye roll while she finished the rest of her tea. As she'd suspected—it was lukewarm at this point, all the lingering bits of loose leaf flavor at the bottom leaving an odd taste in her mouth. Without a word, she held out her hand. And waited. And waited.

And waited, until Severus crossed the space between them and handed her his whiskey. The small sip burned all the way down her throat, scalding the green tea taste in the process, and pooled in her belly, warm and ever-present. She handed the glass back with a muffled cough, a hand over her mouth, and Severus strolled back to his spot along the railing, with its thin wrought iron bars in place to ensure no one tumbled over and onto the stairs below, finishing the rest of his drink in a moody silence.

He wasn't fine. But neither was she.

Once he'd been sure they had no angels tailing them through the back alleys, Severus had cut back across town with Moira in tow. Three streets over from Seraphim Securities, they'd passed the popular university crowd hang, The Inferno, and stopped a little way up the street in front of an enormous, gaping space between two red-brick apartment buildings.

Exhausted from running in heels, Moira had dreaded another detour through the garbage-dumpster lined alleyways. It was then Severus had taken her hand again, and as he pulled her into the alley, she quickly learned what he had meant when he'd said his cousin had spelled his home up tight. One moment they were outside—the next, she was walking into the ground level of a long, narrow building, clutching Severus's hand so tight that he complained he'd lost circulation.

Panicked, Moira had whirled around to find Severus closing the front door, which sat next to an enormous window overlooking the sidewalk—the same view one might expect from a ground floor apartment in any of the buildings around them. Only *this* building had been invisible to the naked eye from the outside.

"You need a special mark to get in and out, to even *see* or touch the building in the first place. The only way someone without the mark can get in is if they're touching someone *with* said mark," Severus had told her, totally blasé about the whole thing as he lifted his shirt to reveal a crudely carved pentagram over the left side of his ribcage. "Alaric and my cousin Cordelia have the same branding. It's her mark. Bit cliché for a witch, but that's the key in and out. No one else, demon, angel, human, vampire, garden gnome, will be able to find us."

To the rest of the world, there was no building. They would walk right through yet another dusty, abandoned alley—the illusion a product of his witch cousin's magic.

It had been a *lot* of information to take in all at once. Unable to get a word out, Moira had just plopped down on the floor, as cross-legged as her skirt would allow, while her brain scrambled to connect the logic dots. Rather than console her, Severus had disappeared to make tea and grab a bottle of Jack Daniel's from the ground-floor kitchen. He then led her up those nightmare stairs to the fourth floor—his floor—and sat her down on a leather couch in front of the window that faced the street.

And there she'd been, almost totally immobile, for long enough that her limbs were starting to stiffen. As she set the little china teacup down on the window ledge, catching a glimpse of the sunny, beautiful spring day outside, Moira knew she should have been thinking. Processing. Coming to terms with everything she'd seen and learned. But her mind had been relatively blank, and she couldn't help but wonder if it was because she had already decided to accept whatever Severus had to throw at her—or if she was just in shock.

Despite not thinking like she should have, Moira had memorized nearly every detail of Severus's home. Four floors. Invisible to outsiders, but tastefully and sparingly decorated on the inside. It made her think of those house-hunting shows she and Ella had shamelessly binged on during undergrad exam seasons. Who didn't want to look at pretty, expensive houses in far-off lands? The shows were like cotton candy—no substance, but enjoyable. The building Severus shared with this Alaric guy reminded her of something she had seen in Amsterdam: tall, dangerously steep stairs, thin but multi-level.

A grey and black colour scheme carried throughout the interior, from the painted exposed stone on the walls to the slick black hardwood on every level. First floor: kitchen and dining area. All the latest appliances. Sleek furnishings. Second floor: Alaric's level. A bit messy compared to the rest of the house. Furnished with a huge L-shaped sectional and an enormous wall-mounted TV. Third floor: empty. Under construction, apparently. Severus hadn't elaborated.

Fourth floor: Severus's domain. Sparsely furnished save for the couch and a trio of black bookshelves, each filled to the brim with books—orderly chaos. A white and grey checkered rug at the foot of the couch. A glass coffee table. No curtains over the windows. Across the space, beyond the stairwell next to the wall, just like on Alaric's floor, was a closed door, which she assumed led to a bedroom.

Moira wasn't sure why it surprised her that Severus kept his personal space neat and tidy, but it did. He just had all that *personality.* She assumed it would carry over into the way he decorated his home. Not so. Not a photo, painting, or decorative vase in sight. No plants either, save for the herb garden growing in the kitchen downstairs.

"Moira?"

"Hmm?" She blinked out of her staring, heart pitter-pattering hard when she found herself the sole object of his attention.

"Really... How are you feeling?"

Her jaw clenched briefly as she considered it. How *was* she feeling? Like her whole world had been turned upside down. Like her body wasn't *hers* anymore. Like their first and possibly only attempt to get into Seraphim Securities had been a *complete* disaster and she was still no closer to finding her dad. So, just peachy.

In no mood to discuss it, not yet, she shuffled to the edge of the couch, elbows propped up on her knees, and rested her chin on one fist.

"What did you do to the receptionist?"

The muscles along his jawline flickered, as though he too were clenching in response to a question he didn't want asked. Silently, he strode across the narrow room and set the glass tumbler on one of the bookshelves. Jacket gone, button-down sleeves scrunched up to his elbows, tie loose, that *face*—he was positively swoon-worthy. Moira hated that she thought that—hated that he had this unspoken method of distracting her.

"I did what I do to all humans," he admitted softly, trailing his fingertips along a few books before turning on the spot and pinning her with that unflinching stare. "I charmed her."

"Care to elaborate?"

"Some demons are born with certain *gifts*," he told her, hands in his pockets as he began pacing back and forth from one side of the room to the other—no more than ten or twelve feet, at the most. "*I* was born an incubus. You know we draw strength from humans to survive, surely, but we give a little of ourselves in the process. Our touch is... electric. It's exhilarating. Exciting. A sexual *thrill* without the penetration." He grinned when she made a face. "Oh, don't look like that. It's what we *do*. You must have felt it."

"Felt what?" Her cheeks warmed. "A sexual *thrill* without the penetration? No. I can't say I did."

He paused for a moment, brow furrowed. "Come now. You don't need to be embarrassed by it. The sensation is perfectly natural. It keeps our, er, *suppliers* compliant. Many humans climax from touch alone."

Moira stood abruptly, moving before realizing she had responded so viscerally to the idea. How nice for all those women—to be able to orgasm just from an incubus touching them. How fucking swell.

"Well, you and I weren't headed that way, if that's what you're implying," she said stiffly, her stomach in knots. His chuckle only made the heat in her cheeks burn brighter.

"Look, I know you've got some angel in there," Severus

pointed to her, waving his hand up and down her body, "but there's human too. I know you felt something that night. It was clear in your...*response*."

Mouth hanging open, Moira gawked at him, no longer caring if he saw her blush. "Wow. *Wow*. You really are full of yourself."

"It's not an issue of being full of myself," he growled back. "It's a fact—"

"No, what I'm telling you is a *fact*." She tugged Ella's bunched-up blouse out of the waistline of her skirt, suddenly too *hot*. "Look, this isn't a challenge to your ego, but I didn't feel like you were, you know, drugging me, or whatever it is you do to humans. I'm sorry, but I didn't."

"You don't need to be ashamed of the way your body responded to—"

"I was just trying to get into it!" she cried, wanting to run her hands through her hair—only to remember it was drawn up in a tight braid. At this point, however, *many* rogue hairs had escaped, likely giving her a half-crazed look. She exhaled sharply and planted her hands on her hips. "I was just trying to get into the moment. I was nervous as hell about hiring an escort, and I just... I just wanted to have a good time for once. I figured that would be doable with a professional."

His eyes narrowed slightly. "And are you telling me that *didn't* happen?"

"Yeah, pretty much."

"That's bullshit," he snapped, starting to pace again. "You and I would have had a grand old time together, just like every other human out there, if you hadn't run off scared."

"No—"

"*Yes*," he sang the word back at her, almost cruelly, and

glared. "It's just a part of your fucking biology. I don't know what you're playing at here, trying to tell me otherwise. Clearly, you've found one of my buttons, and you're trying to *push* it. To what end, I have no idea."

"You are *so* full of yourself!" Moira half shouted, glaring right back. "This isn't about *you*. This is *me*, trying to be honest. If what usually happens when you touch a human was that live sex show with the receptionist, then *no*, that didn't happen!"

"Right." Severus's eyes swept up and down her figure again, almost dismissively, and he snorted. "Of course not."

"What's that supposed to mean?" That, what, there was yet *another* thing wrong with her? She had always been self-conscious about the fact that she'd never fully orgasmed before. *Always*. Now here Severus was, telling her that she should have felt something that she didn't, and Moira didn't have to put up with it. Not from him. She got enough of that crap from her own critical self.

"Look, you're half human," he ground out. "You must have been *close* to—"

"No, I wasn't!" Moira marched right up to him, blocking his path, going toe-to-toe with the demon and refusing to wilt under his glare. "Was I having a good time? Yeah, you give a really good massage, and I was kind of getting into it once the nerves went away. But you're just like all the rest of them. You're the same as every other guy who can't get me off."

His nostrils flared, and in one blink, the whites of his eyes vanished, replaced by an inky black that did strange things to her—things she wasn't ready to admit to. Moira swallowed hard, refusing to be intimidated just because some sex demon was getting a reality check.

"I always thought I was just picky, that the guys I was

with were inexperienced, *something*," she continued, her voice low and carefully controlled. "But then I couldn't do it myself either, and suddenly the guys touching me didn't *feel* like anything anymore. No one does. Every person in my life who touches me, it's like...it's like a gust of wind. It's *nothing*." She stabbed an accusatory finger at his chest, all the while unsure of who she was really angry at here. "You were supposed to be different. And you were! I finally felt like I was being *touched* again, like I wasn't totally disconnected from the world, but then it ended the same as it always does...with me unsatisfied, hating myself, and yet another guy who can't help me close the fucking deal to add to my list."

Mouth suddenly dry, Moira pressed her lips together and realized she was shaking—and closer than she should have been. Hell, she was up on her toes, glowering at him like he was the one who was totally fucked up. And he wasn't. Sure, he'd inadvertently poked the bear by refusing to accept her truth, but—

"I," Severus hissed, his voice like the first rumble of thunder before a devastating storm, "am *nothing* like the little human boys you've no doubt *fumbled about* with through the years."

"Oh yeah?" She cocked her head to the side, eyebrows up. "I've yet to see a single shred of evidence to back that up."

"That night, I was as good as I always am." His cheek twitched, hands curling into fists, and Moira gulped. She knew she ought to back down. She knew now *she* was the one poking the bear, adding fuel to the fire, but she couldn't help herself. He didn't get to win this one. Severus had a leg up on her in just about every other part of their strange relationship, but not this. Because Moira was *right*, and he was being a stubborn, petulant sex-demon *ass*.

"*Are* you good though?" she whispered, tilting her face up and holding that all-black stare. He must have leaned down to meet the challenge, because she felt the buzz of their proximity, the hum of anger and something far more dangerous boiling beneath his skin.

And she liked it, the danger, far more than she should.

"Because, let's think," Moira carried on, their noses nearly touching. Severus continued to glower down at her, still as a marble statue save for the odd twitch in his lips, the flare of his nostrils, the flicker of his jaw muscles. She inhaled softly, her gaze dropping to his lips. "You escort for a living. Your whole schtick is that you use it to sustain yourself. I get it." Moira held her hands up. "I don't judge, as long as you're not killing your clients. But let's be real... You don't have to actually *try* all that hard. Like you said, some of them climax just because you're touching them. It's their biology. So, really, *are* you good?"

"Each and every one of my clients experiences pleasure beyond what she'll ever receive from any man in her lifetime." He over-enunciated his words. Anger-enunciating. It was kind of hot—and she knew, once again, that it shouldn't be. Why couldn't she stop staring at his lips? Drawing in a shaky breath, Moira lifted her head further, tipping it back just enough so that it wasn't their noses about to bump, but their mouths.

"Well, yeah, of course they do...because you're drugging them." She nibbled her lower lip, not missing the way Severus's eyes became heavy-lidded—as though watching her just as she had been watching him. Moira cleared her throat, her anger slipping away word by word. "And, you know what? I don't think you would have made me come. You know why?"

"Why?" he snarled.

"Because you're probably just not used to *trying*," she murmured, grazing her lips over his before swiftly retreating, adding about two feet of much-needed space between them. Severus seemed to lurch after her, but he righted himself quickly as Moira planted her quivering hands on her hips and shrugged. "Just accept it, Severus. You've been showering me with hard truths since we met. I think it's time to swallow a taste of your own medicine. You are a fucking *lust* demon. You don't have to *work* to make women come, so, logically, when you're faced with someone immune to your crap, you trip up a bit. You've just never had to try before. I get it."

What the hell was she even accomplishing here? Pissing off the only creature in town who could possibly help her find her dad, all because he, what, didn't believe her? Had used her as a human shield? It was petty, but damn, did it ever feel *good*.

Severus straightened, rolling his shoulders, his knuckles cracking. She expected to see rage glowering at her again. Instead, she found bemusement. Frowning, she countered his step toward her with one giant step back.

"Oh, sweet Moira, I have been *trying*," he told her, following step for step until the backs of her legs nudged the couch—and still he stalked her. "I've tried to keep it all in. I've tried to push you away, tried to create some *distance* between us, but I suppose that's been my fatal flaw, hasn't it? My error, thinking of you as some silly human who'd be taken by my tricks...by my mask."

"W-what?"

His smile was positively predatory. "I think it's finally time to *stop* trying..."

Moira shrieked when his hands clamped down on her forearms, his grasp so solid and *real* that it made her heart skip a beat, just as it had the first time she saw him. Smiling, his eyes still black as the night, Severus yanked her toward him, and in one swift movement, threw her over his shoulder like she weighed absolutely nothing.

CHAPTER THREE

It was pathetic how little prodding he needed to unleash the beast.

Severus had been trying. So. Damn. *Hard.* To ignore his baser instincts. To dissuade her, to throw her off. Moira had become too comfortable in his company, and she didn't know the danger she put herself in.

But to insult his gifts. To doubt his *power*, the only natural talent Severus possessed... Well, she had crossed the line.

And now she would taste the consequences. She'd feel them, live them, *breathe* them until she begged him to stop, and even then he made no promises.

"What are you *doing*?" she cried, her legs fighting against his arm as her fists pummeled his back. "Are you fucking *serious*? Put me down!"

Scream all you want. It won't do you any good. Moira had made the mistake of thinking she called the shots here—that she could waltz into his house and insult him.

Just like all the others. Insult upon insult upon insult. Incubi and succubi might not be worth much in the grand demon hierarchy, but they had skills. Talents. Abilities that they alone were born with, and, after centuries of honing them, Severus was damn skilled.

It truly was pathetic, to get so riled up over a bit of wordplay.

Perhaps it was just an excuse—the straw that broke the camel's back. The last nudge toward his undoing. Whatever the reason, Severus no longer cared. All thoughts of pissed-off angels vanished. Moira was the only thing on his mind, and by the time he was done with her, she wouldn't be able to shake him from hers.

He crossed the length of his floor in long, quick strides, then wrenched open his bedroom door and stalked in. Over his shoulder, his little angel hybrid continued to fight him, even when he slammed the door and shrugged her off. She yelped again, tumbling toward the floor, but Severus caught her before she had a chance to fall far. The demon's reflexes were stronger, faster—primal. He had her trapped in the time it took her to murmur some incoherent protest, his hand around her throat. She lifted her chin, stiffening.

She truly was exquisite. Severus had battled the allure, the painful *pull* toward her, hoping his leering and sneering would send her in the opposite direction. He had sought to spare her the creature who truly desired her. But she had ignored his warnings. She'd met the eye of the demon, stared into his truest self, and hadn't even flinched.

So be it, sweet Moira. Let her have the demon.

He took her mouth with all the savagery she deserved, his cock stirring at her long, low moan as she slid onto her tiptoes, eyelashes fluttering up at him. In a frenzy of tongue and teeth, of swollen lips and wandering hands, he kissed her with everything he had held back from the first moment he saw her. No holds barred. Lay it all on the table. His hand tightened, feeling the delicate structure of her windpipe, and still she kissed him back. Angrily. Fiercely, as if not willing to be cowed by his venom.

Thin, nimble fingers clutched at his shirt, her tongue shy as his thrust into the sweet darkness of her parted lips. Not once did her eyes close—but neither did his, the eternal blackness boring into her ethereal blues. They didn't quake. No fear, no regret. He saw in them a forbidden desire, surging when her hips nudged against his. A growl reverberated in his chest, and he swore those damn blues *smiled*.

Because if they didn't, her mouth did. So, Severus pushed back, pinning her against the door, those bright blues widening slightly at the feel of his *need*. He ground his hips, driving his cock against her as he dragged his mouth from hers, catching her lower lip with his teeth. She shuddered, retreating somewhat, and he rubbed against her again—harder this time, watching, relishing her response.

She did feel pleasure, the lying chit. He probably could have held her here, one hand on her throat and the other up her skirt, and made her scream ten times over. How terribly sad that no blundering human male had made her come before—even sadder still that she hadn't the faintest idea how to do it herself.

This wasn't a punishment, unleashing the demon upon her—this was a gift.

Keeping his features hard, mouth set in a thin line, he smoothed his hand along her neck and wrapped the end of her braid around his fingers—then pulled, hard. Moira gasped, head shooting up, neck utterly exposed. Grinning, though only because she couldn't see him, he trailed his nose down the column of her throat, inhaling her, burning her scent into his brain so that he could have her long after she fled. Her fingers curled around his shirt, twisting the white cotton. He responded by dragging his tongue from the hollow of her neck to the tip of her chin, nipping at it for good measure.

Her *shudder*. A sigh like silk, a quiver that shot straight to his cock. He wanted to make her do it over and over again until she couldn't *stand* it.

Severus kissed her instead, claiming her mouth once more as harshly as he dared, the hand on the back of her head steering her straight to him. And, once more, she took it, every ounce of it, her hands racing up his chest and gripping the crisp collar of his shirt. His teeth scrapped her lower lip when she ripped the shirt open, buttons cascading to the floor, her nails raking down his bare chest. Before long she had a leg hooked around his waist, skirt hitched up, thigh exposed, and it would have been so easy to drop to his knees right now and taste her. So easy—and so damn *right*.

But that wasn't the plan.

Instead, he gathered both her hands in one of his, pinching them together at the wrists, kissing her deeper, grinding harder, driving her into a frenzied distraction so that she wouldn't realize what he'd done until he'd done it.

Moira tore herself away at last, gasping for air, head turned to the side. He caught the drum of her heart, beating, beating, beating beneath the flesh of her neck.

"I'm not afraid of you," she whispered, facing him again, their foreheads resting together. He noticed her swallow hard, lips parting slightly as she stared into his black abyss. "I know what you're doing, and I'm *not*."

"Not yet." Severus tugged the bowline knot he'd just tied tight, binding her wrists together with his checkered tie. Immediately she stilled, her wide eyes shooting to her bound hands.

"W-what are you doing?"

"A perfect knot—one-handed," he purred back, withdrawing and tugging the tail end sharply. She jerked forward, a puppet at the end of his string, her cheeks blazing. He stood back, watching her wriggle about, fingers trying to slip under the fabric, hands desperate to separate. Little did she realize that the harder she squirmed, the tighter the noose. Severus could undo it in a pinch, by tugging the appropriate section or merely ripping it in half, but he much preferred to watch her panic.

"*Severus.*"

"Oh, hush." His inner demon was positively *beside* himself, delighting in her indignation—and not missing the way her legs had snapped together, as if fighting off a surge of desire. Hell, he could smell her from there. No point in hiding it.

Gripping the tie, he marched her across the long, narrow room, then shoved her onto his bed, his hand on her hip. Down she went. Up her skirt flew. She rolled, trying to wriggle free from his grasp, but Severus put an end to that in a snap. Hopping onto the king-sized behemoth, he prowled to the head of the bed, then looped the tie around one of the wood bars of his headboard. Moira squealed, dragged right alongside him before being trapped in place. Once he had her secure, he sat back on his heels and clapped his hands together, the noise making her flinch.

"*You* look far too pleased with yourself," she stated, her voice adopting a rather low, almost *husky* quality. Severus gritted his teeth; like his cock needed to get any harder.

"It's difficult not to be," he told her, eyes raking across her helpless body. "You make a pretty captive."

"Untie me."

"No." Instead, he went for the waist of her slightly too-tight skirt—and unceremoniously shred the thing in two. His name flew from her lips, half scolding, half crying out. Unfazed, he spread the fabric open, like two butterfly wings on either side of her. Black satin panties greeted him, and a quick look at Moira showed her cheeks on fire and her eyes clenched shut. Before he could make quick work of the final barrier, she managed to roll over, the tether between her and the headboard shortening.

Severus tsked. Like he couldn't rip that flimsy bit of fabric off from this angle too. He watched, head cocked to one side, as she tried to push up onto her knees, grunting softly. The demon grinned.

"Thank you," he murmured. She'd made it *much* easier for him to peel the satin off with her hips lifted—and that was precisely what he did. With a finger hooked under either side, he yanked the material down her hips. Silly thing realized what he was doing too late, her hips pressed flat to his bed again, but it didn't matter; her panties were already down around her thighs. Might as well submit to the rest.

When she wouldn't loosen her locked thighs, Severus helped himself to her perfect, pert little ass, sinking his teeth into her right cheek just deep enough to make her squeal. Like he'd pressed the magic button, her legs flailed, and he was able to slide that damp black satin off without a single tear. Moira lifted her head as the bed creaked, her eyes narrowing when she spied him hanging her panties from the corner of the headboard like a trophy.

"Severus."

"You know, saying my name only makes it *worse*," he told her, swooping down to meet her gaze, his head resting on the bed beside her. Her cheeks sunk in momentarily, as if she was biting them, and he noticed her swallow hard.

Good. A bit of fear, a bit of pain and pleasure, never hurt anyone.

Still, he couldn't stop himself from offering her one last out. The demon fought him, his throat tight as he said it, but this was *Moira* tied to his bed, helpless. "You know what you need to say to end it."

Her eyes narrowed again, glaring, and he returned the look with a smug grin.

"Come on," he cooed, walking his fingers up her back, over the thin material of her chiffon blouse. "Say it. *Do* it. I dare you."

When she turned her head from him, still scowling, he grabbed her braid again and yanked it back, her surprised gasp making the demon purr.

"No?" He wrenched her head back a little further, handling her as he hadn't *ever* dared handle a lover. No demon had gone to bed with him. Humans would break under the same pressure, but Moira merely winced, the strain evident in her neck, her eyes—and still she said nothing. Severus chuckled, then licked the shell of her ear and whispered, "Good girl."

She shuddered as he released her, thighs clenched tight together again—her smell intoxicating. Crawling down to the end of the bed, he positioned himself at her feet, then grabbed her knees and flipped her over with ease. Then, just for good measure, Severus took her by the ankles and pulled her down as far as the tie would allow, her arms stretched taut overhead. Hunger hummed through every fibre of his being. Hunger for her, for the way she would feel wrapped around him.

And not for a second did he hunger for what she could *give* him in return. With Moira, he didn't crave the life essence—he only craved *her*.

Smirking, he took those creamy white ankles, bony, her toenails painted pink, and wrenched them apart. Naturally, the rest of her legs followed, and she fought him with a barely contained huff, wriggling against both her restraints and him. Severus held her there for a moment, legs splayed and lifted, pretty little cunt open to him—his eyes fixed on her face. So determined to break free, so *focused*. He could watch her all day.

But he wouldn't. He'd burst before that happened. So, he nipped at her instep, holding tighter when she tried to draw her legs back, then ran his teeth along her Achilles tendon. Before long, he had her legs tossed haphazardly over his shoulders, and the look in her eye—the resignation, that there was no recovering *now*—was worth every insult she'd hurled at him earlier. In fact, that little episode was a thing of the past. Off his radar. Forgotten. As was the angel, their mission—everything. Severus couldn't tear himself from *Moira*, from the way her thighs quivered, the way she wiggled about when he licked and nibbled the underside of her knees.

She whimpered his name just as he trailed his tongue along the delicate flesh of her inner left thigh, her arousal so overwhelming that it was a wonder he heard her at all. Still, he paused, glancing over the crest of her sex with an arched black eyebrow. Her chest rose and fell in uneven beats, her fingers no longer fighting the restraints, and he thought it a pity he hadn't torn off that damn blouse too.

But then again, her nipples would have been far too distracting, too fun to torment.

"Yes?"

"What are you doing?" she whispered, lips barely parted, her eyes heavy-lidded and her cunt *dripping*. The question was rhetorical, surely, yet he couldn't help but respond to the naivety in her tone, the innocence in her voice.

"Why, what do you *think* I'm doing?" He nudged her legs off his shoulders, then sat up briefly to get rid of his meddlesome shirt. Even if he didn't *get* anything from her, he wanted as much skin-to-skin contact as possible.

"You... You..."

He clucked his tongue at her, scolding, and then settled between her thighs again. This time her legs went over his shoulders easily, limp, but her toes curled.

"Moira, don't be like that," he chastised, pinching her inner thigh. A cry caught in her throat, so he did it again. Another delicious sound to add to his memory bank. "You practically *begged* me for this... So, here I am—*trying*."

He flashed her a sordid smile, and she clenched her eyes shut, head falling back on the bed. His tongue swept across his bottom lip as he studied her—the delicateness of her swollen lips, arousal leaking through them. He couldn't recall if she'd had hair the last time, but up close, he realized she did. Light, thin, short, *faint* hair.

"Consider this a lesson learned, darling," he growled, settling down and eyeing what he truly wanted. He repositioned his hands, using them to spread her open for his greedy mouth. She stiffened, her breath catching, and he let out a dark chuckle. "Be careful what you wish for..."

She gave a shout when he finally dragged his tongue between her slick folds, his name sounding desperate and tortured, her hips arching to meet him. Sweet Hell *below* she tasted fucking *divine*. Severus growled, his entire body igniting as she overwhelmed him—touch, taste, smell, *sounds*. Why hadn't he done this sooner? Why the hell had he walked around like a fucking martyr when he could have given in and done *this* every day?

He groaned, tongue swirling around her clit, her body twitching and shaking and writhing beneath him. His hands cupped her ass, squeezing, and then lifted her up so he could taste her deeper—so Severus could properly *devour* her. He showed no mercy, no signs of slowing, as he worked that sensitive little bud over, honing just the way she liked it by how desperate a cry she made. Above, Moira tugged at her restraints, cheeks flushed—a vision of a woman possessed. His mouth quirked at the sight, cock straining against his trousers.

Pushing up onto his knees, Severus lifted her off the bed, her weight like nothing in his hands, and let the demon truly taste her. His tongue thrust deep into her trembling body, over and over again as he nuzzled her clit. He could eat her all day, all night—if Severus could survive on Moira alone, he would have. He'd forsake all others just to taste her sweet, sweet nectar from night until noon—provided she sang for him as desperately as she did now. Thankfully, they were the only ones home; Alaric might think he was killing someone up here.

And that, in itself, was quite the compliment.

"Oh, *fuck*!" she wailed, the headboard resisting each tug she made. A product of Hell, it was built of stronger stuff than most of the furniture around.

"Such awful language," he scolded, slipping two fingers into her before latching onto her clit again. Her legs fought him, rebelling at last, trying to squirm out of his grasp. Severus held firm, memorizing the expression of blissful agony etched across her beautiful face as he fucked her with his fingers and tormented her with his tongue.

That is, until she locked her ankles and squeezed him with her thighs—hard. His pace faltered, the buildup breaking, and he noticed her tense body relax somewhat in his absence. Scowling, Severus twisted himself out of her leglock, then hoisted her legs up, an arm under her knees, and spanked her as hard as he dared. The sound carried through the thick stillness around them. Satisfying. Moira yelped, flinching away from him, her mouth open—and perfect for filling. She'd deserve it, after all, to be tied up and used to find *his* pleasure, not hers.

Not today. That wasn't the point of today.

"You behave yourself," he ordered, wrenching her legs apart, "or I'll tie your ankles to the bedposts and *really* let you have it."

She closed her eyes tight again, whimpering, and let her head fall back on his pillow. "It's too much. It's too much. I c-can't—"

He chuckled coolly. "Dear girl, you've hardly had enough."

Severus drove two fingers back into her slickness, debating whether or not to add a third as she fought her restraints again. He threw one leg over his shoulder as he leaned down and smothered her clit, employing every tactic in the book to make her squeal. His tongue had long abandoned mercy. Hard. Soft. A flicker—barely there, featherlight and torturous. Meanwhile, he stroked her inner walls, his pace relentless and his stamina boundless. Slowly, with her blouse bunched up beneath her breasts, her body started to clench around him. He kept her other leg pinned to the bed, her quim ripe for his very own picking as he plundered it.

"S-Severus," she whimpered, pushing against his shoulder with her thigh—more insistently now. "Severus, *stop*. Please, please, *stop*!"

He glanced up with a huff, then lifted his mouth from her and glared. She said it again, and that earned her his hand cuffed around her chin, forcing it down to meet his stare.

"*What*?" he growled, noticing the wet smears of her own arousal his fingers left on her cheeks. He nearly slipped them between her gently parted lips, but thought better of the distraction.

"It's... It's too much," she told him again, her eyes watery and cheeks flushed. Scoffing, he brought his hand back to her thighs, then slowly massaged her outer lips, occasionally slipping back in to stroke the inner ones. All the while her body trembled and tightened beneath him.

"Does it *hurt*?"

"Uh, no," she said, her cheeks growing redder. She cleared her throat, floundering. "It's just...overwhelming. Maybe we should, uhm, take a break, or...?"

He pressed his lips together, wanting to laugh but knowing he shouldn't. If what she had said about never climaxing before was true, then he supposed it *would* be rather overwhelming. Good.

"But you aren't in pain?"

"My wrists hurt a bit."

"I don't give a fuck about your *wrists*, Moira." He grinned down at her shocked expression, one that soon burned dark, riddled with pleasure as he slipped his fingers back inside her. "Buckle up, sweetheart. Today's the day you finally come."

"Severus—" She bit her lip, a moan trapped in her throat, when he lowered his mouth to her clit again. She had to be close. So, Severus threw in everything he had to get her there. As she thrashed about, her traitorous hips ground against his hand, his mouth, her words quickly incoherent. He had an end goal in mind, but Severus took his time riling her up and letting her fall, making her realize how foolhardy it was to stop when she was nearly there—that she needed to *push* herself, to careen headlong into the darkness, not retreat from it.

She finally broke with a wordless cry, her eyes shut and her mouth open. She was a fucking *vision*, and Severus was torn between watching, her back arched and her arms perfectly restrained, and burying his tongue inside her to feel the quakes of her first climax. In the end, he did both, first admiring her, burning that image of her ecstasy into his mind forever, then replacing his fingers with his tongue. She tasted even sweeter when she came, and Severus greedily lapped up every drop, prolonging her blissful torment as best he could.

When her body finally sagged, her climax lasting a good minute—which he could only imagine felt like an eternity for his little hybrid—Severus eased away from her. He arranged her legs on the bed, adding a slight bend at the knee while she gasped for air. Severus then sat back and ran a hand through his hair. Her taste lingered on his tongue, and he licked his lips, staring down at her, knowing only one thing was certain.

He had to have her.

Now.

Now or he'd die. He'd combust into starlight or ash or coal or whatever the *fuck* demons were really made of.

"Oh my god," she groaned, chest heaving. "Oh...my *god*."

"I can assure you that he nothing to do with it," Severus muttered, his words clawing their way up his tight throat. The demon wanted to mount her—take her right then and there. Hard. Relentless. Pound her into the bed until the legs gave way, until the whole damn building collapsed around them. He had never felt so close to truly losing control, and he knew that if he didn't give an inch, the beast inside would take ten miles.

Eyes fixed to her, Severus climbed off the bed and strode to the head of it, undoing the knot around her wrists with a simple flick of his hand. Her arms sagged down as she panted, trembled, her cheeks permanently pink and her eyes closed.

They snapped open, however, when Severus scooped her up and carried her as a groom carries a bride over the threshold, not stopping until he had her back pinned against the empty wall across from his bed. Moira stood up on her tiptoes, her lower lip caught between her teeth, and as soon as Severus went for his trousers, her nimble fingers were there too, undoing the zipper as he popped open the button. He shoved the too-tight material down, face pinched in annoyance, then kicked it all off as her hands closed around his cock.

His eyes fluttered closed, a hand planted against the wall to steady himself as she stroked him. Up and down. Curl around the head. Down and up. He let her touch him until he couldn't stand it, until it physically *pained* him to be so still. Then, batting her hands away, Severus hoisted her up, fingertips digging into her thighs, and unceremoniously pushed into her tight channel. Her flighty hands went from his chest to his shoulders, then up to his face, grasping hard as he filled her, a strangled moan tumbling through her parted lips.

He buried his face in the crook of her neck, breathing her in, barely feeling the tentative kisses she peppered along his throat, his shoulder. The inner beast roared to life, a surge of desire coursing through every inch of him until he could hardly think straight. Nothing else existed but his cock inside her. Nothing else mattered. And at the feel of her crossing her ankles against his lower back, Severus finally surrendered.

The surrender of an incubus wasn't gentle. It wasn't all soft moans and lingering kisses and eye contact. It was raw, savage, unbridled—and he gave her nothing else. He pounded into her, moving so suddenly, so harshly, that she cried out against his skin, one hand buried in his hair while her other arm snapped around his neck. Moira clung to him for dear life, because what else could she do? Severus gave her no options, no alternatives—weather the storm or be claimed by it.

And from the way she tried to buck her hips, from the way she clenched her fist in his hair, Moira had opted to weather the storm; he'd never been prouder of her than in that very moment.

He let the demon take the reins, fucking her as he'd wanted to from that very first night—brutally, until the stone wall behind them cracked and splintered. She must have felt it, the coarse backdrop to his surrender, but she only held tighter to him.

"Faster," she whimpered, digging her heels into his back. Severus obliged with a snarl, snatching her hand from his hair and pinning it to the wall. He gave over completely, raking his teeth along her neck, rolling his hips as her body started to tighten around him.

"Moira, you—"

"*Fuck,*" she cried, her body convulsing against him—and her teeth sinking into his shoulder. He hissed again, pain blooming through the intense fog of pleasure collecting in his brain, and released her trapped hand in favor of clutching her neck instead. Severus wrenched her away from his shoulder and held her against the wall, her body still rippling through her second orgasm in the most fucking amazing version of *come hither* he had ever experienced.

But it was her mouth that was his undoing. He could leisurely fuck for hours, but the sight of her heady smile, her heavy-lidded gaze—and his bright red blood smeared across her teeth—was his downfall. Cursing, Severus clamped his mouth down over hers and tasted metallic as he spilled himself into her. He thrust hard and stiffened, and she kissed him like it was the last time. An earth-shattering pleasure overwhelmed him, unlike anything he had ever experienced before—and Severus briefly wondered if he had died.

But his shoulder throbbed. Ecstasy coursed through his veins. And the hybrid in his arms cradled his head in both her hands before nipping sharply at his lower lip.

Knowing he was likely shoving her against cracked stone and jagged edges, he somehow managed to walk them both back to the bed. She giggled softly, the sound cutting through the high-pitched whine ringing in both his ears, and sat up with her hands on his chest after Severus flopped back on the bed.

"Thank you," Moira whispered. Her smile wobbled when he caught the tear sliding down one cheek, then the other, her eyes watery and his blood on her lips. He wiped that away too, licking his thumb clean as he stared up at her.

"For what?"

"You know what."

Ah, yes. *That*. It was a crime that she hadn't experienced such pleasure before, and if he had it his way, she'd have an orgasm a day until she caught up with her peers. Severus merely smiled weakly, seeing no reason to point it out or talk about it.

"I can assure you... It really was *my* pleasure."

She replied with another kiss, one that turned languid and slow. Unhurriedly, Severus tugged the hair tie off the tail of her braid, then freed her white locks from their constraints. When she pulled away, hovering over him with her hands planted on either side of his head, her hair fell around her face like a halo.

And—angel and demon politics aside, a millennium of fear and disdain forgotten—she truly was the most beautiful thing he had ever seen.

"Moira?" Severus leaned against the closed bathroom door, listening to the shower run inside. When he heard no response, he rapped his knuckles against the wood, then pushed in. Steam plumed over the glass shower divider, the heat fogging it enough to obscure the naked figure on the other side, the entire room like a sauna. Even the enormous ceiling window had fogged over. "Moira?"

Her head turned sharply in his direction, and he watched her shuffle to the end of his rather large shower area, then poke her head around the end of the glass wall. Much to his amusement, she had her arms crossed over her breasts. "Yes?"

"I think the time for modesty has come and gone, darling," he teased, arching an eyebrow and looking pointedly down at the offending area. She scowled back for a moment, then cleared her throat, lips threatening to lift into a smile.

"What do you want?"

"Oh, just dropping off supplies," Severus mused. "Fluffy towels to your liking? Are the scented shampoo bottles adequate? The water pressure doing it for you?"

After he had forced himself to stop kissing her, Severus had suggested a bath in the claw-foot tub. His bathroom was nearly as big as his bedroom; Verrier had spared no expense in furnishing his son's home, and that generosity had extended to his roommate too. Pricey grey tile lined the walls of the shower, the tall, slightly tinted glass barrier dividing it from the rest of the space.

He would have preferred to climb into the tub with Moira, still mildly concerned that he had hurt her back in the throes of the best sex of his life. Much to his surprise, she had insisted she had a seminar to attend in a half hour—and if there was no imminent threat of angels hunting either of them down, she needed to get moving.

A lesser man would have taken it as a snub, but he had seen the look of longing she cast the large bath when he'd given her a quick rundown of how the shower worked. While she seemed a bit shy around him now that they had both come down from their high, Moira didn't appear to *need* the kind of coddling a hot bath might bring, the two of them wrapped in each other's arms, processing what had just happened.

She had been quite annoyed, however, that he'd torn her skirt in half.

"What the hell am I supposed to wear?" she had moaned after she'd finally climbed off him, the time for unhurried kissing over, and shoved the damn thing in his face as Severus tried to concentrate on her, still in a post-orgasm haze. He'd muttered some unintelligible nonsense, then showed her to the shower. And now he was back, more in control of his faculties, the demon satiated—for now.

"I've got twenty minutes to get to campus," Moira stated. "Do you have something for me to wear or not?"

"My cousin Cordelia left a dress ages ago," he told her,

holding the garment by the shoulders and letting it unfurl. From the wide-eyed look on Moira's face, it was not to her taste.

"Is your cousin in a Tim Burton movie?"

"Her tastes are rather eclectic for Earth," Severus agreed with a glance down at the dress, "but quite on trend in Hell, I'm afraid."

Moira blanched, then offered a small nod. "Right. Okay. That'll work. Thanks."

"I'll leave it next to the sink."

"Thank you." She disappeared back inside the shower, her lithe figure strolling to the water, the cascading stream altering its echo as it pummeled her body.

He set the all-black garment down on the counter, wondering how Moira would pull off so much lace, never mind the corset ties at the back. Just as he was about to offer his assistance, he caught his reflection in the steamed mirror, and wiped the condensation away with a frown. His cheeks had a veritable *flush* to them, and while his demon eyes had retreated to something more realm-appropriate, the irises looked the same as they did after he'd taken energy from a human. Severus leaned closer, eyebrows furrowed. He didn't *feel* stronger, yet his body showed all the signs of increased vitality.

He swiped at the reflective surface when it started to fog over again, taking a better, longer look before glancing at the shower. Moira certainly was a puzzling creature, one he no longer wanted to keep at an arm's length. The inner demon had proved he could have her without breaking her, and that felt more reassuring than Severus cared to admit.

Curious, he tugged the neckline of his navy blue T-shirt to the side. There, plain as day, was the mark she had left on his shoulder. He swallowed hard, then winced when he traced a finger over it, pain twinging down his arm. She had looked so beautiful with his blood in her mouth, across her teeth, her features wild with pleasure, and her eyes—her eyes belonging to him.

Severus realized in that moment that he *wanted* her. Not just her body. Not just her smart mouth. All of her.

And he wasn't just helping her because he thought it a pity to see her killed by an angel, but because he felt something stir in the pit of his lonely, black soul whenever he looked at her. Moira wasn't a danger to him. She was a storm, the kind he couldn't run from anymore, not after today; the kind of storm he needed to chase, to succumb to in all its brilliant, blinding glory. He needed *her*—and not because she had she bitten him.

But because she could make him bleed. Because she could withstand the force of him, his raw nature, and then joke with him ten minutes later like they were any ordinary pair of lovers. Because after Severus's lifetime of solitude, of drugging and tricking and stealing from the women in his bed, she'd come to him willingly. Eagerly.

He stalked across the bathroom and stopped at the opening of the shower. Moira peered back from beneath the powerful spray of the showerhead, bubbles in her hair, trickling down her back, and tiptoed toward him when he beckoned her with a crooked finger. Once he could reach her, he caught her forearm and dragged her the rest of the way to him, smothering her protests with his lips. She tensed briefly, then melted, wrapping her wet little self around him, mouth opening like a flower in bloom.

"I'll call a car," he rasped, clutching her arm between them, their mouths close enough that he could still taste her. "And I'll drive with you to campus...just to be sure."

She nodded, gaze slowly lifting from his lips to his eyes. "Okay."

"Okay."

"Get out," she whispered with a grin, "or I'm going to miss my class."

"Fuck class," he growled, going in for another kiss that he knew would make her knees buckle and her toes curl—only to have his little hybrid *shove* him out of the shower, giggling. He let go begrudgingly, with the knowledge that he could have had her again if he really wanted—and again, and again, until class was the last thing to *ever* cross her mind.

Instead, Severus readjusted his annoyingly firm erection, forced the rumbling demon back in its cage, and marched out into the bedroom to call for a town car.

CHAPTER FOUR

Severus only exhaled when the smoke had started to burn his lungs, his throat, the back of his tongue. It plumed in front of him, a great grey cloud, before dissipating into the night air—gone forever. He glanced down at the cigarette in hand, then flicked it with his thumb, ridding it of the smoldering ash at the tip. A burning red glow flickered back, and he brought it to his lips for another drag.

Humans smoked for all kinds of reasons, but he knew many did it to calm their nerves. If only nicotine worked its magic on demons, too, then he would have a real excuse for smoking the damn things. It was a habit he'd picked up in the 1920s, one he hadn't been able to shake. Not because it *did* anything for him. He just liked it. He wanted to smoke. Severus had come to accept that.

Moira was his latest cigarette. She didn't *provide* him with anything when they touched—no essence, no strength, no power. Yet he had come to accept that he wanted her, desired her, longed for her because of all she offered *besides* her life force. Her charm. Her intelligence. Her smart mouth and delicious cunt.

And her reliability. While Severus was always exceedingly early, another habit he'd developed since living in the human world, Moira tended to be five minutes ahead of schedule—always.

Standing in the alley between the Inferno and Rose's Corner, Severus checked his wristwatch. Ten minutes to go until their designated meet-up time; five minutes until Moira strolled around the corner, bypassing the already large line of humans waiting to get into the building's more palatable street entrance, drawn like moths to a flame. She and he had business in the much darker core, the demons-only bar and nightclub where Alaric would be bartending in about an hour. Severus found that the Inferno, owned by his roommate's father, was one of the few places where demons congregated en masse that he wasn't blatantly hassled for being an incubus.

No, the discrimination was subtler here, with snide looks and muttered insults, but being Alaric's friend and roommate offered him *some* pull. Tonight, however, he would need to prove his worth to the main man himself: Verrier, Alaric's father and a former prince of Hell. Severus seldom ever spoke to the creature face-to-face, and he couldn't remember a time when it had been *just* the two of them, alone in Verrier's office. He'd also never brought a date to the Inferno; it was going to be a night of firsts.

He puffed the smoke out in rings this time, leaning against the warm red brickwork of Rose's Corner, another of Verrier's establishments, while he waited. The restaurant was just as full as the nightclub next door, humans drawn to the high prices and lush liquor without understanding *why*. It was booked up months ahead of time, and Verrier made a pretty penny off both his Farrow's Hollow businesses. Not that he needed the money, per se; as a prince of Hell, retired or not, he commanded respect everywhere he went. While the demon gangs and mafia families ran the city's underbelly with an iron fist, Verrier outranked all of them —period.

It was Verrier's knowledge and expertise that Severus would rely on tonight. Clutched under one arm was his sketchbook, filled with detailed drawings of the ten angels he and Moira had seen around Seraphim Securities over the last two and a half weeks. Severus had asked Alaric to arrange a meet-up with his father so he could show him the sketches. Hopefully, the most powerful demon in town could put names to the faces—and offer whatever other information he saw fit to provide in the moment.

Because they needed all the intel they could get, and Severus had hoped to bypass the tedious task of sneaking around and buying information from demons who would grossly overcharge him. Their run-in with the angel the other day made the matter time sensitive, and while Severus hadn't heard the flutter of angel wings around every corner, he couldn't be one hundred percent certain they would let him and Moira slip away unquestioned. He had even taken to following her around campus these the last three days, just to ensure no one else had decided to do the same.

This time, however, he was quite obvious about his stalking. He made sure she noticed each and every time, and Moira played right into the little game with a sly smile. Hands in her pockets, a wool cap on her head, she would brush by him, bump into him, *graze* him in passing. The little minx usually had him so riled up by the end of the day that he needed to take a handful of cold showers afterward just to think straight. He would have loved to have dragged her into a discreet alley somewhere at any given time and fucked her raw—as punishment, of course, for being such a tease—but she had asked him to keep his distance so she could get this week's coursework out of the way.

"If we're going to be surrounded by demons at the Inferno, I don't want to be thinking about essays and seminar prep," she'd insisted Monday evening, lips swollen, a firm hand on his chest as he bore down on her. "So, keep it in your pants until Wednesday."

And he had, respectfully. But now that Wednesday night was here, and she was two minutes out, Severus found he wasn't as in the mood as he could have been. This was dangerous—all of it. Tangling with angels. Getting Verrier involved. Bringing Moira to *the* den of sin and vice in Farrow's Hollow—the *it* place to be if you were a hellion in the mood for revelry. Usually the weekends were busier; he hoped that hump day would produce its usual crowd of loners, stragglers, and grumpy assholes who just wanted to drink in peace.

Still, he couldn't let his guard down for a moment. Even though Alaric had promised to keep an eye on Moira if his meeting ran long, and Severus intended to pay off several others to mind her safety in his absence.

He still couldn't decide if this was a mistake or not. Going to the Inferno to meet Verrier alone would have been ideal—it wasn't like the princely demon would allow Moira, a stranger whom he couldn't read, into his office—but his little hybrid was persistent. She wanted to be involved. She wanted to get her hands dirty, even if she hadn't come right out and said it. This was *her* father they were hunting. She deserved to be there, even if her only job was nursing a drink at the bar and looking inconspicuous from the sidelines.

Severus just needed to get her in and out in one piece, and hope no one took a special interest.

He snorted and glanced toward the road. Guaranteeing no one took a special interest in her was easier said than done when Moira looked like—

"Holy fuck." The exaltation tumbled off his lips, his sketchbook falling to the ground before he could even process what he was gawking at—she was that damn beautiful.

Standing at the entrance of the alleyway was a lady in red—garnet, actually, rich and succulent like expensive wine. Moira was supposed to be coming from her office hours on campus, and Severus had prepared himself for jeans and *maybe* a cute shirt with a low neckline. What he got was a vision in deep red, wearing a fitted, high-waisted pencil skirt and a little bralette with a lacey trim that dipped down over the exposed skin of her abdomen. A thin black choker sat midway up her throat, and her legs in those black high heels were to *die* for; he almost asked her to walk across his wretched body just to feel their bite.

"Well?" She held her arms out, a small black purse hanging off her shoulder. "Do I look demon-bar appropriate?"

Her voice snapped him back to the moment, and Severus shook his head as he marched over to her, closing the distance between them in a few long strides.

"*More* than appropriate," he rumbled, his eyes sweeping over her figure at his leisure. Red and black. Classic human attire when they wanted to blend with the demon crowd. He bit back a smile, because he couldn't poke fun at her like he did the others. Even dressed as she was, Moira was ethereal and splendid, her limbs willowy and her hair a crowning halo. The stark white locks were tossed up in a ponytail today, bouncy and tempting, a siren call for Severus's fist. She had managed to style it so that a little hair still framed her face, a slight curl to it—like she had taken the time to primp.

For *him*, maybe?

The inner beast all but salivated at the thought.

"It, uh..." Moira smoothed her hands down the skirt, and her cheeks coloured when Severus grasped her hip so he could admire her further.

"You're *too* delectable," he murmured. "Every villain in there will want to sink their claws in you."

He caught her swallow hard as she fiddled with the white waves around her face.

"I take it you approve then?"

"*Very* much." Did she know how difficult it was to ignore his baser instincts? All he wanted to do was throw her up against the wall and have his way with her right then and there. Screw the appointment with Verrier. Fuck the people waiting in line just around the corner. When he was with Moira, touching her, breathing her in, the rest of the world had a knack for going quiet.

"It used to fit better," she said quietly, tugging at the skirt. "All my clothes did. They're too big now."

He forced himself to study her with a more critical eye, only for a moment, and could acknowledge that the bralette would better suit a bigger bust. Some excess fabric puckered over her ass. But to him, she was exquisite.

"You know, you should probably be eating more these days," he told her, the thought popping into his head out of nowhere. When she looked up at him with a frown, he shrugged and traced the thin strap of her top, slipping a finger under it and following it to her protruding collarbone—eager to yank the strap all the way down and expose the creamy breast underneath, topped with its perfect pink nipple. Instead, he forced his hand back to his side, into his pocket. "If our theory is correct, and you are changing into an, er—" He cast a quick glance down the alley to confirm they were alone. "Well, changing into *that*, then your metabolism has probably spiked too. If you're losing enough weight that it makes you unhappy, increase your food intake. I'm sure you can afford to do it."

Young demons were positively *ravenous*, gluttonous to a fault; Severus could only assume that Moira's body was going through something similar as her angelic side made itself known.

"That seems," she paused for a moment, brow furrowed deeper, "logical."

"Hmm." He leaned down and pressed a quick, hard kiss to her cheek, not wanting to ruin the ruby-red lipstick making her mouth so delectable. She'd added a bit of black shadow to her eyelids too, but not enough to distract from her natural beauty. "Sometimes I can be logical. If only you'd just listen to me when I talk, you'd see—"

He exhaled sharply when she smacked him square in the chest, her grin making his heart beat just a little faster.

"Ouch." Severus tossed his cigarette aside and pressed a hand to his chest, donning a dramatically wounded expression—although it did smart a little. He wasn't used to lovers hurting him. In fact, Severus had spent the last two centuries on Earth trying not to break anyone; it was odd, to experience the opposite. The dull ache dissipated as he rubbed at it, Moira's grin morphing to something brighter, and he felt a slight twinge in his shoulder when she flashed teeth.

In Hell, demons healed from most injuries in a flash. On Earth, healing times varied, depending on the severity. Moira's teeth had left a mark on his shoulder that hadn't healed yet, days later—and Severus didn't want it to. He relished each stitch of pain, each dark reminder of that day in his bedroom.

"Do I actually hurt you?" she asked quietly, her hand settling over his, her skin warmer than he remembered. When he nodded, throat too tight to speak, she pulled back, the playfulness gone. "Oh. I'm sorry—"

"Don't be." Knowing they needed to get moving—because he could exchange hushed flirtations in a dark alley with Moira all night—Severus shrugged off his jacket and hung it over her shoulders. "I like the pain. I haven't felt it in years."

"I know the feeling."

They studied one another briefly before she slipped her arms into the jacket sleeves. The piece was far too big for her, but it covered her up enough so that her outfit wouldn't elicit the same response from other demons as it had from Severus.

With a firm clearing of her throat, Moira looked up at him, the tenderness in her expression gone. "And why am I wearing this?"

"Like I said, you look good enough to eat," Severus told her as he grabbed her hand, only her fingertips poking out the ends of the sleeves, "and if we're not careful, someone might just try to take a bite."

She opened and closed that ruby-red mouth a few times before muttering a soft, "Oh."

"*Oh* indeed." Severus led her down the alley, snatching up his dropped sketchbook on the way. Just before they reached the steel door without a handle, Moira slowed, tugging on his arm insistently enough to stop him.

"So, what exactly am I supposed to do in there?" She nodded toward the black-brick building, sounding a little nervous for the first time since she'd waltzed into the alley looking good enough to mount.

"You," Severus said, yanking her toward him and catching her when she tripped over her heels. His arm snaked around her waist, and the height difference forced her to tilt her head back to meet his gaze. "You are going to sit at the bar. Enjoy a drink. Take in the *ambiance.* Verrier won't even entertain the idea of letting you into his office, unfortunately, so that's about all you can do."

She didn't bother to hide her disappointment. "Right. Okay."

"If all goes according to plan, we'll be out of here in a tight forty-five," he promised. Severus had wasted many nights away inside the Inferno, but with Moira on his arm, he wanted to get in, get the intel, and get out as fast as possible. He would have preferred to do this after Alaric had started his shift, but Verrier had one time and one time only to meet with him, and Severus couldn't exactly say no.

Nor could he be late. So, he bestowed another sharp kiss upon her, this time catching the delicate flesh at the top of her throat, then turned and pounded a fist on the steel door. He tapped out this month's secret knock and tugged Moira inside as soon as it opened.

"Leech," Dartanious greeted, the prickly bastard of a doorman giving him the usual sneer. Towering over both of them at nearly seven feet, the grey-haired demon drew a breath, likely to insult him further, but his words seemed to die on the tip of his tongue when his black-eyed gaze landed on Moira.

"Hello," she said, offering a shy smile before Severus steered her toward the nearby bar. He rolled his eyes, feeling the doorman's gaze clinging to him as he escorted the most beautiful woman present—succubus waitresses included—toward a barstool. Moira followed slowly, absorbing the place with a wide-eyed stare, her hand clasped in his and hanging between them, arms stretched taut.

Just as he'd hoped, it was an ordinary Wednesday night. Unlike the last Wednesday he'd stopped by, the place was half-empty and quiet. Music tinkled out of the overhead speakers, but the floor vibrated from the bass beats pounding through the nightclub on the lower levels. Alaric's usual post at the back bar wasn't even open yet, the lights over the shelves of liquor dimmed, so Severus had no choice but to plant Moira at the main bar next to the front door.

A few eyes followed them, but Severus felt the heat of their stares falling squarely on *him*. They could sense him, an incubus, a lowly creature among the other demons. Moira would be a black hole to them, a void without the usual vibrations. Hopefully that, and his much-too-large leather jacket, would shield her from any curious onlookers. After all, hybrids gave no vibration. Alaric was the same—just a bunch of nothingness. Severus thought it an advantage; no supernatural beings could read them. He'd kill for that kind of anonymity.

"Now, sit here," he urged, helping her onto the high stool with a hand around her waist, "and order whatever you like."

Their arrival caught the attention of the succubus he had hoped would be working tonight, and she sauntered over with an exaggerated sway to her hips—wearing nothing but bright pink nipple covers over her generous breasts and a pair of skimpy cut-off shorts below. Moira's eyes widened with each step, but her incredulous, mildly horrified expression disappeared when Severus gave her waist a sharp pinch.

"This is Madeline," he said with a nod to the purple-haired succubus, her silky mane rolling down her back in exaggerated waves tonight. "She'll take care of you while I have my meeting with Verrier."

He caught the succubus's eye as he said the last part, raising his voice just enough for her to catch his meaning.

"Of course," Madeline purred back, though she only smiled when Severus shook her hand and slipped a hundred-dollar bill into it, just for added security. She knew she'd get a second when he returned to find Moira still in one piece where he'd left her.

"We're the same, she and I," he added to Moira, and she nodded at the very slight, hardly noticeable lift of his eyebrows, as if catching his meaning. *You don't need to be frightened of her.*

"Hardly the same," Madeline protested, sprawling across the bartop and propping her chin up on her fists. "I'm much, *much* better."

"I can see that," Moira said, a faint quiver in her voice. "Nice to meet you."

"Oh, she *is* a precious thing," Madeline cooed as she straightened, the movement so sudden that Moira all but jumped back against Severus. He held her in place, not wanting Madeline to know she startled easily.

"Keep an eye on her," Severus remarked. He then snatched her wrist, *hard*, when Madeline appeared to be reaching across the bar to cup Moira's chin. "And *don't* touch her."

"Men." The succubus snorted and tossed Moira a quick eye roll. "So possessive. What can I get you to drink, honey?"

"Uhm." Those haunting blue eyes darted to the drinks board overhead. "A martini?"

"Sure thing. Olive?"

"Please."

"So polite," he heard Madeline coo, as if speaking to a toddler, while Severus checked his watch. "Wherever did you find her, Sev?"

He scowled; no one but Alaric was allowed to take such liberties with his name. Unfortunately, he hadn't the time to snarl back, so he kissed Moira's cheek instead, told her to drink slow, and headed for the staircase at the far side of the bar. He shot one last glare over his shoulder, catching and holding Madeline's eye, and she waved him off with a huff he could feel across the room.

Sketchbook in hand and heart in his throat, he took the stairs two at a time, hoping that Verrier was in a pleasant, helpful mood. One could never be certain with a prince of Hell—they smiled when they liked you, but they supposedly smiled just before they slit your throat, too.

And Severus had no idea how to spot the difference.

CHAPTER FIVE

Moira wasn't sure what she had expected a demon bar to look like—but this wasn't it.

Delving into Severus's world of angels, demons, and the supernatural over the last several weeks had been *thrilling*. Not only were they so much closer to finding her dad than she could ever have been on her own, but she was finally starting to feel like a *person* again. Not a pasty freak. Not a human oddity. When she looked in the mirror this week, she no longer saw a walking corpse staring back at her; at the very least, she didn't see something grotesque *every* time. She hadn't rid herself of the insecurities completely, but she was trying. Because this new body wasn't the result of an illness, of a secret, lethal disease. Moira was *becoming* something—something real, something worthwhile.

And Severus had had a huge hand in helping her discover who, and what, exactly was lurking inside her. For all his snark, leering, and eye rolling, Severus was the most helpful, considerate, *patient* person—demon—she had been with in a long time. With him, she could be herself, or whatever her "self" was transforming into.

It was liberating.

And the *sex*. Sex with Severus was unlike anything she had ever experienced before, and it took all her self-control not to move into his bedroom permanently. Not only could she touch him without worrying she'd snap his bones, but he had opened her eyes to a world of pleasure she'd never thought possible before. Orgasms? Pretty incredible. Outstanding. Two thumbs up. Gold medal. A++. Tens across the fucking *board*. Moira still couldn't wrap her mind around the fact that her body could *do* something so ridiculously pleasurable. The hype was justified.

Best of all, Severus grounded her back in a reality she thought she'd been fading from for almost a year now. When people touched her, brushed across her, accidentally knocked into her—Moira hardly felt it. Being with Severus only made her realize just how different she was becoming from the people she had known her whole life, but she wouldn't change what she had with him for anything, not when his touch was so very *real*. Every caress, every nip, every grasp of his hand, fingertips biting into her skin—Moira felt it, and it felt damn *good*. Grounding. No longer was she disappearing into the ether as the rest of the world carried on without her. Severus had brought her back to life simply by being himself; she'd never find the right way to thank him for that.

Awesome sex seemed like a pretty great start.

Her eyes drifted along the stone staircase, trailing after him as he disappeared upstairs. He might be moody, and she might still need to learn how to properly interact with him—with the darkness behind his penetrating stare—but Moira didn't mind the work. To her, Severus was worth the effort, whether he knew it or not.

Because he made her feel safe in this new, foreign world

of angels and demons—and he made her feel *real* surrounded by humans.

Moira needed him.

"Here you are, honey." Madeline, the curvy succubus he'd left her with, set a freshly poured martini in front of her, that smile dazzling. "One martini, with an olive."

"Thank you." Moira brought the drink to her lips for a quick sip, trying not to wince as the gin burned down her throat. She wasn't a fan of martinis, but, put on the spot, she had panicked and said the first drink that came to mind. Usually Moira preferred beer—or something deceptively fruity with a high alcohol content.

The succubus leaned on the counter, breasts shoved up to her chin. "What's the verdict? Scrumptious? Positively *divine*?"

"Delicious," Moira insisted, muffling a cough after her second miniscule sip. Unable to hold the demon's black-eyed stare, she busied herself with a quick study of this new facet of the Inferno.

During their undergrad years, she, Ella, and all their friends had visited the two-storey human side of the bar every other week; they advertised *aggressively* on campus, offering students deep discounts and ladies' nights dripping with free booze every Friday. While Moira had all but ceased socializing since starting grad school, too overwhelmed with her body to bother with it, she knew for a fact her housemates still went at least once a month.

And, honestly, the human side was a lot more fun. The music was better, the crowds were livelier, and the décor looked like it belonged in this decade—this *century* even. The demon side was just depressing, with all that exposed black brick and dark furniture and just dark everything.

Well, not everything. The three ladies manning the bar were a breath of fresh air, but none of the patrons seemed to bat an eye at their outlandish outfits or their come-hither stares.

Overall, she gave the bar a solid B+: nothing special, but clean and efficient enough that she'd feel comfortable getting semi-drunk here.

"So, tell me," Madeline purred, placing a hand over Moira's to recapture her attention. "How did a cute little thing like you end up with a dull *wretch* like Severus?"

Flustered, Moira retracted her hand somewhat forcefully. Madeline would expect a reaction, and Moira had proven that she couldn't be drugged by a sex demon's touch. However, it seemed stupid to let *her* know that, so she batted her eyelashes dreamily and took another sip of her martini, hoping the act was convincing.

"Well, we, uh, met..." Damn it. She and Severus hadn't worked out a cover story yet. With the demon's unflinching stare boring down on her, she straightened on the barstool, kept any exposed bits of skin—the few visible with Severus's giant leather jacket over her shoulders, the fabric soaked in his delicious cologne—to herself, and decided to tell a half truth. "I'm a client, actually. We just had to make a pit stop tonight."

"A client who...knows his true nature?" Madeline asked, an eyebrow lifted. In an instant, Moira's hands went clammy. Did Severus's clients not know he was an incubus? Probably not. Shit. Shit. *Shit.*

"Well, I guess you can say we run in similar circles," she managed, then took a much, *much* too large gulp of her drink. She coughed before she'd even swallowed it, gin coming out her nose. Madeline merely stared, unfazed, and made no effort to help.

"You do give an *odd* vibration. Hardly one at all, in fact... What are you, exactly?"

"Didn't your mother ever tell you that's a *rude* question, Madeline?" Severus countered, appearing out of nowhere by Moira's side as she grabbed a napkin and wiped at her nose. Her watery gaze shot up to him, and Moira offered a weak smile as he patted her back.

"Hi," she croaked, pleased to see the purple-haired demon vanish from the corner of her eye after Severus shot her a withering look. "You weren't gone long."

"He's running late tonight," Severus told her, holding his sketchbook loosely at his side, dashing as ever in the black cotton tee and fitted denim. He just had the perfect ass for jeans.

"So, what does that mean for us?" Her cheeks warmed when he caressed the side of her neck, his arm circling somewhat possessively around her shoulders.

"We," he said with a sigh, "now have an hour to kill. Would you like to go somewhere else? Rose's Corner might have a booth open."

Moira scoffed and shook her head. "That place is *way* too expensive for the food they serve."

"Now, darling, be nice," Severus warned with a tight smile. "Verrier sets the prices and I'm sure they're more than fair."

She glanced around them, wondering if someone might be listening, but that didn't seem to be the case.

But then again, what did she know? Severus had proven to her that she was still *way* out of her depth in his world, so she had stopped arguing with him—about most things, anyway.

"Okay," she said slowly, her tight smile matching his. "I'm sure I'm mistaken about the...pricing structure." At his nod, Moira could almost imagine him murmuring *good girl* in his sultry, husky sex-god voice, and she found herself crossing her legs as desire shuddered through her. "Anyway. We don't have to leave. We can just wait here, can't we? Have a drink together?"

His smile vanished, though the tightness didn't. Severus's dark stare bounced around the room, taking it all in, before he let out a long sigh—almost in defeat. "Sure. That'll be fine. We can..."

At the sound of a commotion coming from the main door, Moira looked over her shoulder. In spilled a group of loud, laughing, *shouting* men, all swathed in black suits and what Moira could only describe as *bling*.

"We'll sit it out downstairs," Severus remarked curtly, grabbing her hand and pulling her off the barstool. Moira stumbled after him, her heels higher than what she usually wore, and only noticed she'd left her half-drunk martini behind when Severus stopped at the closed-down bar on the other side of the room. She watched, brow furrowed, as he tucked his sketchbook behind the counter.

"Are you sure you want to leave that there?"

"Alaric will be here in fifteen minutes," he muttered, scribbling something down on a napkin with a pen. "It'll be safe here."

She bit her lower lip, wondering if she ought to question him. Those sketches had taken two weeks to perfect, and they were the whole reason she and Severus were even *here* tonight. However, when he caught her expression, he flashed one of those sinful smiles that made her knees weak, then steered her toward a staircase that led down instead of up.

"Don't fret, pet," he insisted. "I leave things back there

all the time. They'll be *fine*. No one wants to get incubus *cooties* by snooping through my things, I promise."

"Right." Well, she had trusted him about pretty much everything else so far—why not this? Moira still cast one last look back, noting the empty stools and dimmed lights—the complete opposite of the bar she had nursed her martini at. The new arrivals flocked to Madeline and her cohorts, the din they created worse than the neighbourhood frat assholes who lived across the street from her in the campus suburbs.

Soon enough, however, the chorus of rambunctious male voices was replaced by a pounding, whumping bass beat. Descending the dark path into the lower level of the Inferno was like stepping into an entirely different world. It was a wonder the sound didn't carry upstairs, and Moira gasped at the sight of torches—real, flickering, fiery torches —illuminating the bottom half of the winding stairwell.

Her eyes nearly popped out of her head when she and Severus happened upon two half-naked individuals in the throes of rabid, aggressive sex at the last turn of the stairs. Stunned, Moira slipped on the last step, smacking face-first into Severus's back, and then pressed a hand to her burning cheeks as she all but ran from the live sex show. Her demonic companion's chuckles reverberated in her ears, and she only slowed when he wrapped a hand around her waist and pulled her back.

"I'm afraid this isn't the Inferno you thought you knew," he rasped in her ear.

No, it most certainly was not. They'd waltzed right into a dungeon, torches illuminating the stone floors, walls, and ceiling as far as the eye could see. There were triple the number of people down here than there were upstairs, and it fleetingly reminded her of the dance floor in the human Inferno—only with a lot more nudity. Black eyes everywhere, demons on full display. Moira swallowed hard, trying to find her nerve.

"Are you sure you don't wish to go anywhere else?"

"Are any of them going to touch me?" she shouted back, gripping the fabric of Severus's shirt so tightly that she was surprised she hadn't ripped it. When he frowned and shook his head, Moira squared her shoulders. "Then no. I can handle it."

Once she realized that no one had so much as glanced their way since they arrived, the scene of writhing bodies, the air thick with sweat—among other curious smells—became slightly more palatable. The music, however, was kind of a nightmare, and Moira plugged her ears with her fingers as Severus steered her into the madness.

With such low ceilings, Moira found this level more claustrophobic than the last, but spying things like a DJ turntable perched up on a stage and a bar manned by three other beautiful creatures had an oddly calming effect on her. It was just a club—a more gratuitously sensual club than she was used to, but it wasn't like they'd strolled into Hell or anything. These were just people—demons, whatever—who were forking over their hard-earned cash in exchange for a good time.

They might as well be university students.

Severus led her around the mob, rather than through it, and soon had her seated at a tall table, one of many, along the back wall. Her feet dangled about a foot and a half off the ground, and she crossed her ankles, fingers drumming anxiously on the black—was that granite?—tabletop.

"Would you like something to drink?" He was forced to ask the question directly in her ear—but he wasn't shouting. No, it was the same sinful rumble that always made her heart flutter and her panties damp, his lips brushing the shell of her ear. Moira found herself leaning into him, taking a few seconds too long to clue into why he'd even asked.

"Oh." She looked up, startled. "I forgot my martini. I didn't *pay* for my martini!"

"I have a tab," he remarked, waving off her concerns when she turned her wide-eyed stare toward him. "Shall I get you another?"

Moira shook her head, suddenly shy: Severus fetching her a drink when it was just the two of them at, well, a *sex* club, felt strangely intimate. Then again, it was no more intimate than Moira arching herself up to whisper in his ear, her hand settling on his chest. "I don't really like gin. Can you make it, uhm, something sweeter?"

The muscles along his jaw flickered, as though clenched, and Severus tugged the front of his jacket up to cover more of Moira's figure. Her breath caught at the way he rustled her about, rearranged her. When their eyes met again, blackness stared back. She still wasn't sure how to feel about it—the demon inside. The *true* Severus, if she understood all his vague comments correctly. All she knew was that it aroused her *far* more than it should have, and she hastily retracted her hand when she realized it was clutching the neckline of his T-shirt.

"One *sweet* drink, coming up," he purred in her ear, and she shuddered when his tongue trailed along the shell this time, teeth catching the lobe. "Don't move."

"No promises," she managed, but only when he eased away, every inch of her on fire. Severus cast one last sinful grin over his shoulder before disappearing into the crowd, headed in the direction of the bar.

Left to her own devices, Moira took the time to calm down, massaging the colour out of her cheeks as she gave herself a mental pep talk. They were here tonight for *serious* work. Sure, she had spent nearly a full hour in the library bathroom after office hours tonight, primping and prepping, wearing actual makeup that took actual time to apply in order to enhance her looks, for the first time in *ages*. Yes, some of it had been for Severus's benefit, and some of it stemmed from the desire to start feeling like her old self again, but Moira had wanted to *fit in* more than anything. She had wanted to appear cool and collected—surrounded by demons, but totally at ease with it.

Thus far, she wasn't sure she had been successful in that respect—but Severus certainly seemed to approve of her outfit. So. That had to count for something?

Get a grip, girl. She leaned back against the prickly stone wall behind her, willing herself to act normal. This was just a bar. Upstairs was *just* a demon who might be able to put a name to her dad's face—no big deal. Get in, get out, and get the job done. That's what this was supposed to be. A job. Not...fun sexy times with Severus.

She nibbled her lower lip, then sat up and rubbed at her teeth, worried her ruby-red lipstick might have transferred by her annoying little habit. When she was done, she noticed a few figures on the edges of the sex pit watching her, and she rolled her shoulders back, lifted her chin, and adopted an air of nonchalance that she assumed would go unquestioned in a place like this.

The façade worked, boosting her confidence and soothing her nerves—until her wandering gaze stopped on a couple *literally* fucking no more than ten feet from her. The woman—human, if her eyes had anything to say about it—suddenly bent over in front of the tall, dark-eyed demon man behind her, jean mini-skirt hitched up and hands planted on the floor. Moira watched, horrified, as the demon undid his pants, whipped out his cock, and plunged it into her.

"Oh my god." She couldn't look away. It was like a car accident—she *had* to watch, no matter how uncomfortable it made her. No one else around them seemed to notice, or mind, that two figures were just...having sex. Right there. Right on the dance floor. Brazen as anything.

Suddenly, Severus's looming, smirking figure blocked her view, and he handed her an ice-cold glass of something.

"Sangria," he told her. "Extra heavy on the fruit."

"Thanks." The word snagged in her throat, and she shoved the straw between her lips and sucked half the white wine mix down, her cheeks flaming. Severus, rather than settling onto the stool on the other side of their table, stayed right there, planted in front of her so that she couldn't see the dance floor anymore, a hand on her knee. Slowly, as his wandering hand drifted under the fabric of her skirt, Moira forgot what was going on around them—lost in the sensation of his thumb tracing slow, lazy circles across her thigh.

"We've still got another forty-five minutes," he told her, leaning down again—and this time blatantly dragging his tongue from the nape of her neck to her ear. "Whatever shall we do to pass the time?"

The crux of her thighs tingled as his caress grew more insistent, more obvious, and Moira found herself widening her legs as much as her pencil skirt would allow.

"Oh, I don't know." She downed the rest of her sangria in near record time, though she hardly felt the usual buzz in her head or in her core. Severus's touch, figuratively, seemed to intoxicate her more than alcohol these days. She set her glass on the table, then fluttered her lashes at him, adopting an air of innocence. "Did you have something in mind?"

The sensual quirk of his mouth, steeped in desire and

concerningly predatory, nearly made her swoon, and Moira gasped when he cupped her face and kissed her. Harshly. Roughly, his tongue sweeping between her parted lips, tasting like peppermint and risk. She adored the taste of his kiss—of every single one of them, all different but all equally dangerous. Equally *thrilling*. Her toes curled in her heels, legs desperate to wrap around his waist as she strained to keep pace with him, with his tongue that wouldn't let her rest, that seemed to want to stroke every inch of her before the night was through.

Her fingers curled around his shirt, her body rising up to his as he cradled her head. Two large hands caged her face, leaving her feeling both cornered and protected, a willing captive in his embrace. He seemed to want to work those hands into her hair, but her meticulous styling held him at bay. Instead, Severus tore himself away, eyes blacker than ever and mouth lifted in a snarl.

Before she could get a quip out, knowing he'd enjoyed their verbal foreplay before, he snatched her hand and all but hauled her off the stool. She teetered after him, determined to keep pace without falling flat on her face or getting her heel wedged in the dusty cobblestone flooring below.

Once again, Severus led them around the pit of writhing bodies, wherein many couples appeared to engage in something more risqué than dancing. He slowed when they reached the other side, and stopped completely in front of an arched wooden doorway. He gripped the wrought iron handle and gave it a good rattle. Then, when it opened unhindered, he dragged her inside and slammed it shut behind them.

Moira blinked rapidly, trying to adjust to the complete and utter darkness around her. The scent of sweat and sex had vanished, and in its place was a damp, cool airiness. When Severus let go of her hand, she wrapped her arms around herself, feeling uncomfortably off-balance—until a smattering of light trickled in from the ceiling. She looked up, squinting at first, the little dots like starlight—it was oddly beautiful, given the abrasive environment outside.

With the lights growing brighter, she had the chance to quickly take in the new room. While small, its ceiling was higher than the dungeon-esque dance floor they had left behind. Made entirely of stone, it was a round little room with bench seating lining the walls—and a giant wrought-iron hook hanging from the ceiling. She gulped, lips parting as she stared at it, but before she'd had the chance to ask a question, Severus had her pinned back against the door, his mouth on hers.

And, in a heartbeat, she forgot about the hook, about the people fucking outside, about all the black eyes and his abandoned sketchbook. All that mattered was him and her, the heat rising between their bodies—the way their mouths fit so perfectly together that it made her heart hurt.

Kissing her harshly, desperately, Severus all but smothered her with his powerful frame, his hands first gripping her backside, then sliding up, purposefully, over her hips, her breasts. They stopped at her shoulders, where he finally wrenched his leather jacket down her arms. It crumpled at her feet, forgotten, and her skin prickled, kissed by the cool, dark air.

How strange—to suddenly feel so exposed, so on display, while still completely clothed.

She could feel him fumbling about between them, the sensation accompanied by the crisp snap of his leather belt as he tugged it free from its loops. Her lower lip caught between Severus's teeth, Moira whimpered when he finally withdrew, half dragging her off the door by that lip, half daring her to wriggle free. She wouldn't. She had never been one for pain in the bedroom, but something about the way Severus delivered it was heavenly. So, she let him pull her, an ache skittering below her skin as a much deeper, much stronger pulse of desire throbbed between her thighs.

When he finally did release her, she fell about a foot back against the door, her heart racing. Belt gripped in hand, Severus arched an eyebrow at her, the starlight above casting unnerving shadows across his face, across those obsidian eyes. Only a fool would lean into the fear—and with Severus, Moira had become quite the fool.

He waited, the thumping beat vibrating the door behind her, Moira's breath coming hard and fast. He waited until she settled, until her eyes finally lowered to the belt held taut between both of his hands. Knowing he'd track the movement, she swept her tongue across her lower lip, then offered her wrists. She placed them together, daintily, and reached out to him. She hadn't been one for ropes in the bedroom either, but Severus seemed to enjoy restraining her.

And Moira enjoyed letting him.

The demon eased forward with a smirk, a lift of his lips that she knew ought to make her cower, and then, slowly, with great care, looped the belt around her wrists. He took his time deciding which notch to use, and not once did his gaze leave her face. Moira stared back, chin lifted, only to gasp when he yanked her forward suddenly, the leather's bite harsher against her skin than she'd expected.

She toppled into his chest, her bound hands between them, and Severus wrenched her head back by her ponytail. Her little squeal of surprise, dragged out by the sharpness of his kiss, earned her a growl in return. He held her flush against him, his arousal prominent, unabashedly pressed to her abdomen, even as he walked them into the center of the strange little room.

He left her breathless once more, ending the kiss too abruptly for her liking and yanking her bound hands high above her head. Moira winced, shoulders protesting only slightly, and was forced onto her toes as Severus hung her from that iron hook. Just for good measure, she tried to free herself, squirming about as he stepped back, but once again he had proven his ability to trap her in one place.

From a distance, Severus admired his work, those black eyes betraying nothing—the noticeable bulge in his pants did that just fine. Mouth smug. Hands clasped behind his back. Severus was the vision of a man too pleased with himself.

He cocked his head to the side, watching her tiptoe in place. She wanted him back, his lips dragging across her skin and hands doing torturously wonderful things to her body. The distance left her uneasy.

"Is the door locked?" she asked, voice cracking.

"What's wrong, darling?" He grazed a finger from her cheekbone down, over her lips, along her neck, across her collarbone. His eyes seemed to glitter, catching the individual stars in the ceiling. "Not an exhibitionist?"

"No," she said firmly. Severus pursed his lips, then huffed and marched around behind her. Moments later, she heard something heavy click into place. The nerves drained out of her—only to be replaced by nerves of a different kind entirely. Locked in—just her and the demon. Unable to turn around, the hook unyielding, she was forced to listen to the gentle click of his shoes, each footstep sending a prickle of excitement, anxiety, *need* across her entire body. Her nipples hardened, poking through the thin, velvety fabric of her bralette—a garment designed to be both a bra *and* a shirt. She'd bought it years ago and had never been brave enough to wear it.

Now, she wondered if Severus would do her the courtesy of leaving it in one piece. He hadn't been all that thoughtful with her clothes last time.

Severus circled her slowly, each step precise and measured. He did it twice, the second time trailing his finger down her spine—gently at first, then roughly digging into the dip of her lower back. She squirmed out of reach, only to be pulled back by the little zipper at the top of her skirt. Biting her lower lip, she inhaled sharply as he unzipped the garment, then pushed it over the swell of her backside, down her thighs, until she stepped out of it and kicked it away. She expected her panties to come next—red, lacey, the mildly scandalous crotchless ones he had found so interesting that first day in her bedroom. She had been mortified then that someone so stunning—and terrifying—had taken an interest in her panty drawer.

It seemed the fascination remained, because he paused for a moment, running his hands along the lace before delving between her thighs, his fingers ghosting over her slick folds left exposed by the slit. Moira pushed up higher on her toes, gasping shakily as pleasure fluttered out from her core. Then, just like that, he retreated—no more than a torturous tease. She licked her lips, her entire body feeling flushed, as he smirked.

"You remembered my fondness for them. I'm flattered," he rumbled, his voice thick with desire and maybe —affection?

"And you have expensive taste. Keep that in mind if you decide to rip anything this time," she told him, though the firmness had evaporated from her tone. A shuddering, trembling breathiness replaced it, and she tried to square her shoulders, tried to find the fire again, but she could already feel herself melting as his dark chuckle washed across her skin.

"I do so enjoy that smart little mouth of yours," he cooed as he grasped her face. She thought he might kiss her as he swooped in, but he merely scraped his teeth over her chin and down her throat. Moira hissed softly, pain intermingling with the pleasure slowly gathering deep within her. She should have held back a little—not played so easily into his hand. But Moira couldn't ignore the heat between them. She didn't *want* to.

So, she arched her back, rising up just enough to meet his open-mouthed wandering down the planes of her body. His lips plucked at each nipple through her bralette, and she squirmed, wetness palpable now between her thighs. He murmured her name, painting it across her skin in broad, sweeping strokes, until he finally stopped. With a gulp, Moira peered down to find a demon kneeling before her, hands on her thighs, eyes drinking her in.

"Severus, you—*oh!*" She giggled, not meaning to, when he lifted her up and all but sat her on his face. With her legs dangling over his shoulders and down his back, her arms found instant relief, the pressure easing as he took the brunt of her weight.

Every slow, even breath, a torturous exhale tumbling between his parted lips, burned her sex. She thought he might torment her. After all, they had a *lot* of time to kill before his appointment with Verrier. However, Severus pushed the lace aside quickly instead, then cupped her backside, fingertips bruising, and guided her aching heat straight to his mouth. Her body spasmed with the first sensuous lick between her swollen lips, her eyes wide.

Something straddling the lines of a gasp and a sob slipped out, pleasure radiating through her, so swiftly, so *suddenly*, that she almost told him to stop.

She'd told him to stop last time too—right before she'd had her first orgasm. It had been...life-changing. And uplifting, honestly. Not because a man had showed her how to pleasure herself—but because he had taken the time to prove that she wasn't broken. He had taken the time to prove her fears *wrong*. All she needed was the right pair of hands, the right mouth, on the right places.

Humanity had been fading from her ever since her changes began, and with Severus, she was finally starting to understand why. She wasn't defective. She wasn't doomed for a pleasureless existence. She had just given up on herself, beaten down from *everything*—too despondent to even try.

That same night, Moira had locked her bedroom door, turned off the lights, and touched herself as he had. Harder than she had ever dared before, she explored her body, this *new* body, imagining his hands, his tongue, those blazing black eyes swallowing her whole—and she had come just fine on her own, too. Her climaxes with Severus had been better, but she was determined to outshine him someday with enough solo practice.

Someday—but not today. Not with the way his tongue looped around her clit, each sweep drawing out a sweet pain that reminded her of lightning. The searing, burning, crackling kind that cuts across a black sky in the middle of a storm—so too did her pleasure slice across the steadily swelling fog of desire building within her, threatening to burst, to rain down and drown her.

She let her head fall back, helplessly trapped and in no mood to escape anytime soon. Hands bound, unable to move her hips away from his greedy mouth—only able to grind them up and down, only able to *take* the ecstasy of his touch, not deny it.

It felt like hours—but it must have only been minutes—before Moira finally broke. Eyes clenched, she whimpered through the pleasure lapping across every part of her like a rushing, thundering river. Her heels dug into his back, and Severus bit her thigh in response—but neither let up. Not until the high of her undoing cracked and splintered, and Moira's eyes fluttered open, lost in the twinkling starlight above.

Slowly, the music filtered through the fog, and her body sagged when Severus set her feet back on the ground and stood. He wiped around his mouth, then licked his fingers clean. Moira expected the smugness again, the triumphant grin, but his lips were set in a thin line instead, jaw clenched tight enough that the muscles flickered. Fear crept through the pleasure, coaxing her out again, her breath starting to quicken as he strode around her and disappeared from sight.

She didn't need to turn around to know he was still with her. Moira felt him, the soft, barely-there vibration of his being—something she had never understood before, but the deeper she sank into this world, the more she embraced it. She heard him too, the pop of his pants button and the hiss of his zipper. Fingers bit into her hips again, her thighs, as he eased her legs apart—and then filled her with a single, brutal thrust.

Her cry bounced off the walls, eyes wide and fluttering as she adjusted to the sheer size of him, to the fullness. Pleasure bloomed within her again, tendrils of pain laced throughout, and Moira turned her head only slightly when she felt his lips on her shoulder.

"You are," he growled, briefly biting down hard enough to make her yelp, "*the* most exquisite creature I've ever seen."

When words failed her, she simply let her head fall back against him, lips parted and eyes closed—the ultimate trust, a calculated risk. He nuzzled against her neck, her skin erupting with goosebumps in response. Firmly, his hand wrapped around the base of her ponytail again. Her toes could no longer reach the floor, but she still tried anyway, straining, and Moira shuddered softly when his other hand trailed across her bare stomach. He did so gently at first, tickling her, chuckling as she squirmed, until he finally slipped under her top's lace trim, under the red velvet, and pinched her already painfully hard nipple. She flailed out a little, legs kicking, hips bucking in response, but he stilled her with a harsh tug of her hair, his teeth on her neck.

"Are you ready, sweet little Moira?" he rasped in her ear. She kicked back, savoring his grunt of pain when her heel collided with his shin. His fingers moved to her other breast, just as ruthless with that nipple, and he nipped at her earlobe. "So be it."

"Big talk—"

He tore another sharp, startled cry from her with the first thrust, then the next, and the next, pounding into her. Her wrists screamed and her sex *ached*, the build toward another climax making her bite down on the insides of her cheeks. Muffle the cries, the whimpers, the *moans*. Severus reprimanded her by latching onto the nape of her neck and sucking until she kicked him again.

"Don't be quiet," he hissed, his voice thick, the words savage. "I want them to hear you. *I* want to hear you."

Moira wanted to keep the sounds to herself—but she

couldn't. Not when he took her harder, faster, hammering into her, tweaking her nipples, wrenching her head back—until she saw stars again. Earnest, true stars. The pleasure of her second climax dulled her senses, the twinges of pain fading fast, only ecstasy in their place. Tears rolled down her cheeks as thick, molten *heat* leisurely swept across her body.

"Moira?" She heard his voice distantly, through the fog—barely. "Am I hurting you?"

"N-no," she managed, her body tight and trembling.

"You're crying."

"I'm *happy*." Happy to be normal, to experience *normal*. To be kissed and taken by a man who didn't see the changes—who didn't fear them. In that moment, she was happier than she had been in a *long* time... Tied up in what could very well be a sex dungeon, being pounded into by a demon. Moira was *happy*.

"*Fuck*." He hissed a string of incoherent curses against her skin, releasing her hair and wrapping both arms tightly around her waist. The brutality of his final thrusts punctured the post-orgasm bliss settling in, but he stilled moments later, choking out her name.

They stayed there, pants and soft moans filling the room, until Moira realized her fingers had gone numb. She nudged his shin this time, and Severus needed no words to lift her, then detach her bound hands from the hanging hook. A little unsteadily, he carried her across the small chamber and sank onto one of the stone benches, still buried inside her.

"You know," Severus murmured, kissing up her arm, her shoulder, her neck, "we still have another, oh..." He held up his wrist, a thick, expensive-looking watch staring back at them. "Twenty-five minutes."

"Do we?" Moira asked, settling in, ignoring the dreamy quality that clung to her words. "How ever will we pass the time?"

"Oh," his hands trailed up her thighs, rearranging her on his lap so she could feel him hardening again inside her, "I think you'll find I'm *very* creative when it comes to killing time..."

Moira pressed her hands to her cheeks, hiding the blush, and laughed.

CHAPTER SIX

"Are you sure I can't get you something stronger to drink?"

"No, water is fine," Moira insisted, smiling when Severus's roommate Alaric set the glass in front of her. He'd filled it to the brim with ice, just the way she liked it, without needing to be told. "I think I've had enough to drink tonight."

"I very much doubt that," he said with a chuckle, leaning on the counter, long fingers threaded together. "I'm sure you'll find your tolerance for most things is higher these days, if Severus's theory is correct."

She shrugged. "I guess so."

He was right, of course. She didn't feel the least bit drunk from the drinks she'd had before she and Severus found a scandalous way to kill time down in the sex pit. Not even tipsy, which was what two strong drinks would have done to her a year ago. Food never seemed to satiate her these days, not even her favourites, and she could handle all the savagery Severus had to throw at her in the bedroom. It would be a fun experiment for another night—to see just how much it would take to get her good and drunk. Tonight, however, Moira wanted to keep her wits about her.

Taking a long sip of her water, she glanced over her shoulder toward the staircase Severus had climbed nearly an hour earlier, his trusty sketchbook tucked under his arm. By the time they had resurfaced, the scene had picked up, and he'd deposited her at the back bar with a guarantee that his roommate would look after her. Unfortunately for her, Alaric had been busy tending to patrons for much of her solo hour, so she wasted time away on her phone, no longer in the mood to demon-watch as the minutes ticked by.

Now that the seats alongside her had emptied, however, she finally had the tall, sinewy figure all to herself. A delicate smattering of barely-there freckles painted the bridge of his nose. They matched his copper-red locks, which were swept back and arranged with some sort of styling product. He was a handsome guy, complete with a very posh English accent to boot, but she didn't feel the same hum vibrating off him that she had come to associate with Severus.

"So, how long have you and Severus been living together?" she asked when she realized he was still watching her.

"Well, my father moved me over here when my mum died, and I was seventeen," he told her. Moira schooled her features as she always did when someone mentioned the death of a parent, but she still felt that stab of longing, that slash of emptiness, deep inside her. She might not have been actively grieving for her mom anymore, but she missed her—always.

"I'm sorry," she said quickly, hands curled around the huge glass, "about your mom. Mine died when I was twenty-one. It's... It sucks."

"Not my best year, no." Alaric swallowed hard, eyes everywhere but her. "But it was good to reconnect with my father. He wanted me close. Back then I thought it was because I looked so much like her, but then he gave me a job here, and I met Severus, and... Well, we've been roommates ever since."

"That's sweet."

"Well, I wouldn't throw that term around when you're referring to a demon," Alaric told her with a slight grin, one that grew when her cheeks colored. "He's a good guy though. He'll never admit it, of course, but he's one of the few demons I've met who didn't give a shit that I'm a hybrid."

Her eyebrows shot up, curiosity piqued. "Do demons generally have a problem with hybrids?"

"Sev didn't tell you?"

"No." Moira huffed. "He's a bit stingy with information. It seems like I'm still operating on a need-to-know...thing."

"Right." He straightened and grabbed a spray bottle and a roll of paper towels, then started cleaning the counter. "Look, hybrids are a bit of a...taboo subject in the demon community. Most demons don't acknowledge any children they have with humans. I was lucky my father loved my mum as much as he did, otherwise I'd be on my own."

"But why?" She hadn't put much thought into being a split between a human and an angel, but from the tone of Alaric's voice, perhaps she should. "What's the issue with hybrids?"

"It all depends on how the demon views humans," Alaric told her, throwing himself into a particularly troublesome spot, his brow furrowed. "Some see them as a, well, a lesser species, if you will. Others look at them as food. A few see them for what they are—people. But the majority of demons just think themselves *better* than humans." He glanced up at her, his eyes a lovely emerald hue. "So, you take an apex species, then mix it with the bottom of the food chain... No one really likes the outcome, especially when you don't know if the demon side'll even show until they're adults."

"Has yours started to show?" she asked, not missing a beat. She couldn't imagine those wholesome green eyes going black, but then again, there were *many* stunning creatures walking around this side of the Inferno. Just because you were pretty on the outside didn't mean there wasn't a beast dripping with darkness on the inside.

"No. Not yet, anyway." He chuckled, rolling his shoulders back when he straightened. "I think he's shy. Having Verrier for a father would probably give any demon a complex."

Before she had the chance to ask *why*—because she still didn't understand what the big deal was with this Verrier guy, beyond the fact that it was clear Severus feared him—a cluster of noisy men settled along the barstools, filling all but the one beside her. Tucking away his cleaning supplies, Alaric shot her another grin, then mouthed *be right back*. Moira nodded and smiled, then took another generous gulp of her water. Hopefully he wasn't gone for too long. While drawing information out of Severus was like pulling teeth, Alaric seemed all too happy to talk.

And she *wanted* to talk with him: he was the first hybrid she had ever met. If what he said about the demon community's prejudices were true, she still had a lot to learn —and she needed to learn it fast. For all she knew, angels could be just as biased against *her*, and if that was the case, she definitely needed to know. Moira needed to *prepare*.

Not that she hadn't been preparing all her life for her

absentee dad to reject her the first time they met, but things felt different now. Somehow the thought of an *angel* rejecting her, tossing her aside like she was nothing, hurt a whole lot more.

"Now, what sort of cruel creature would leave a pretty little thing like you all by your lonesome?"

Each word fluttered over her, trickling in one ear and tumbling out the other. She winced, goosebumps prickling to life uncomfortably, even under Severus's leather jacket. Distinctly male, the voice had a snake-like quality to it, hissing and whispery, and Moira nearly toppled off her stool when she found the source of it—seated directly beside her, too close for comfort.

"Hi," the demon cooed, his pitch-black eyes a stark contrast to his clean-shaven porcelain skin—skin that could give hers a run for its money. "Is this seat taken?"

"Uh, yes." Moira glanced back to the stairs, then positioned herself for a cold shoulder brush-off, ignoring the way he sat facing her, legs open and arm resting across the bartop in front of her. He smiled, flashing a set of exceptionally sharp teeth.

"By me, right? Taken by me?" His laugh made her stomach roil, and Moira shot him an incredulous look.

"Not exactly."

"Well, perhaps just for a little while then, eh?" He reached out, as if to brush the loose bits of hair from her face, but she recoiled before he could. Disappointment flashed across his features, but she couldn't detect a single genuine thing about it. Dressed head-to-toe in black, the suit expertly tailored to fit his lean physique, the demon's hair matched his eyes, and his smile glittered dangerously like the mishmash of silver crosses and necklaces hanging around his neck. Each cross was adorned with pearls, which she thought odd—for a demon.

"I don't—"

"Now, now, no need for that," he crooned, offering her his hand. "Let's just be friends, shall we? You can call me Diriel, sweetness."

Moira swallowed thickly and tried to catch Alaric's eye, but the band of clucking idiots at the other end of the bar were keeping him busy. She huffed, staring pointedly at Diriel's extended hand for a moment before pinning her glare to his face. "I'm really not looking for more friends, but thanks for the offer."

"*Feisty*," he growled, inching to the edge of his barstool, his presence humming unpleasantly into her personal space. "I do enjoy that in a woman. Why don't I buy you a drink? I'll let you talk mean to me all you want."

"No." Seriously, demons were worse than human men at bars; neither could take a hint. But she couldn't physically ward off a demon. Severus had already proven that her strength wasn't exactly up to the task.

"Hasn't anyone ever told you that the more you say *no*, the harder we work for your attention?" This time, the demon managed to sweep his fingers, talon-like nails and all, up her cheekbone and into her hair. Not wanting to cause a scene, Moira merely pulled back as much as she could, then tried to slide off the stool and leave. Alaric was too busy to step in—and she didn't want to bother him with some jerk, anyway—so she figured Madeline might be better company. Surely *any* guy here would choose to harass a half-naked succubus instead of Moira.

However, just as she started to rise, Diriel's hand slammed down on her shoulder, shoving her onto the seat again. Panic skittered through her, her hands pulsing with an onslaught of adrenaline, her skin growing hot.

"Stay," the demon urged, his voice laced with a sharper edge this time. "Chat. I think we'll get along just *fine*."

Lips pressed tightly together, she leaned forward to call for Alaric—only to see another bartender in his place, the hybrid's figure disappearing through a door at the back of the bar.

"It's just you and me, sweet thing," Diriel whispered, his words washing over her again, the sensation making her gag. Finally ready to throw her new strength around, and sensing that she had no other choice, Moira balled her hands to fists just as his nails bit into her, cutting right through the leather jacket and into her shoulder.

"Come on, Diriel. No one likes a bar perv who can't take a hint."

Her whole being lifted at the sound of Severus's voice, paired swiftly with his hand wrenching Diriel's off her. While the cross-covered demon retracted his hold on her, he stayed right in her personal space, lips lifted in a sneering sort of smile that made her blood run cold.

"Severus, always a pleasure."

"Let's go," Severus urged Moira, his arm curling around her waist. "We're finished here—"

"Hardly finished," Diriel snapped, grabbing the too-long leather sleeve and yanking Moira back into her seat. "As I recall, *leech*, you stole a girl from me the other week. Plucked her right out of my grasp when we were going to have such *fun* together. I think it's time I returned the favor."

"Fuck off, Diriel," Severus snarled as he situated himself between Moira and the other demon—no easy feat, given his proximity. "You know Verrier hates when demons brawl in his bar."

"Ah, yes, but wasn't that him I just saw you walking out the front door?"

No longer able to see Diriel with Severus's body blocking her, Moira gripped the back of his shirt, pinned in place between him and the foot of wall sticking out from the bar, and searched frantically for a friendly face. Alaric was nowhere to be seen, and there were too many people crowded at the other bar for her to find Madeline.

"He and I had business this evening—"

"And now your business has concluded," Diriel purred, "because he *was*, in fact, the man surrounded by an entourage that just sidled out. Probably off to grab a midnight bite at Rose's Corner, eh? Terribly habitual, that Verrier."

"Severus, let's just go," Moira murmured, trying to slide off her stool, but there were too many fucking demons in the way to get her legs out.

"No, sweet thing, you're going to stay *here*." There was a brief scuffle between Severus and Diriel, and the incubus's body was forced back into her suddenly. "And good ol' Sevvy and I are going to have a proper chat now that Daddy's left the playground. Eh? No one to run to when the other kiddies pick on you tonight."

"Get fucked, Diriel—"

The sound of Diriel's fist colliding with Severus's jaw reminded Moira of thunder. The demon moved so quickly, so brutally, when he leapt off his stool and followed a staggering Severus, fists flying as the incubus tried to both block his face and get a few good hits in himself.

"Severus!"

"Moira, go!"

Diriel whirled around after shoving Severus into a nearby table, the onlookers jumping to their feet as he shattered their drinks.

"Moira, eh?" Those black eyes practically glittered. "So, it's got a name—"

Fear coursed through her, chest tight and limbs stiff—until Severus threw himself at Diriel from behind. The other men along the bar were already off their stools, forming a semicircle around the fighting pair, and she gasped when one delivered a well-aimed kick to the back of Severus's knee, knocking him down. Another managed to land a blow to his temple, his rings leaving a river of blood oozing down the side of his face.

"Leave him alone!" she shouted, but her words were drowned out by the steadily gathering crowd of laughing, jeering, black-eyed demons—most of whom appeared to be rooting for Diriel. Without a friendly face in sight, she threw herself into the ring, stumbling off the stool and teetering in her heels. "Get off him!"

A hand with an iron grip grabbed her by the elbow and wrenched her back, and she screamed, kicking out as more hands started to grab at her, threading her through the crowd. Too many bodies between her and Severus for her to do much good now, she turned to the bouncer.

"Do something!" she demanded. The enormous fellow stood at the back of the horde, still and silent, expressionless —until he met her gaze and smiled.

Fucker.

The chorus of screams and jeers and cruel laughter had become deafening. Through the gaps of demon bodies in front of her, she saw vague flashes—Severus on the ground, Diriel wailing on him. Blood everywhere.

Moira had to do something—or her only true friend in this new world was going to die.

So, she grabbed the hand clamped down on her shoulder, yanked it forward, and sank her teeth into the underside of the demon's wrist. He cursed in a language she didn't understand, but she kept biting until she tasted metallic blood—and the demon shoved her off him. She stumbled into a few onlookers, spitting out warm viscous blood as she went, and when none of *them* tried to grab her, she shouldered her way through until she was right back in the thick of things.

"Go!" Severus screamed at her. "Get out!"

Just as she'd thought: he was on his back, knuckles torn apart, face so covered in blood he was hardly recognizable. And Diriel, standing over him, towering—his relentless fists paired with the odd kick from his little group of cheering friends. Fury made her burn, her cheeks hotter than they'd ever felt.

"I said," she cried, staggering forward in her tight pencil skirt, her too-high heels, "leave him *alone*!"

Diriel whipped around just in time for her to slam her hands against his shoulders, hoping that her new strength would at least knock him off balance.

A blinding flash of pure white light surged from Moira's palms—and hurled him clear across the bar.

The crowd fell silent. Diriel's limp body crashed into something, creating a ruckus of shattered glass and splintered wood—but that too went quiet. Trembling, Moira stared down at her hands, palms up. *That* had never happened before. They looked the same as always, but her head had started to spin and her knees felt less than stable.

Whispers erupted around them as Severus rolled onto his side and spat out a mouthful of blood. Slowly, he lifted his gaze to her—no longer pitch-black, but the one she had first met. Lighter even, his irises a murky grey.

"What the *fuck* is going on here?" Alaric demanded, slamming the door at the back of the bar shut and striding to the counter. Eyes wide, he leaned over. "Sev?"

In an instant, Severus was on his feet and scooping Moira up with an arm under her knees. She squealed when he tossed her—*literally* threw her—over the bartop and growled, "*Go.*"

Alaric barely managed to catch her and stay standing, the pair crashing into the shelves of expensive, rattling liquor bottles. Voices started to rise, calling after Severus, but it all blended into one awful roar, cinched together between her ears by a high-pitched whine she could feel in her teeth. The incubus flung himself over the bar, leaving a trail of blood behind him, grabbed Alaric by the shoulder, then shoved him and Moira toward the back door.

"*Go!*"

"And where the fuck were *you*?" Severus's words echoed through the main floor of his home, and Moira could hear he and Alaric both pacing, marching about, heavy-soled shoes tapping against the hardwood.

"I was signing for a delivery! Father was gone, and it needed to be dealt with. I *told* Seamus to keep an eye on her," Alaric bellowed back. "I couldn't have been gone for more than five minutes!"

Seated on the top step of the first narrow, steep staircase in the four-level invisible house just up the street from the Inferno, Moira watched the lingering rain droplets roll down Severus's leather jacket. It was still wrapped around her shoulders, just as he'd left it. The spring storm that had appeared out of nowhere continued to hammer the window that overlooked the street, and she glanced toward it when light split the darkness. It was fleeting, flickering, a lone bolt of lightning—and she couldn't help but think of the power that had shot out of her hands when she had pushed Diriel.

It had been like that. Lightning. A spotlight. A burst of something raw and primal that somehow managed to both frighten and comfort her.

Just like Severus. He had all but yanked her out of Alaric's grasp when they retreated into the sterile back-of-house area of the Inferno, which was nothing more than a series of winding corridors situated between the human and demon side of things. Although her heels made it next to impossible, Moira had kept pace, running alongside the two roommates until she was falling through a heavy metal door on the opposite side of the building, straight into Alaric's parked white Lamborghini.

It was the last thing she had expected a sweet, chatty guy like Alaric to drive, and she had been forced to sit on Severus's lap, soaked to the bone from the downpour, as they raced out of there. The rain made the roads slick, and Severus had held tight, smearing his blood—still hot, even now—on Moira's neck when Alaric had skidded to a stop in front of the seemingly empty alleyway. Clutching at Severus's hand, she had fled alongside the pair into their magically hidden home, the door slamming shut soundly behind them.

All she had wanted was to grab a wet cloth and clean Severus's face, but the pair had started bickering as soon as Alaric locked the front door. Numb, Moira had climbed the stairs in silence with the intention of waiting out *that* particular storm—all the while knowing she was bound to dive headlong into another when it blew over.

"I told you not to leave her alone. I *told* you—"

"And I'm sorry! I didn't think five minutes would be an issue!"

Their shadows stretched across the dark wood flooring, the light over the stove still on in the kitchen. Biting the insides of her cheeks, Moira slowly slipped off her heels and lined them up on the step below her. If Alaric hadn't been there, she would have started peeling off her soaked clothing too, in need of a hot shower and a stiff drink. But he was there—and he wasn't backing down from Severus's shouts, even though the demon's voice was raspier, more animalistic than she had ever heard.

Good for him. Moira wasn't sure she'd fare that well if Severus used the same tone on her.

"You know my father's thoughts on brawling in his bar—"

"Diriel threw the first punch!"

"*This* is why I've been telling you to take clients. She can't be such a distraction that it's a detriment to your health...to *her* safety."

"Alaric, don't—"

"But never mind that," the Englishman growled, the volume of the argument finally lowering. "You brought a hybrid *angel* into my father's bar? Do you know how insane that is? Have you lost your head?! Every fucking demon in Farrow's Hollow is going to know about her by sunrise tomorrow!"

"I know, Alaric."

"And they're going to come for her—"

"I *know*."

The sudden, tense silence had a shiver racing down her

spine. Moira wanted to blame herself; it was her random burst of light that had been a dead giveaway. But she hadn't known. She still didn't know what she was capable of, and no one, Severus included, had been all that willing to tell her.

"I need to go," Alaric grumbled, his heavy footsteps stomping about, followed by the rattle of keys. "I need to speak with my father. I need to fix this. I need to...ban Diriel and his fucking lackeys before they..." He stopped in the space between the front door and the bottom of the staircase, glaring in what she assumed was Severus's direction. "Don't bring her back to the bar. *Ever*. You know Father wants nothing to do with angels. You *know,* Severus. Why the fuck didn't you tell me what she was? A hybrid, sure, I knew that, but the other half could have been *anything*. She's fucked all of us, and she's not even a full angel. You should have warned me that..."

He trailed off, his coppery brow furrowing, before he slowly looked up the stairwell. A lone tear spilled down her cheek, and Moira brushed it away, blinking hard. She hadn't even noticed that they'd been gathering. Alaric sighed and ran a hand through his shaggy hair, all that styling product soiled by the rain.

"I'm sorry, Moira," he said softly—kindly, at the very least. Then, without another word, he stalked out the front door and slammed it behind him. Moments later, the roar of his expensive engine filled the street, and she watched the tail end of it race out of sight through the front window.

Moira wiped at her cheeks again, not wanting another tear to fall, only to stop when she found Severus standing at the bottom of the stairs. The split lip she had seen in the car had healed, but his face was still covered in bloody smears, his eyes lighter than usual. She waited—waited for him to say something, waited for the anger to seep out of his features.

When neither seemed likely to happen anytime soon, she grabbed her shoes, stood, and started up to his floor. Heavy footfalls followed on the stairs behind her, and together they climbed the remaining two flights in silence.

Once she had reached his level, she peeled off his jacket, hating the way it clung to her now, and hung it over the railing. She set her purse on the ground beneath it, shoes beside that, and waited with crossed arms for Severus to join her. When he finally did, the anger was still there, written across every inch of him, from the stiffness of his walk to the tightness around his mouth.

"Why the fuck didn't you tell me you could do that?" he growled, a hand resting on the railing. She bit the insides of her cheeks, swallowing the immediate flash of anger inside *her* at the accusation in his tone, and waited. When there was no follow-up, no additional words—no inquiry as to how she was feeling—Moira glared at him.

"Because I didn't *know* I could do that," she said. There was no point in trying to hide the way her voice trembled—so she just let it. "In case you've forgotten, I literally know nothing about this. About me. I'm relying on *you* for this stuff."

His eyes narrowed, and he turned away. Two steps later, he faced her again, pointing at her as his mouth opened and closed wordlessly, then shook his head and stormed across the sparsely furnished space and into his bedroom. Temper rising, Moira followed, her skin littered with goosebumps and her soaked clothes feeling tight and uncomfortable. She'd been able to clean up in the club's bathroom after their sex dungeon romp, but now she just felt—horrible. Moira felt horrible in every sense of the world.

Inside the dark bedroom, illuminated only by the barely-there bits of nighttime Farrow's Hollow filtering in from the skylight, she stopped at the end of his bed. Her fingers grazed the blankets, memories of that day, that wonderful day, bringing a blush to her cheeks.

It vanished, however, at the sound of *him* inside the bathroom. Water running. Splashing. Footsteps on the tile—and then his looming figure in the doorway. He swiped at something on the wall of his bedroom, and suddenly soft yellow lighting erupted from all four corners of the long, narrow room.

Even in *that* cozy lighting, he looked angry with her.

"I should have realized," he said, each word slow and deliberate, like it took real effort to say, "the other day... When you burned my hand, you were angry. You..."

Severus started pacing, leaving faint wet outlines of shoeprints on the ground, his face almost clean, excluding the bloody marks along his hairline. Like unwashed hair dye staining his skin. Unsure of what to do, where to sit, Moira stood there, perfectly still, until he whirled around to face her—then she started picking at her nails.

"Moira, why the fuck did you do that?"

"I didn't do it on purpose," she argued, less defensive than she could have been after the shift in his tone. Still, his *I'm just disappointed* tone of voice was almost as insulting as the *I'm fucking pissed* attitude he'd adopted only moments earlier. She forced her hands to her sides, curling them into fists. "I was trying to help you. I didn't know that would happen. I just meant to shove him off."

"You should have gotten the fuck out of there like I told

you to," he insisted, the demon eyes reappearing at last after one hard blink. "I told you to go. I was *fine*."

"Not from where I was standing." She lifted her chin a little, refusing to be cowed by the blackness. "You were getting the shit kicked out of you."

"I'm a *demon*. I'll heal!"

This time she flinched—but only because he'd shouted. Severus picked up his pacing again. If he'd had even a smidge of decorative crap to throw around his room, things probably would have started to shatter. Instead, he just radiated anger—and all the petty emotions that went with it. Moira could feel it standing five feet away, the heat rising all around her with no escape.

Her lower lip wobbled—noticeably now, so that she could feel it—and finally she let the tears come. Fat, heavy, *livid* tears that left hot streaks down her cheeks. She didn't bother to wipe them away, but she didn't let her face screw in despair, either. Moira kept her emotions in check, the tears her only giveaway—and the trembling fists.

When Severus finally stopped stalking back and forth, he looked up at her, the demon eyes gone again, and frowned. In that moment, it was like he had only *just* seen her, truly seen her, since the fight at the bar started. Her hands stopped shaking, and she closed her eyes as he marched over and engulfed her in a hug—a wet, hard, unyielding hug, one that, in spite of everything, she still found comfort in. Slowly, she brought her hands up and gripped his sides, fisting them around the fabric of his damp shirt, and let him hold her. The tears ceased shortly after, and she sniffled when he started to rub her back.

"I'm sorry for shouting," he murmured against her temple. "I just shouldn't have brought you tonight."

"But I wanted to come," Moira said against his chest. "I

wanted to be there."

"And I should have known better." He exhaled sharply, his breath hot on her skin. "I'm sorry, Moira, for everything. Tonight was my fault, not yours."

She nodded. Although it crossed her mind to argue, to insist that *she* was the one who had outed her abilities, she didn't. The argument would fall on deaf ears for *both* of them. Moira was still learning. Severus should have known better.

She didn't belong in a demon bar—no matter how *real* it had made her feel again.

Severus held her a little while longer, rubbing her back, disturbing the damp bralette clinging to her until she couldn't take it anymore. He then let her change into something dry—not warm, but good enough. Charcoal grey eyes, almost human in appearance, watched as she stripped out of her clothes, tossed them aside, and dragged one of his baggy old T-shirts over her head. His scent soaked the material, and she brought it to her nose under the guise of wiping at it—but really, she was holding it there so she could breathe him in and think of him in a different light. When he was on top of her, inside of her, pleasuring her because he seemed to get a thrill out of the act itself, out of watching her climax against his mouth.

Wearing his shirt, the hem stopping at the top of her thighs, Moira could pretend that they were just regular people who'd spent the night at the bar. She could pretend, just for a moment, that she was drunk and he was too, that they'd danced the hours away, laughing with friends, before crashing in each other's arms, in his bed, with plans to do brunch tomorrow morning, hungover and miserable—but still happy, too.

"Here," he murmured, and the illusion shattered. "Get

in. Your skin's ice cold."

Letting his shirt drop, Moira padded across his room and climbed under the sheets. Her head knocked back against the wooden bars at the top, the ones he had tied her to that first time, and her cheeks warmed. Severus seemed not to notice as he tucked her in, then sat too far away, perched at the end of the bed.

"Severus?" She licked her lips when he glanced her way. *Are you scared of me?* Scared of her power, of what was simmering just below the surface. He didn't seem to be a big fan of angels. Moira wanted to ask, to confirm that nothing had changed between them—and that nothing would, no matter what kinds of abilities sprung up from her depths. Instead, she chose an easier route and picked at her nails—nails that grew quickly these days and were becoming harder and harder to trim with her regular clippers. "So, what now?"

"Now... You stay here."

She looked up sharply. "What?"

"You heard Alaric... By morning, *every* demon in Farrow's Hollow will know there's an angel hybrid running the streets. They'll know you're with me, and they'll come looking for you. You can't leave this building."

"That's insane." A little half smile tugged at her lips, hoping this was just some joke, but Severus wasn't smiling—and hers died too. "Severus, no. I don't see why I have to—"

"Because they'll take you," he said sharply, turning away. "They'll take you, and use you, and pick you apart, hoping to find something inside you that will help them hurt the *real* angels."

The thought made her stomach turn, Diriel's glittering black eyes flashing across her mind. She hugged herself, sinking deeper into the plush pillows beneath her. "Oh."

"I'm not trying to keep you all to myself," he said softly. "This is for your own safety."

"But I have a *life*," she argued, knowing it was a weak one at best—but it was true. "Can't I just go home? I'll stay in my room. I'll have Ella—"

"You'll put all of them in danger." Sharp as a whip, his words snapped across the gaping distance between them. "You'll put Ella in danger. You need to stay here until I figure things out...until I can put an end to the rumors and say you're something else. Something they'll believe. Something from Hell, preferably. Something that isn't so shiny and new and *appealing* to them."

"Severus, I don't want to be put on lockdown in your house—"

"And why not?" He stood and scratched at the back of his neck, still not looking at her. "No one knows this place exists save for Verrier and the witch who enchanted it, who just so happens to be my cousin. They can't find you here. This is the *only* place in the city you're safe, Moira, so you're just going to have to accept that."

"Yeah, well, I've been accepting a lot of shit lately," she told him thickly. "A *lot*. And I could do with a little more patience from *you* while I come to terms with everything. Is it really so unbelievable that I wouldn't want to be locked in here?"

"What's unbelievable," he growled, *finally* facing her, his features hard again, "is that after all this time together, after all we've done together, you still don't trust me. I want to keep you *safe*, Moira. It's what I've wanted from the beginning. Now it's just from all of the demons in Farrow's Hollows, too, for fuck's sake."

Biting the insides of her cheeks, Moira looked to the skylight, to the heavy droplets of rain hammering it relentlessly. She had nothing left to say that she hadn't already said. Actually...

"Did Verrier give you the names?" she asked in a very small voice. Naming the angels who worked at Seraphim Securities had been the entire *point* of this evening's outing, yet it felt so insignificant now.

"Yes. He named all of them, though he had no interest in divulging anything further. In fact, he told me to mind my own business when it came to angels, but that was expected." His response was tight—restrained. "We'll get back to searching for your father once I've...*fixed* this new little situation of ours. One life-threatening problem at a time, hmm?"

Moira's lips wobbled, and she pressed them together, determined not to break down. If the situation really *was* as dire as he made it out to be—and what reason would he have to lie?—then she had to stay here. For the sake of Ella and everyone else she cared about, Moira couldn't set one foot outside until the demon glowering at her fixed what had happened tonight—what had happened in about ten seconds.

Ten short seconds that had changed her life.

She ought to be used to it by now.

But she wasn't. Not in the slightest.

"Look, just...try to sleep," Severus muttered as he headed for the door. "I need to think."

He caught the light switch on his way out, the warm yellow glow disappearing, followed by the click of his bedroom door closing. Moira sat there for a moment, listening to the dull roar of the storm outside, to the individual droplets pounding against the skylight—before drawing her knees to her chest and sobbing into Severus's blankets.

CHAPTER SEVEN

"Fucking...ridiculous thing," Severus grumbled. The digital interface on the oven beeped angrily back at him, and he heard Alaric snort from across the kitchen. Refusing to be goaded into anything, he squared his shoulders and tried again, the user manual spread open in front of him. He would conquer this damn oven timer—one way or another.

Why did it need to be so bloody complicated, anyway? All he wanted was to set it for an hour—simple. Normally he wasn't one for any complex cooking; brew a pot of lentils and he could be full for days. Most of his sustenance came from humans anyway, not food. Unfortunately, demon bodies weren't quite as robust on Earth as they were in the hellscape below. It was part of the deal for being allowed in the human realm, the price you paid for going topside. Demons on Earth were weaker, healed slower, and operated at about sixty percent of their usual capabilities, power-wise. The farther you went from a hell-gate, the weaker you became. It was why cities located near the portals were so inundated with demons, Farrow's Hollow included.

"Aha!" He stepped back when the timer started ticking

down, then hastily threw the skillet with the wrapped pork tenderloin onto the middle shelf. "Pork is in."

"Only took you fifteen minutes to figure the oven out," Alaric announced, shattering his moment of triumph. "Pretty sure that's a record, Sev."

His roommate hovered by the breakfast bar on the other side of the L-shaped counter. The tenderloin, however, was not for Severus's consumption, but for Moira's. The building's newest resident was seated at the dining table that separated the first-floor seating area from the kitchen. Papers spread everywhere, she was nearly finished marking all the essays due for her teaching assistant job at the university. As Severus strode over, Alaric sliding off one of the barstools after him, she didn't glance up.

"Everything's taken care of," he told her, pausing at the other side of the table, his hand gripping the back of a chair. He tried not to smile when she savagely crossed out an entire paragraph and scribbled something in the margins. She had become ruthless with her grading since moving in almost a week ago, and given that her frustration was partially his fault, Severus felt he ought to make an apology of some kind to the students affected.

When she was done, she set the pen down with a sigh and looked up.

"Side dishes too?"

"What do you take me for?" He cocked his head, grinning. "Of course the sides are done. You just need to heat them up."

Steamed vegetables and a very generous helping of mashed potatoes. Since Moira had been forced to move in against her wishes—for her own *safety*, but never mind—Severus had tried to soothe her temper by keeping her well fed. In just a short week of *his* meal regime, her cheeks were already a little less gaunt; as he'd suspected, she hadn't been eating enough to match her new body's needs. If this forced imprisonment lasted a month, Severus estimated he'd be able to completely get rid of *all* her figure's sharp, pointy edges that she disliked so much.

At the sound of Alaric getting his shoes and jacket together by the front door, Severus dug Moira's phone out of his pants pocket and set it on the table.

"Please only use it to call me," he said, predicting the roll of her eyes before it happened.

"I know, Severus."

Severus keeping the device on his person at all times hadn't helped make her transition to full-time resident any smoother. Unfortunately, Moira just didn't seem to understand the true severity of her situation, and he couldn't risk her calling Ella and inviting her over. The fewer people who knew about his home, the better. It was logical. Rational. *Reasonable*, given all the chatter in the city's demon community about the new angel hybrid in their midst. However, all that logic and reason wasn't much help to Moira, who he knew felt like a prisoner. Getting in contact with Ella would likely lift her spirits, but he couldn't chance it.

Besides, Ella hadn't exactly been his biggest fan when he'd showed up on the front porch with a bag for Moira's things a week ago. It was the only time he had allowed Moira to contact her, and his little hybrid had sold the lie that she was staying at her new boyfriend's house for a little while—or so he'd thought. Ella had looked like she wanted to skin him alive, even more so after he answered her thousand questions as vaguely as possible while he puttered around Moira's bedroom, filling the bag.

The curly-haired human, short in stature but fiery in

nature, had to suspect *something*. It was why Severus had sent the occasional text message from Moira's phone to let Ella know that she was *fine*, and that she would fill her in on everything soon. After all, he had agreed to it—Moira would have to eventually bring her best friend into the world of demons and vampires and angels and everything else that could rip a human in half. It was a stipulation she'd made in exchange for staying with him quietly, without a fight. Ella needed to know the truth—she needed to be protected, and knowledge *was* the first line of defense.

Fine. Severus would see to all that, but only after he had quelled the rumors circulating Farrow's Hollow about Moira and her abilities. Until he could guarantee the safety of the woman who *actually* mattered to him, Ella was at the bottom of his priorities list.

The inner demon had become increasingly protective of Moira with every bit of new intel Alaric privately shared with him. Farrow's Hollow was abuzz with news of an angel hybrid, and nearly every demon wanted a piece of her, just as he'd feared from the moment she blasted Diriel off him. He had never been possessive over a woman before, but his inner demon was addicted to the bored, occasionally cantankerous woman sitting at his dining table—and he would eviscerate anyone who touched a single white hair on her beautiful head. Severus was on the same page for once, and some of his inner self's aggressive protectiveness had seeped into his everyday behaviour—hence the phone hoarding.

"So, still won't tell me where you're going, huh?" Moira asked as he rounded the table and swooped down to plant a kiss on her cheek. She leaned into it with a soft sigh, eyes drifting closed. Severus lingered, breathing her scent, fighting to control the beast within.

Understandably, Moira had been less than forthcoming physically since he had trapped her inside his home. He and Alaric had bought some furniture and converted the previously empty third floor into something Moira could feel comfortable in during her stay. Sometimes she did her schoolwork on the couch set, but despite having a perfectly apt queen-sized bed of her own, she slept in his every night —with or without him present.

His lips parted when she smoothed a hand up his cheek, nails grazing his recently trimmed scruff. Alaric's less than subtle throat-clearing from across the room had him straightening with a growl.

"You don't want to know where we're going," he assured Moira as he cupped her chin, thumb stroking her cheek. She had been getting warmer to the physical touch since that night, but, not wanting to worry her, Severus had kept that to himself. When Moira shot him a skeptical look, he sank down to her eye level. "I promise. You *really* don't want to know."

One of Verrier's informants had told Alaric that some of the demon mob families would be getting together tonight to have some drinks, eat some food—and then *bid* for ownership of Moira. None of it mattered, because Severus wouldn't let them find her, but he couldn't stand the idea that someone out there would think they *owned* her. Legally. He had no doubt that someone would be up from Hell to administer the binding blood contracts and everything. So, he and Alaric—well, *just* Alaric—had landed themselves on the guest list and intended to outbid every sick fuck present. Severus had a sizeable fortune after working for years as an escort, but it was Alaric who had a limitless supply of credit in every currency, courtesy of his father.

Verrier might have been retired, but every demon within his jurisdiction was required to pay the same tribute to him on Earth as they would pay to the princes of Hell below—and it was a testament to just how much Verrier had loved Alaric's mother, and Alaric by extension, that he had handed over his little black card the moment Alaric requested it.

Meanwhile, to say that Verrier had been less than impressed with Severus when he had waltzed into his office at the Inferno, begging for angel names, would be the world's greatest understatement. While the former prince had provided them, he'd done so with the assurance that *that* would be the last he heard of this angel nonsense.

And then Moira had thrown Diriel across his bar, damaging tables and chairs and glassware in the process. While Verrier refused to become directly entangled in the fallout of that night, he *had* allowed Moira to stay in his son's secret building, and now Alaric had a blank check to bid on her tonight. He might have wiped his hands clean of angel affairs, but Verrier would still do anything for his most beloved son.

It was a weakness Severus knew he had exploited far too often in the last week, but he had no other choice. Moira's life was at stake. None of the demons searching for her would kill her—just gleefully torture her until her life expired, however long *that* would be. Hybrid life spans varied depending on what the human was mixed with, and no one had much experience with angels. At this point, even Severus was just making it up as he went along.

"How long will you guys be gone?" Moira asked as he crossed the room and swiped his shoes from the rack in the coat closet.

"Apparently the..." Alaric pressed his lips together, the

word "auction" likely on the tip of his tongue. Severus shot him a *look* as he sat on the stairs and stuffed his foot into one of his polished wingtip oxfords.

"I believe we should be back by eleven," he told Moira, looping the thin laces. "I'll send you a message should things run later."

"And then we can start our movie night," Alaric added, the enthusiasm in his voice failing to draw more than a half smile out of Moira. "Right? *Right*? I can't believe you've never seen any of the Indiana Jones films. Harrison Ford is a *legend*."

"So I'm told," she said flatly, then offered a more genuine smile when she caught Severus's eye. "Pick up some snacks on the way back?"

"Certainly. Text me your preferences."

"Have fun tonight," she called as they headed out the front door, "with whatever it is you're doing."

"Trust me," Severus told her, gripping the knob tight and scowling at the thought of what was to come, "we most certainly *won't*."

~

Moira waited until the final lock was set and Alaric's gaudy car had pulled away from the curb before she sprang into action. The chair's legs scraped across the hardwood as she shoved back and scurried into the kitchen, lowering the temperature on the oven and quickly checking on the tenderloin to ensure it wouldn't burn. Pork took forever to cook, right? At such a low temperature, she could get to campus and back before it was done—and well before her demon guards returned from whatever they were doing tonight.

Nibbling her lower lip, she returned to the dining table that had been her essay-marking hub for the last few days, then gathered all the corrected essays—due at midnight tonight from *all* teaching assistants, no exceptions—and set them in a neat pile. Heart pounding, she looked to the door, half expecting Severus to come thundering back in with an *aha, the jig is up!* All she got instead was the very gentle evening traffic cruising by the front window. Still, she waited a moment longer, her palms starting to get clammy, before grabbing her phone and ordering a taxi to the address of the apartment complex next door.

With an estimated arrival time of five minutes, she packed her shoulder bag—graded essays, wallet, phone—and hurried upstairs. Her lungs burned by the time she reached the third floor, still no more accustomed to scaling the thin, narrow stairwells today than she had been a week ago. It had been very thoughtful of Severus and Alaric to give her an entire floor to herself while she was stuck here, even if she spent every night in Severus's bed rather than the squishy queen they'd had delivered on her first day.

In fact, as she changed out of her sweats and into something more campus appropriate, Moira had to acknowledge that her new roommates had been *very* accommodating—despite her moodiness—from the very beginning. Sure, the night of the incident had been tense. Alaric had apologized for what he'd said the following morning, citing stress as the reason for blaming her for all their problems, and Moira had forgiven him without a second's hesitation.

Alaric had turned into a welcome ally in the week that followed, always up for playing video games with her, watching movies or shows, and drinking well into the early-morning hours with expensive liquor from his dad's bar when Moira felt like getting drunk. She hadn't succeeded yet, but Alaric made it fun to try.

Even Severus, for all his phone-stealing and lecturing, had put in the effort to make her comfortable. He hadn't apologized for his behavior that night—for storming off and leaving her sobbing in his bed—but his actions had suggested as much. By day, he saw his human clients, bolstering his strength for the nights he spent in the demon underbelly of Farrow's Hollow, supposedly trying to quash whatever rumors were flying around about her.

He had even faced Ella's wrath, both in person and over the phone, when he had gone to their house and packed up some of Moira's things for her. The incubus took care of all her meals, and he hadn't once tried to fuck the tension away —as much as Moira wished he would. All in all, he had been a perfect gentleman, which made what she was about to attempt ten times harder.

As Moira pulled her black wool cap on, carefully tucking all hints of white hair beneath, she hesitated again. Severus *had* been great, even with her sullen pouting and frustrated glares. Moira had made it very clear she didn't want to stay here, locked up like a prisoner, but she understood the logic behind it. Unfortunately, understanding didn't translate to acceptance, and her mood had been up and down—mostly down—all week. Alaric had suggested that she might finally be processing, *really* processing, everything that had happened to her since she met Severus, all the hard new truths she'd had to swallow. It made sense, and she *knew* she shouldn't have taken her mess of emotion out on Severus—but he had proven to be an easy, willing target.

And it made her feel awful. Just—downright shitty, honestly.

This—sneaking out—made her feel worse. The essays were due back, however, and Moira was determined not to let that stupid *incident* derail her life completely. All she needed to do was get to campus, take all the back routes to her professor's building, then leave the stack in her mailbox. Hail a cab, somehow figure out how to get back inside the magical building that no one but her, Severus, and Alaric could see, and then bam. She'd be good to stay indoors for another miserable week.

Wearing a thin beige knit sweater and a pair of old skinny jeans, the waist still too big, Moira slipped her feet into her beat-up runners, then hurried down to Alaric's room. Violating his privacy didn't make her feel any better—nor did the distinctly *boy* smell of his dark, cluttered bedroom—but the bathroom on her floor had no windows and the skylights in Severus's didn't open, so she needed this one to get to the fire escape that spanned from the roof to the ground floor of the building. The front door wouldn't open for her after Severus had locked it, and she wasn't sure *why*, but in a pinch, the fire escape would do just nicely.

While the lock on the window latch was trickier than she anticipated, Moira managed to get it open. About a foot to the right, the ladder ran parallel to the window, and she climbed on top of the toilet, her heart leaping into her throat as she peered down. Why hadn't she thought it would be this high? The building was narrow and tall; Alaric's second-floor bathroom looked like any regular fourth-floor drop. Taking a deep breath, she maneuvered herself as nimbly as she could, adrenaline making her movements somewhat uncoordinated.

Once she had a hand wrapped around a black metal ladder rung, she managed to swing herself over, a little squeal slipping out when she didn't immediately find her footing. As soon as she did, Moira took a moment to catch her breath, heart pounding between her ears now. There. The hard part was over, right? All she had to do was climb down. The alleyway was silent behind her as she descended, one rung at a time. Beyond the usual downtown chorus of car tires on cement, the occasional honk, and the *very* distant chatter of pedestrians, she felt alone behind the building.

When the tip of her shoe touched cement, she hopped down but kept one hand firmly on the ladder. She peered up, squinting at the still-open bathroom window, then flinched when her phone started to ring from the depths of her bag.

Moira turned to dig it out—and in that moment, as soon as she broke contact with the fire escape, the building disappeared.

She gasped, despite having known that was exactly what would happen, then reached out. Her long, grasping fingers didn't collide with anything as she swiped her hand through the air. Gone. Like it had never existed.

"Oh, Moira," she said, sighing like Severus did whenever he was mildly exasperated with her lack of otherworldly knowledge, "you did *not* think this through."

When she had concocted this little scheme of hers a few days ago after reading a terse email from her professor reminding all TAs that the essays were due, it had been easy to just throw her hands up and decide she would figure out how to get back inside Severus and Alaric's magical home when she returned. Now, however, she could acknowledge the folly in that logic.

What could she say—this former honor student had zero experience breaking the rules. Moira had been punctual and obedient all her life, sometimes to a fault. Sneaking out was unexplored territory.

She pursed her lips, knowing and accepting she'd have to call Severus on the way home to explain what she'd done. He'd be angry—and rightfully so—but she knew he would let her in. Hopefully. And then deliver a well-deserved earful of lectures about safety and how terrible demons were and how much of a risk she had taken and blah, blah, blah.

Fidgeting, Moira checked her wool cap one last time, now aware that her *tell* as an angel hybrid was the startling white hair she shared with all the others at Seraphim Securities. Then, because curiosity prompted her to, she took another swipe at where the building ought to be standing. Nothing. A little smile tugged at her lips. *Amazing*.

She *really* wanted to meet this witch cousin who had enchanted an entire building to vanish completely, not only from sight, but from every other sense too.

Unfortunately, there were more pressing issues to take care of. With her phone still bleating at her, she fished it out and answered somewhat breathlessly.

"Daisy's Taxi here for Lara?" a woman's voice remarked as Moira held the phone to her ear with her shoulder, now jogging through the vacant, dismal, rain-soaked alley where a building had once stood.

"Coming now," she managed. She might have made a mistake in using her real name when she booked a night with an escort, but Moira had learned since then. Her mom's name, thankfully, was common enough not to arouse suspicion, and she kept her head down when she blitzed from the shadows of the alley and into the awaiting taxi in front of the neighbouring apartment building.

The driver in the front seat smiled at her in the same palpably disinterested way most taxi drivers did when they picked up a student headed for campus, and as the car—its interior positively *reeking* of cheap, sharply floral perfume—eased away from the curb, Moira flopped back in the seat, and only then noticed she was shaking.

Shaking, but free at last.

Even if it was just for the next half hour.

The end of this term marked Moira's *fifth* year on the FHU campus—and it was strange to realize she actually missed the old place.

Standing at the bottom step of the stairs to her professor's sprawling gothic tower, a building which housed all the offices for the art department, Moira studied the familiar campus with a smile. She shouldn't have missed this place. It drove her nuts on a good day, all the clueless undergrads milling about. Always too busy, lines too long at the coffee bars, nowhere to sit in the library when she wanted to work. But she had missed it.

Eleanor Grimsby, the professor she had been assigned to TA for this year, had roped her into a conversation when she'd caught Moira dropping off the graded essays in the mailbox outside her office. Apparently, she had been the last TA to do so, but Grimsby hadn't chastised her for it. Instead, she'd asked if everything was all right, noting that some of her colleagues had been chatting about her absence from seminars this past week.

"Oh, just caught that flu thing that's going around," Moira had insisted, a part of her pleased that her professors noticed when she didn't attend their classes. But then again, with her new looks—how could they not? The pair had chatted in the dimly lit hallway for a good fifteen minutes about essays, exams, and her thesis, due next year, which Moira still hadn't started. It had been oddly pleasant to discuss academics like nothing had changed, and now as she stood on that step, the horizon painted amber and gold and purple with the setting sun, Moira could forget that the entire demon population of Farrow's Hollow was out looking for her.

She could forget that she was turning into a *creature*, angel or not.

She could forget about Severus's warnings and Alaric's cautious hybrid chatter. Moira was just a graduate student again. A teaching assistant. A twenty-three-year-old with her whole life ahead of her.

However, as soon as she forced herself off that step, breaking into a brisk march toward the campus bus terminal —taxis were known to loiter around there too, even at this time of night—it all came flooding back to her. That she *wasn't* just a normal university student. That her whole life might or might not still be ahead of her. That Severus was going to ream her out—and that she hadn't spoken to Ella face-to-face in a week.

Abruptly, she stopped, ignoring the grumbles of the lanky asshole who walked into her because of it. He carried on, enormous headphones over his ears, and Moira grabbed her phone with trembling hands. This was the longest she and Ella had ever gone without seeing each other, excluding that one summer Ella had been forced to visit some cousins in New York. It had been the summer between eleventh and twelfth grade, and that had been the longest three weeks of Moira's life—or so she'd thought.

The distance had a purpose, of course. As she stared at

Ella's display picture on her contacts page, grinning at the crossed eyes and the tongue poking out between her full lips, Moira knew that bringing her into this very real, very supernatural world was damning her.

But she couldn't go on like this. Ella had known something was up, something was *different* in her life, ever since the changes started, and Moira hadn't done much to include her in that. She knew it hurt Ella. She knew her best friend suspected Moira was keeping secrets—and she couldn't stand it.

Beyond that, if the demons matched a name to Moira's face, Ella was at *risk*. And in Moira's mind, there was being at risk and being oblivious to it—and then there was being at risk and knowing the dangers. At least with the latter, Ella could be protected. She could make her own decisions—maybe even move in and share Moira's new digs.

At least then, she wouldn't be left in the dark until something that haunted it finally took her.

So, Moira pressed the call button and brought the phone to her ear. At the first ring, students spilled out of the nearby chemistry building, the seven-to-nine evening classes finally letting out. The bus terminal would be busy, and Moira slowly drifted toward it, her smile vanishing when Ella's voicemail recording started to play. She hung up, tapping the disconnect button harder than necessary, and went to her text messages instead. Ella *lived* with her phone. Even if she was in a class, she always answered.

Unless something from Moira's new world had taken her, Ella was screening her calls.

Frowning, Moira fired off a quick text to let her best friend know she was on campus if she wanted to grab coffee.

I'll wait for the next fifteen minutes—until the next bus

arrives. Just let me know. I'm so sorry, Ella. I really need to talk to you.

After she hit the send button, she called Severus too, her heart pounding faster with each ring. That call also went to voicemail, and this time she left one.

"Hi. So. It's me. Don't be mad, but I'm on campus because I needed to drop off these essays with my prof. So far, so good. No black-eyed creatures following me. I was discreet. I'm just waiting to see if Ella wants to grab coffee with me, and then I'm going to head back. If you guys are done with whatever you're doing, you could always pick me up. I fully anticipate a lecture. I know. I deserve it. I just had to get out and do this." She paused, breathless, and then cleared her throat. "See you back at your place."

When she hung up, something inside of her deflated a little to see that Ella hadn't texted her back. She deserved that, too.

The bus terminal was a nightmare around the time classes got out; nowhere to sit, no one looking where they were walking, smokers brazenly lighting up in defiance of all the *no smoking* signs. The hustle and bustle had been annoying to endure *before* the changes. Now, it was downright awful.

Moira's every sense faced a continuous assault these days, the clamor of crowds just a little too loud, the clashing scents of perfume and body odor making her just a little too queasy, and the array of color and clothing making it just a little too hard to focus. Nothing crazy. Nothing she couldn't handle. It was just—a little too much. She wasn't sure if her senses were *heightening*. She could hardly feel it when humans knocked into her, not like she had with all the demons manhandling her at the bar. But the rest of her senses were on overload tonight, more than usual, and she zipped around the corner of the nearby science library, in need of a brief reprieve.

An empty street greeted her—not a car, bus, or student in either direction. A quick check of her phone showed nothing from Ella or Severus, and Moira finally stopped her aimless pacing, leaning against a fat, heavily graffitied campus security post—*press the big red button if being attacked!*—and frowned.

Should she be concerned that neither were responding to her?

"Excuse me?"

Moira looked up sharply at the figure standing in front of her. Dressed in a salmon-pink collared tee and jeans far lighter than hers—ugh, and *very* white shoes—the guy was the physical manifestation of every douchebag who partied in the frat house across the street from hers in the suburbs.

"D'you know where Morrisey house is?"

Typical. It made sense that a guy who looked like that, with a six-pack of beer in one hand, was headed directly for said noisy frat.

"Uh, yeah." Moira pushed off the security pole, strolling toward him and pointing back toward the FHU campus core. Something hummed in her ear, and she swatted at it distractedly—were the mosquitos out already? Wasn't it still spring? "You're just on the wrong side of campus. You can cut across the Hills, then through the pass between the biology building and the greenhouses. It's like four streets over from there. You can't miss it."

Especially if those assholes were having a party. The whole place would be lit up like Christmas, lights strung along the balconies and porch railings. Kegs delivered the day of. Police arriving by 2 AM, right on schedule. They always invited Moira and her roommates to join them, but thus far no one had ever taken them up on the offer—excluding the one time last September that Moira and Ella'd had to drag a belligerently drunk Lee away from the party house, but that had only been because she thought the frat house was *their* house and she just wanted to go to bed.

"Oh, shit, really?" Frat Boy Junior, young enough to *maybe* be a year out of high school, scratched at the back of his neck. "Damn. Okay."

"Okay." Moira looked down at her phone again. Nothing. Where the hell—

A startled cry caught in her throat when the guy backhanded her—*hard.*

Demon hard.

Moira staggered into the pole, her phone clattering onto the sidewalk at the same time the six-pack of rattling beer bottles did, forgotten. Her hands warmed as they shot up defensively, Frat Boy Junior closing in with black eyes and a horrible smile.

"Lights out, half-breed," he sneered, moving faster than she anticipated. He skirted her outstretched hands and pressed a wet, scentless rag to her face. She lashed out at him, trying to duck out of reach, but found her movements instantly sluggish. Her mind slowed. Her hands cooled. Her knees buckled.

And as she felt his arm coil around her, darkness clouding her vision, the last thing Moira heard before she lost consciousness was the sound of tires screeching across pavement—headed straight for her.

~

"Sir, a moment of your time?"

"*What*, Thompson?"

Severus smirked at the sharpness of Alaric's tone. Just about every demon present was on edge now that the auction was over an hour behind schedule, and having his vampire babysitter loitering outside, constantly checking in on them, had been driving Alaric up the wall.

Generally, Alaric's watchers kept their distance, but only because Alaric's nights mostly consisted of bartending at the Inferno. No risk there, not with his father working one floor above. Any demon who tried to hurt, maim, or kidnap his roommate would be on a suicide mission. However, when Verrier had learned they'd be attending this auction, it had taken all of two seconds for him to *insist* they bring Thompson with them. Severus wasn't a fan of the bloodsucker either, but he had learned to tune him out a long time ago—the same with all of Verrier's babysitters. As far as Severus was concerned, they were nothing more than the hired help. Flies on the wall. Insignificant and easily replaceable.

Alaric rolled his eyes and stepped into the hall, leaving Severus all by his lonesome in a small room stuffed full of demons representing the three demon mob families of Farrow's Hollow. The number of mob families had fluctuated through the decades, but there were currently five key players running the city's dingy underworld. Five groups who sometimes played nicely together, but usually did not.

At the moment, there was Verrier's posse in the legitimate private sector, usually there to quash larger conflicts before an angel was forced to step in; Diriel's ragtag band of thugs, whose sole purpose in life was to party like it was their last night on Earth; and finally, the three mob families, each specializing in either the sex, drug, or weapons industry. Most of the Farrow's Hollow demons fit within one of those groups—being alone was oftentimes worse. Severus would know.

It was Alaric's contacts who had rooted out the auction's time and location, and while Severus had been *disgusted* at first to be stuck in this small space, nothing more than an empty stockroom at the back of a demon-run clothing boutique, he was now getting a kick out of the fact that the auction had fallen on its face before it even started.

The mobsters were all eager, of course, whispering and gossiping with one another about Farrow's Hollow's only human-angel hybrid. Everyone had had to sign a treaty, blood signatures only, at the front of the room that stated all would honour the outcome of the auction. Whoever won Moira tonight had first dibs on acquiring her. Alaric had his black card ready to go, and had even signed his father's name just for some additional security. The rest of the black-suited, low-jean-wearing cretins hadn't said a single word to Severus since he'd arrived, and only a few dared ask Alaric why his father was so interested in a hybrid. Naturally, they had received no response—only a withering glare that would make Verrier proud. The questions stopped shortly after that.

Sighing, Severus retrieved his phone from the deep pocket of his black trench. An hour and *five* minutes late—and still no signal. With a clenched jaw, he lifted the phone, moving it about, hoping to see the bars fluctuate at least a little. Nothing. He scowled. One of the families had probably used their witch to block reception to the building tonight.

It was quite hush-hush, this auction. All the proceeds were to be held in a trust at the lone demon-run bank in the core of the business district. Once the winner claimed Moira for himself, the funds would be transferred to the communal fund used to pay off the city's human authority figures. No one *liked* groveling, but the cooperation of some key players was essential to ensure demon comings and goings went on unnoticed by the general public.

The mass hysteria of humans learning demons walked among them... It would be a mess. A mess most demons would relish, mind you, but it would certainly make things more taxing on those who just wanted to assimilate.

"Sev?" Alaric's face appeared in his peripheral view so suddenly that he jumped.

"Something wrong?"

"We need to go."

Without questioning it, Severus slipped out the propped-open stockroom door, then followed Alaric down the dingy back corridors, not speaking again until they were out the fire exit. Thompson had picked them up from the Inferno, changing from Alaric's flashier vehicle to something a little more low-key—as low-key as a burly black Lincoln Navigator *could* be, the enormous SUV taking up nearly the entire width of the alleyway they'd parked in.

"What is it?" Severus demanded now that they were out of earshot. His first thought was Moira, but Alaric would have been in more of a panic had that been the case, surely.

"Chatter says angels are breaking up the party in about two minutes," Thompson remarked, a black earpiece with a wire trailing down under his suit giving him quite the federal-agent vibe. All he needed was a pair of sunglasses and he'd be set.

Lean, pushing six-and-a-half feet, with skin whiter than freshly fallen snow, the vampire had been Alaric's nighttime watcher for about seven years. Given the fact Verrier hadn't seen to replace him, he must be damn good at his job—and that meant angels were, in fact, headed this way.

Still, Severus couldn't help but ask, "Are you sure?"

But Thompson was already standing at the back door of the SUV, gesturing for them to get moving—stiff and expressionless as ever.

Alaric, however, hung back, hands in his pockets. "You want to wait around and see? Thompson's sources are usually pretty on point."

Did he want to sit tight and wait for an angel to gate-crash? Not really, but the idea that someone had leaked the intel just to get Severus and Alaric out, knowing they had been spotted with Moira, made the inner demon anxious. The beast had prowled to and fro all day in anticipation of tonight, stalking the breadth of its cage—demanding to be set free. Severus couldn't risk it. Even if he *had* been bolstering his strength with daily client visits, plus touching any human he could in the meantime, he'd be outmanned at the auction—outmanned by demons whose brute strength *didn't* rely on humans. No, the inner demon could gnash its teeth and stay put.

"It might be a trick," he said after a moment's consideration, his voice low—though he knew Thompson's sensitive vamp ears would hear every word anyway. "You know, to get us out of the way?"

"Yes, but..." Alaric fell silent when Severus distractedly pressed a finger to his downturned lips. A high-pitched whine, like the sound of an incoming bomb strike, grew louder and louder with each passing second. A quick look to Thompson showed that the vampire heard it too, and in an instant he was by Alaric's side, making the hybrid jump and curse under his breath.

"We need to move—"

Whatever was falling collided with the top of the building, everything from the walls, the bricks, straight down to the foundation rattling on impact. It all happened so fast—the crashing of a lead weight between the floors, windows noisily bursting on the street side and the odd two at the back shattering into the alley. Severus yanked Alaric aside to avoid the fallout, only to stagger back as a blinding white flash of light radiated throughout the building. Short-lived screams from the demons inside assaulted his ears.

"Sir, we must—"

The fire exit door, purposefully weighted like a dying star to keep humans out, flung open, the angelic light bathing the alley. All three cried out, Severus falling to his knees and curling into a ball to shield his face—and Alaric crawling on top of him like a hybrid shield. The holy light seared whatever bits of skin it touched, and Severus gritted his teeth through the agonizing pain. Had Alaric's body not been covering him, he'd be a blistered *nothing*.

Just as swiftly as it arrived, the light vanished—someone had turned off the juice. As darkness cloaked the alley once more, Severus pushed Alaric off him and flopped onto his back, gasping and writhing. What skin *had* met the angel's light bubbled in a manner akin to a human's third-degree burn. His body would heal, even if it took a little longer on Earth than in Hell—and hurt a whole lot more.

"Are you all right?" Alaric whispered, crawling back to his side, that bright green stare sweeping up and down his body. "Did it get you?"

"We should have just gone," he muttered. The largest knuckle on every one of his fingers was a scorched, bubbling disaster. The skin around it had also reddened, but nothing worse than a severe sunburn. Severus would survive. The demons inside wouldn't be quite as fortunate. "You good?"

"Fine," Alaric insisted as he helped Severus sit up. "It did sting a bit, though."

"Well, look at you." He patted his friend's shoulder, the movement searing across his damaged skin. "Seems like you're growing into your demon skin yet."

"Doesn't seem like a benefit in these circumstances." The strain of lifting him flashed across Alaric's face as he hauled Severus to his feet.

"No, I'm afraid not. Better hang on to that h-humanity until all this is settled." Over his friend's shoulder, Severus spied what was left of his vampiric babysitter. "Didn't do Thompson much good either."

Alaric whirled around. "*Fuck.* Father's going to be *so* annoyed."

Touched by the angel's light, the vampire had become nothing but a pile of black ash—truly dead at last. He had to hand it to the guy; at least he'd stayed behind in a foolish attempt to protect his charge. Severus would never speak ill of him again.

"He really hates interviewing new handlers," Alaric continued as they shuffled toward the SUV.

"What about—" Severus gritted his teeth when his hand closed around the passenger-side door handle and one of the blisters burst. Acidic puss oozed between his fingers, and he wiped it off on his pants—only to burst two more in the process. Breathing deeply, evenly, he wrenched the door open and climbed inside as the engine roared to life. He didn't bother with the seatbelt like Alaric, and instead stared straight ahead, his entire body quivering as he tried to ignore the agony coursing through him. "What about K-Kingsley? He's been gunning for Thompson's post for," he swallowed hard, eyes clenched briefly, "years."

"Yeah, I'll put a recommendation in. Kingsley's just a

real boring old sod, you know? Dresses like it's still 1896, and I don't think I've ever seen him smile," Alaric muttered, and the SUV jerked backward when he slammed his foot on the gas. Hightailing it down the vacant alley in reverse, he handled the enormous vehicle with an impressive amount of finesse.

"Yeah, b-because Thompson was such a *hoot*," Severus fired back, his smile dropping as soon as he saw that fire exit door burst open again. Before he could catch a glimpse of the creature responsible, Alaric slammed on the brakes, kicked the SUV into drive, and made a sharp turn into an alley between two buildings that would take them onto the street. He lost the passenger-side mirror for his effort, and Severus watched the rearview until they were back on Flemming Street—expecting to see an assailant at their heels. Nothing.

Instead, they were greeted by the wail of sirens and the stunning flash of red and blue lights; fire, ambulance, and police vehicles were already hurtling down the street toward the scene, the boutique on fire and glass everywhere. Alaric pulled over to let the brigade pass.

"What a mess," he said with a shake of his head. Both he and Severus turned back to watch the rescue efforts unfold through the SUV's tinted back window.

"They got here fast," Severus noted thickly. While demons paid off their fair share of human officials, he figured angels had their hands in many of the do-gooders' pockets too. Fire and ambulance were a given, though he had always thought the police force could go either way. "Probably tipped off that they'd be needed for cleanup."

"Gotta look like an accident," Alaric agreed as he slowly rejoined the stagnant flow of traffic. Across the street from the boutique, a crowd had already started to gather, many with their phones out to film the aftermath. "Do you think anyone survived?"

"Not at the auction. I know there are human apartments above. They'll be untouched...by the angels, anyway. The fire is a different story."

Fire wasn't supernatural. The angel responsible for that light wouldn't do much to stop it—hence the call to the fire department. Additional emergency response teams raced by them on their way back to the Inferno, but when Alaric bypassed the nightclub completely, Severus nodded in its general direction with a grimace.

"Don't you want your car?"

"I'll drop you off first," his friend insisted, making a U-turn on the relatively empty street and parking in front of their building. "I'm sure Moira's annoyed that we're not back yet. Start the movie without me. I need to tell Father what happened tonight."

In no mood to argue, Severus offered a curt nod before all but falling out of the vehicle. As he was closing the door, Alaric's phone went off, its ringtone muffled once the door shut.

Severus wasn't sure what prompted him to check *his* phone. The inner demon was eager to get back indoors, desperate to rub up against Moira so she could coddle him through his injuries. The redness in his skin had already started to fade, but the blisters still screamed as he retrieved his phone. Service at last—and a voicemail from Moira.

Severus stared down at the screen for a moment, his physical aches fading to background noise—anxiety swiftly taking their place. He tapped his knuckles on the window as he dialed into his inbox, motioning for Alaric to wait a moment, then brought the phone to his ear.

"One new message, I know, I know," he hissed at the

automated voice recording. He never had messages. No one but Alaric ever communicated with his personal phone—work phone was a different story, of course. As he tapped around to open the first unheard message, his concern spiked, a flood of adrenaline pounding through his limbs—and only made worse by Moira's message.

"Hi. So. It's me. Don't be mad, but I'm on campus because I needed to drop off these essays with my prof. So far, so good. No black-eyed creatures following me—"

"Fucking *woman*," Severus growled, throwing himself at the front door. He called for her as soon as he got inside—but first addressed the smoking tenderloin in the oven. He yanked it out without oven mitts, hands fried enough that he didn't care about the additional burns, and then raced through the building, shouting her name.

By the time he reached his floor, he sounded frantic even to his own ears. "*Fuck.*"

The building was empty. Not a pretty little hybrid in sight. Severus slammed his fist against his bathroom mirror, hissing as the shattered bits sliced into his hand. The pain didn't matter—and it couldn't compare to the *anger* the inner demon expelled, burning him from the inside out.

He had to find her. Nowhere in Farrow's Hollow was safe for her—hadn't he drilled that into her thick fucking skull enough this week?!

How had she managed to get out? He'd asked Cordelia to enchant the front door before she went to Hell last week, and his cousin provided a talisman to lock it completely from the outside whenever he needed.

It didn't matter. Moira was out there. She was vulnerable.

Severus needed to find her—*immediately*.

He hurled himself down the stairs, tripping on each

landing before thundering out the front door. He'd been moving so fast that he ended up slamming into the SUV while reaching for the door, which then pushed the whole vehicle off-balance, tipping it onto the two wheels on Alaric's side. His friend scrambled for the wheel, dropping his phone in the process, and stared wide-eyed as Severus flung himself into the passenger seat.

"Campus," he growled, pounding the dashboard with bloodied, pus-ridden hands, nearly all his blisters torn open. "She went to *campus*."

The tires screeched as Alaric raced away from the curb, narrowly missing one of those ridiculous two-seater smart cars in the process. The driver slammed on the brakes and the horn, and Severus glared back with black eyes, his lips lifted into a snarl.

"We'll find her," Alaric said, sounding uncharacteristically tense as he ran the nearest red light. "I'm sure she's fine."

"Just *drive*."

He hadn't the patience to be nice about it—to hide the inner beast, which had fled its cage at the first whiff of her missing. Because with his history of having the shittiest luck on both worldly planes, Severus had a gut-wrenching feeling that his pretty little hybrid was already dead.

Or worse yet—taken.

CHAPTER EIGHT

Moira felt it before she opened her eyes—the stabbing, burning, ripping *agony* in her shoulders. She tried to move them, to reach for them, but something sharp and cold bit into her wrists with the slightest movement. Arms forcefully outstretched, she couldn't feel her fingertips. The sandpaper lining of her throat held her groan in, keeping it down, and each hard swallow only made the sensation worse. Like knives. Knives running down her throat. Her stomach churning. Her eyelids heavy. They wouldn't lift at first, but as the fog started to clear, she knew she needed to face the consequences of her actions.

Soft lighting greeted her when she finally managed to open her eyes. As she'd guessed, her hands were bound and pulled out in either direction—handcuffs leaving bloody marks on her wrists, connected to chains embedded in the stone walls, stretching her arms to their limits. Her prison cell was circular, made of limestone, the floor dirt. No windows, but there were dozens of small circular lights in the ceiling, emanating just enough brightness to let her see where she was—to make her queasy.

Directly in front of her was a door. Black. Metal. No window either. And to its side—a camera mounted on a tripod. She blinked at it, trying to make sense of it at first, her mind slow on the uptake. Had Frat Boy Junior drugged her? Kidnapped her? And was he now *filming* her?

All signs pointed to yes.

Moira's lower lip quivered as she bowed her head to her chest. A tremor skittered through her, starting at her core and working its way out. With her knees slightly bent, all her weight had fallen to her arms, to her poor shoulders—they positively *screamed* when she finally found it within herself to stand up straight.

A sob slipped out before she could stop it, and while the intense pain hadn't dissipated completely, it had lessened. Slightly. She rolled her shoulders, then tested the strength of the chains holding her there. They rattled with each tug, but didn't budge. Not an inch, not even when she pulled with everything she had.

Trapped. Hopelessly, utterly trapped.

Was it worth it? Dropping off those fucking essays?

The voice sounded like Severus—a disappointed Severus at that. She closed her eyes again, tears gathering, falling, streaking down her cheeks.

No, she told him. *It wasn't worth it.*

Moira waited, a tidal wave of feelings *pounding* at her. Foolish. That was the primary one. Moira felt foolish. Frightened. Angry. Panicked. But mostly foolish—for ignoring Severus, for thinking all demons would be like him.

She lifted her head with a sniffle at the sound of something clanking on the other side of the door—locks. Not wanting Frat Boy Junior to see her cry, she dried her face as best she could, lifting her stiff and achy shoulders to rub her cheeks.

When the door creaked open, its hinges in serious need of an oiling, Frat Boy Junior wasn't standing on the other side. Moira's eyebrows furrowed, squinting somewhat as the figure stepped out of the shadows and into the gentle light of the room. Dressed in white linens, from the baggy pants to the flowy long-sleeved shirt, he wore a mishmash of silver crucifixes, all varying in style, each one bedazzled with tiny pearls.

The demon who had attacked Severus at the bar. Diriel. Gaunt, with high cheekbones that looked especially sharp in this light. Black hair—wavy but short, styled perfectly around his head to distract from the fact that he looked like some strung-out hippie otherwise. And those eyes—black as a starless sky at midnight. Moira swallowed hard, straightening as best she could while her heart plummeted right down into her stomach.

"Oh, come on, why the long face?" The door swung shut behind him, slamming with a foreboding sense of finality that made her knees quiver. "No tears, Moira. We haven't even *started* to have fun yet."

If she'd thought her mouth had felt dry before, it was like a desert now. She lifted her chin, hoping to mask her fear, her *panic*, as Diriel strolled toward the mounted camera and checked its settings. With his hands clasped behind him, she couldn't see what he was holding until he showed her his back—and when she spied the knife, long and serrated, she yanked at her restraints again, the panic slipping through.

"Right," he said softly, turning on his toes—his feet bare—to face her again. "And we *are* going to have fun. I can promise you that."

"I think our definitions of fun might vary," she choked out, shrinking as far back as she could with every precise step he took forward. The chains only had so much give, however, and her knees threatened to buckle when he finally stopped directly in front of her, no more than a foot or so of space between them—knife hanging limply at his side.

"You know..." His hand moved so suddenly that she yelped when it clamped down on her chin, nails digging into her flesh. "I really ought to thank you." Diriel tugged the gaping neckline of his flouncy white shirt to the side, revealing two severe burns, one on each shoulder, each about the size of her palm. "I never knew I could scar until I met you. So, thank you for teaching me something new. It's been *years* since one of you upright mammals surprised me."

Moira tried not to recoil, to even *flinch* as he bore down on her, all her concentration going to her hands. But nothing happened. No blinding flash of light. No warmth—no exquisite burn. It had made her feel powerful, the fire. She'd realized it days after the incident, lost in thought, moping about her situation. She had protected Severus from a monster—and it had made her feel *strong*. For once, she hadn't completely loathed her new body.

Now, however, she couldn't even get a spark going.

Pathetic.

"My father is an angel, you know," she blurted when the demon dragged the tip of his knife along her side, the sharp point poking through her knit sweater here and there. "And when he finds out what you've done to me, there will be c-consequences—"

"I'm going to go ahead and stop you right there," Diriel remarked, finally removing his clawlike hand, bony and sharp, from her chin—and holding the knife to her lips instead, "before you embarrass yourself."

Moira flinched back, pressing her lips together when the blade's jagged edge brushed against them.

"Simple girl," Diriel cooed as he leaned closer, his breath hot and foul, "we all know your daddy's an angel." He licked her cheek, tongue rough as a cat's. "Who d'you think hired me to do this to you?"

She exhaled sharply, the news knocking the wind out of her. Diriel pulled away, pressing the flat side of the knife to her cheek.

"It was Daddy dearest," he whispered, then swiped a finger under her eyes, its frighteningly sharp nail catching her tears. "In case you're a little slow on the uptake... One can never tell with half-breeds."

Her dad had hired a demon to hurt her? If Diriel was telling the truth—and there was no guarantee of that, a little voice at the back of her head insisted—then that meant her dad knew who she was, where she was...and just wanted her out of the way. It could have all been lies, but what would that gain him? If he wanted to hurt her, clearly all the demon needed to do was tell the truth. The truth was bad enough. Had Diriel's knife not been shoved up against her face, Moira would have let her head drop, using her hair to hide her tears.

"Oh, chin up, buttercup." The demon patted her cheek twice before retracting the blade, tossing it back and forth between each hand. "There's always a silver lining. Your da' hired me to *kill* you, and I haven't yet. Eh? Eh? Not so bad yet, is it?"

Moira's eyes narrowed at him, though her glare lacked venom, as a soul-crushing *sorrow* slashed at her insides. She had spent her whole life preparing for the fact that her dad —well, the guy who had donated a bit of sperm—might not want her. She had given herself dozens of speeches. She had read books on the subject, joined chat forums as a teenager. Moira had thought she'd prepared enough to take the news and not flinch—to be able to run with it, roll with it, and keep going.

Her knees folded at last, her body sinking as far as the chains would allow.

Clearly, she hadn't prepared enough.

Because this hollow feeling, this ever-expanding black hole in the pit of her soul, hurt far worse than anything Diriel had done to her.

"See, this is what the winged *fuck* gets for not adding the specifics to our contract," Diriel continued, his unadulterated glee the cherry on top of this nightmare. "He said I had to kill you, and I *will*, of course, but he didn't say *when* I needed to do it."

She coughed, eyes widening, when his hand wrapped around her throat and hoisted her into a proper standing position.

"So," soulless black eyes wandered up and down her figure, "let's see what we're working with here, shall we?"

He hooked a finger through a belt loop on her jeans, then slashed it open with the knife. Moira stiffened, a sick feeling creeping across her when she realized what he was about to do, and watched, every muscle tense, as he slipped the knife under the waistline, smooth-face down, then turned it upright and ripped. The jagged blade tore right through the fabric, and she tried to wriggle away, a squeal catching in her throat.

"Now, be a lamb and try not to move," he said, crouching down and fingering the rip. "Don't want to nick you...yet."

He proceeded to slash through her clothes with near clinical precision. First went her jeans, cut along the side seams and tossed aside in two neat pieces. He needed to crouch to do it, and, biding her time, waiting with bated breath, Moira struck.

She managed to knee him right in the nose, sending the snarling demon toppling backward, the array of necklaces crashing down with him. Growling, he wiped the blood away on his precious white linens, and then returned to work with a far rougher hand.

Huh. That was less satisfying than she'd expected.

Her panties came next, cut open on either side. Moira crossed her legs instinctively, but Diriel assured her he wouldn't be parting them; he took the longest of his pearl necklaces and looped it around and around her ankles, binding them—*prettily constrained* was his exact wording—seeming quite proud of himself when he was through.

Her sweater came next, hacked and slashed with less finesse, as though he was getting impatient. Last but not least, her bra; he undid the clasp with his teeth as Moira fought back a gag, then, with dramatic flair, slithered around her and ripped it off from the front, the straps snapping at her skin as they broke.

"Well, don't you look..." He pursed his lips as he considered her, tossing her bra aside with a sigh. "Painfully ordinary. Not sure what I was expecting..."

Diriel did a lap around her as Moira shivered and fought back a fresh onslaught of tears, her skin burning with what felt like a head-to-toe blush.

"Does he fuck you?"

She twitched when he prodded the backs of her thighs—as a judge might when rating a show dog. Diriel stopped his circling after two loops around, mouth twisted in distaste. "Severus? Does he? Just ghastly creatures, incubi. They fuck anything with a pulse, and then there's *you*, this...*abomination*. Human and angel. Worst combination of half-breed, in my opinion." He held up his hands, smiling again. "But I suppose I'm not here to pass judgement. I'm here to decide if I'll be slitting your throat now or later." Diriel clapped his hands together, the sound of flesh colliding like thunder. "Let's begin."

Moira wanted to talk. She wanted to sneer something back at him—like heroines did in all the adventure books once the villain had them cornered. She wanted to be brave, to be snarky, to find a weakness in Diriel's cavalier, sadistic armor and exploit it for everything she had.

But she couldn't. She just stood there, shaking, unable to feel her arms, her toes, as her heart pounded between her ears. Any time she *did* part her lips, no words rolled off her tongue—no snippy retort, no nonchalant comment about how she was so totally *fine* and he didn't frighten her one bit. Because he did. Diriel had her naked and chained up who knows where. Her angel light had decided to be shy, and her strength wasn't enough to break her restraints.

She felt naive, small, and foolish in equal measures now, finally aware just how out of her depth she had been in this new world.

Unwanted, too. Unwanted by the man, the angel, who was responsible for what she had turned into.

With Diriel standing behind her now, she let her tears fall as silently as she could, trying desperately to stop her body from quivering. Two fingers jabbed at her back, walking up and settling between her shoulder blades. She inhaled sharply when he applied more pressure, pushing about, as if searching for something.

"Now, right about here..."

Moira screamed—the sound ripping her throat raw—when Diriel sliced into her with that serrated knife. The bite of each sharp tooth, tearing into her skin—agony. One hand gripped her shoulder as she thrashed about, but he continued to dig, continued to cut into her. Warmth rippled down her back, over her backside, down her thighs; she didn't need to look to know it was blood.

Another scream as he started in on the other shoulder—and then another and another. Every inch of the blade, every poke, every gash. She felt it all. Moira had been searching to *feel* again. Severus made her feel in the best way possible—and Diriel the worst.

"W-what are you *doing*?" she cried, sagging when he finally stopped—when he finally seemed to step back, perhaps to admire his work. Moira needn't ask; she knew what he was doing. Torturing her. Getting his jollies. Seeing if he could scar her just as she had him.

Diriel tsked at her, his hand on the back of her hip as his gaze burned across her shredded skin. "Stop complaining. You'll heal. Now, let's have a proper look..."

A voiceless scream tore from her this time, after the knife clattered to the ground and his fingers took its place. She squirmed and twisted, her nerves on fire, her head hazy, as Diriel *dug* into the fresh wounds. Moira kept waiting to pass out, to finally lose consciousness and wake up hours later, sore but alive.

Her new body endured. It met the pain—it felt every bit of it.

"Aha!" She heard him clap again behind her, fingers probing back into her seconds later. "There they are! So little. So *precious*."

Her knees had given way completely now, and she hung there, head bowed, shaking, her entire body burning. "W-what?"

"Your *wings*, simple girl. Your *wings*!" Anchoring

himself on the left chain, Diriel swung around in front of her, the motion making her wrist *scream*. He cupped her face with blood-soaked hands, the rest of it running down her back. It had reached her ankles now, the bright red liquid, hot and ever-present. Diriel forced her to look away from it when he gave her head a little shake, grinning, his laughter hyena-like. "You live another day, Moira Aurelia. You've got angel wings growing back there, just as I suspected you did the second you flambéed me at the Inferno. What luck!"

She blinked up at him, her sluggish mind failing to compute. "Wings?"

"From your dazed stupor, I take it you *don't* know how powerful angel wings are?" He stroked her cheeks with his thumbs—roughly, like an unwanted massage that grated her gums. "One *feather* can sell for millions, and you're going to be my never-ending supply. Angels get their *juice* from their wings. Their brain *and* brawn, if you get my drift. Everybody wants them. Spells. Potions. Rituals. The raw, untapped power of a single feather... Well, it boggles the mind!"

He was spitting on her now, practically foaming at the mouth as he ranted on.

"Now, this can go one of two ways, half-breed," Diriel told her, his voice dropping—suddenly too serious for her liking. "You and I can work together. I'll put you up in style. You'll grow me wings, and I'll harvest for the highest bidder. We can be a *team*."

The very idea made her want to retch, and this time she didn't hide it.

"Or, you can continue to be petulant. I'll keep you tied up...and *still* harvest them for the highest bidder. All that changes is your compliance, eh? I'll have to kill you eventually, I signed a contract, but until then, who says we can't make the most of it? Have a little fun?"

He had gone back to rubbing her face, blood smeared across her lips, and as he stood there, one eyebrow arched expectantly, Moira inhaled the metallic liquid in—and spat it back out at him as hard as she could. Spittle and blood dappled his pale cheek, his chin, and still those awful black eyes gave nothing away.

After a moment of tense staring from both parties, with Moira finally finding the nerve to really *give* it to him with her glare, Diriel let out a long sigh and brushed the blood away.

"You're getting a bit predictable, Moira. A bit *boring*."

He ducked behind her momentarily, then returned in a flash, the knife in hand again. She tried to keep her eyes open, but they blinked hard when he tapped the smooth side of the blade on her nose, blood droplets splattering across her face.

"I'm going to give you some time to think on it," he told her as he strolled backward, casually, toward the door. "You know, weigh your options. And *I'm* going to be thinking too." He gestured toward her with the knife, blood flying everywhere. "We'll find a way to jazz up this very *ordinary* body—not to worry."

And just like that, he was gone. Out the door, which slammed shut behind him. Moira listened to the locks clink back into place. She looked down at the blood pooling around her feet, still lashed together with pearls. The pain hadn't gone away. It clung to her, the emotional and the physical—sank its hooks in and wouldn't let go.

So, she bowed her head, strung up by limp arms and burning shoulders, and finally let the dams burst.

CHAPTER NINE

"She's late," Severus snarled, pacing in front of the ground-floor window, glaring at unassuming pedestrians. Like a caged animal, agitated, he had prowled to and fro for the last half hour in anticipation of his cousin Cordelia's arrival. "She's *never* late."

"Technically she still has three minutes," Alaric said from the kitchen. The clatter of plates suggested he was nearly done unloading the dishwasher, an obtrusive ruckus that made Severus's lip curl.

"She should be here by now. Doesn't she know how important this is? *Time* is of the essence!"

He heard Alaric sigh, but his friend offered nothing further—he knew better than to argue with Severus at this point. Moira had been missing for three days. Three *agonizing* days. Severus had searched high and low for her, calling in favors and paying people off. A hundred grand—gone, now lining the pockets of demon slime whose tips hadn't even amounted to anything. It was only last night, after threatening to get Verrier involved—an empty threat, of course, as Verrier couldn't care less that Moira had been kidnapped—that he had been able to extract useable intel from a demon who worked maintenance at the FHU campus, who finally had the security camera footage to prove it.

Diriel's boys had taken her. Drugged her, stuffed her in a car, and driven north.

As insignificant as Diriel had been in Hell, with no renowned family name to speak of and no particularly special demon abilities, he had built a small empire for himself in Farrow's Hollow.

How he'd done it was anyone's guess. One day he had just *appeared*, influential and filthy rich, with men and ammunition at his disposal. Unlike the other mob families, he seldom threw his weight around, preferring to spend his time torturing and partying. But he had strength in numbers, and Severus knew it would only waste more time if he worked through the levels of the demon's network.

And time wasn't his friend, not after he had finally realized who had taken Moira.

Severus needed to locate her *now*—if she had even survived three days in Diriel's hands.

Unfortunately, the one witch who would assist, no questions asked and no fees charged, was in Hell—on holiday. And not answering his personal summons. The only way Severus had been able to get his cousin topside was through Alaric. The hybrid had told his father there was a glitch in the magic hiding their home, and Verrier put a request in for her to return to Earth *immediately*. Naturally, there was nothing wrong with her enchantments; Cordelia's skills were legendary, and she offered them only to Verrier and her family.

However, when both parties realized it was all just a ruse to get her back to Earth, Alaric had earned a mild tongue-lashing from his father, and Severus had woken up from his two-hour nap this morning, the first he'd taken since Moira disappeared, to a phone call from a shrieking Cordelia. Still groggy, he had let her rant on and on about her professional integrity and how he'd made Verrier question it. When she was through, a bleary-eyed Severus had explained *his* predicament, and after some hemming and hawing, she offered to stop by around nine that morning to help.

"*Finally*," he growled when he spotted her very distinct figure strolling across the street. Swathed in black lace, she was no more than a shadow navigating the bright, bustling spring morning, and she wore a smile when Severus wrenched open the door to find her waiting on the other side.

"Good morning, cousin," she greeted, rasping at him in that sultry voice of hers—she always sounded like a bluesy jazz singer from another decade, or a chain-smoker with a touch of elegance. "You look *awful*."

When Moira had asked if his cousin was a character from a Tim Burton movie, her style assessment hadn't been far off. While rather fashionable in Hell, it was all a bit gothic and heavy for the modern times of Earth.

Her heavily cinched corset gave her a teeny waist and generous hips, despite her already slim figure. Today, she had waltzed straight out a Victorian funeral, from the black skirt with its frilly silk bustle to the fitted black button-up jacket over her petite midsection. Lace everywhere, including the soaring neckline that climbed up her throat and flared out delicately beneath her chin. Finally, the tiny hat that sat just off center, a black net dripping down to cover her sharp, angular features, was just plain *ridiculous*, even for Cordelia.

Her face appeared clear today, much to Severus's chagrin, the porcelain skin unblemished, and the thick black-blue mane that reached down to her hips had been tamed into an uncharacteristically tidy chignon.

Cordelia grabbed his chin as she stepped in, giving it a little squeeze and shake in passing. Ah. Rosewood-red gloves—not entirely black today.

"Thank you for your *promptness*," he hissed, twisting his face out of reach and slamming the door. "I've been waiting—"

"Do not speak to me about *punctuality* and decorum." She whirled around, her demon eyes narrowed as she pointed an accusatory finger at him. "I was summering in Pandemonium with Mother when I received Verrier's summons—his rather *annoyed* summons, at that. You're fortunate I'm even *here*."

"Yes, yes, I've already received the lecture," Severus grumbled, though he paused to kiss her on the cheek, which she offered with a demure tilt of her head, before stalking toward the kitchen. "Let's get to work, shall we?"

"Alaric, *darling*, you're looking well," Cordelia all but sang as she toddled along after him, the click, click, click of her heels across the hardwood making Severus's eye twitch.

"Hello, Cordelia. Nice to see you again."

"More than nice, darling. Tell me, are you still a barman? A creature of your talents is *destined* for greater things! I really must do your cards... In fact, I brought my deck if you're interested."

Severus pinched the bridge of his nose; he knew he should have had Cordelia over when Alaric was out. The witch was positively infatuated with Verrier's son, and she made it known to everyone in the room, Alaric included, that she'd snap him up in a hot second if he so much as smiled at her. His roommate professed to be uncomfortable with the attention, but all his blushing, stammering, and fumbling whenever he was around her suggested otherwise.

Today, however, was *not* the day for flirtatious banter. Severus had been out of his mind with worry since his little hybrid disappeared. He'd been impatient, snippy, and fidgety, unable to sit still for more than five minutes before throwing himself into another half-cocked scheme to find Moira. The thought of another demon taking her, using her for their own perverse purpose, made his insides boil, but the fact that it was *Diriel* only made the matter more dire.

Beyond feeling his own special blend of fear and rage, the inner demon had been giving him outrageous heartburn ever since they'd found Moira's discarded cell phone next to a security pole on the FHU campus. The beast wanted her back just as desperately as Severus did, and if they didn't find her soon, Severus worried he'd be boiled in acid from the inside out.

"Really, with those good looks, you ought to be a *senator*," Cordelia cooed, in the process of peeling off her gloves at the breakfast bar when Severus joined her. Alaric stood on the other side of the counter, at the sink, fiddling with a dishrag. His roommate's flushed cheeks and nervous smile were *telling* as ever, and on any other day Severus would have joined the conversation for a bit of merciless teasing.

Not today.

"*Focus*," he snapped, slamming his hand down on the granite. Alaric jumped, but Cordelia merely shot Severus an exasperated look before delicately removing her headgear. His gaze darted up to her gloveless hands, littered with scars, many decades old. It was a badge of honor among hell-born witches; magic came with a price, and

Cordelia wore her scars with pride. Her face ought to be covered with them, big and small, thick and thin, deep and surface-level, but she always cast an illusion when crossing through the hell-gate.

After all, scar-ridden humans were few and far between these days, and if she wanted to go about her business on Earth without attracting an insane amount of attention, she needed to look normal. It was the same for each and every demon who went topside; the magic of the hell-gates hid their horns and claws, altered their skin. In short, hell-gates made creatures of the underworld palatable.

Alaric, however, had always seemed fascinated with Cordelia's scarring. When he spied the man eyeing her hands, his lips parted as if to ask a question, Severus put an end to it at last.

"You two can flirt and eye-fuck *later*," he growled, looking pointedly between them. "*After* we find Moira."

"All right, all right," Cordelia muttered, waving Severus off as a flushed Alaric glared daggers from across the counter. The witch piled her discarded clothing, which now included her Victorian overcoat, off to the side, revealing the intricate scarring climbing up her bare arms like one mammoth tattoo in varying shades of crimson. She then produced a folded map of Farrow's Hollow from the depths of her skirt pocket and opened it. "I'll need something of hers. Something she has recently used."

Seeing no need for her to elaborate, Severus charged up the two staircases from the first floor to the third. He had left Moira's belongings as they were, as if that would help him forget that she had been kidnapped and was likely being tortured right that very moment. Unsure of what *specifically* Cordelia needed, Severus stuffed everything—

clothes, sunglasses, toothbrush—into Moira's duffel bag, then carried the lot downstairs.

Just as before, he found Alaric and Cordelia mid-flirt, with his cousin half sprawled across the breakfast bar, the huge map of Farrow's Hollow crinkling beneath her. His roommate had moved much closer in his absence, and darted back with a hasty clearing of his throat when Severus dropped Moira's bag on the dining table—loudly.

Cordelia sprang into action, muttering for him to get out of the way as she rooted through Moira's belongings. Severus stood nearby, closer than she would have liked, surely, and crossed his arms as he watched. It felt wrong for someone Moira would consider a stranger to touch her things—*especially* when Cordelia settled on a white bra with pink and baby-blue hearts across the cups.

"A brassiere?" he asked dryly.

"It was closest to her heart, you absolute *child*," she sneered back. Had they been children, she would have stuck a forked tongue out at him before stomping off. Now that they were fully grown demons, she merely turned in a whirl of black lace and stalked back to the counter without another word. Rolling his eyes, Severus followed, his hand pressed to his chest at a sudden flood of acid reflux.

I'm trying *to find her, for fuck's* sake.

Cordelia tossed her head from side to side, cracking her neck noisily with each throw, then rolled her shoulders back and took a deep breath. After instructing Alaric to turn the kitchen light off, she extended her arms over the map, the bra gripped tightly in one hand, the other palm up, and closed her eyes.

Watching his witch cousin perform spellwork was an acquired taste. Her frantic muttering—ancient Aramaic, if he wasn't mistaken—was akin to the possessed speaking in tongues. If she hadn't closed her eyes, you'd be forced to watch them roll back in her head. And her voice—guttural and hoarse, the demon within doing all the casting for her. It was old hat to Severus by now, but he'd thought Alaric might find it distasteful; instead, his friend watched with rapt attention, hanging on her every word.

Over and over she murmured the incantation, the air thickening around them. She held Moira's bra so tightly that her knuckles went white, and suddenly, she hissed, eyes shooting open. Severus and Alaric watched, totally mute, as her palm split, blood pooling in its center. With the tip of her tongue caught between her teeth, lips peeled back in a snarl of pain or delight—or, more likely, *both*—Cordelia turned her hand, whispering the ritual softly now as bright red blood dripped onto the map.

When she finally closed her hand into a fist, the new gash stretching the entire breadth of her palm, the drops of blood on the map unified. Any wayward droplets shot toward the largest, as if summoned magnetically, and Severus moved in closer as the blotch danced around the map—leaving no bloodied trail in its wake. Finally, it stopped, quivering, before the red blob collapsed in on itself, forming a single precise dot that sank into the paper.

Cordelia exhaled, the breath sounding more like a death rattle than anything, before withdrawing both arms and pressing the back of her bloodied hand to her forehead.

"There," she said, her usual rasp back. "She's there."

"Isn't that just forest?" Alaric asked as he and Severus each leaned over the map. Situated north of the university, the area it would appear that Moira had been abandoned in was a forest at the very edge of the city's limits—near the hell-gate, actually, which gave Severus a start. However, logic prevailed, and he shook his head, heart thundering, when he recalled what was *actually* out there.

"No, no, Mammon built an estate there after he created the hell-gate," he said, hoping his recollection of the city's history was correct. Master of magic and wealth, Hell's prince Mammon had built every hell-gate on Earth, and occasionally he wasted a few years away in the nearby cities —should they pique his interest. "The castle was abandoned when he returned to Hell, but I believe it is still functional."

"Demons preferred to live in town when they migrated," Cordelia agreed, her words taking on a somewhat dreamy quality as she strolled around the counter and into the kitchen. At the sound of water running, his cousin humming over the sink, Severus turned and bolted for the door.

"What are you doing?" Alaric hurried after him, grabbing his arm. "You're going out there?"

"We know where she is now," Severus argued. "I have to go. I have to bring her back—"

"Yeah, because running in blindly seems like a perfectly reasonable thing to do."

"And what would you have me do instead? *Sit* here and twiddle my thumbs, as I've been doing all this time?"

"No, but some sort of planning would be helpful," Alaric remarked with a frown. "Don't be stupid, Sev. We know where she is, sure, but we don't know how many demons he has guarding her. Diriel's a twat, but he wouldn't leave someone *that* valuable unguarded, and they will *gut* you the second they see you. Don't. Be. Stupid. Moira doesn't need a heroic idiot—"

"Right, right, right," Severus muttered, silencing his friend with a scowl of his own. Alaric was right, of course.

While every fiber of his being urged him on, desperate to get Moira out of whatever hell she was likely enduring, he couldn't charge in there blind. Besides that, he needed to fuel up; his physical strength was seriously lacking after spending the last three days searching for her. Even a ghoul would be tough to defeat in his current state. "You're right, but Moira—"

"This *Moira* certainly has a hold on you," Cordelia purred, her heels clicking toward them. Severus peered around Alaric, huffing at her, but she remained unfazed by his temper. "I've never seen you so flustered before, cousin."

"She's...important," he said, swallowing hard, "to me. She's important to me, and Diriel will make her suffer."

"Hmm." Cordelia stopped beside Alaric, then brought her hand out from behind her back, the other still dripping blood onto the floor, and held up a small, perfectly innocent cupcake. Her eyelashes fluttered as she offered it to him. "I made you a gift."

"Just... Just now?" Alaric hesitantly accepted the baked good as she nodded. "Well. That's very...efficient of you."

Cordelia hummed in agreement, then sauntered toward the stairs, an extra sway in her bustle. "I'll help you two find this Moira woman, but only if you acquire the building layout to that castle. I can find her exact location to save us some time." She paused halfway up the stairwell and leaned over the railing. "Until then, I'll be napping in your room, Severus. Bit jet-lagged...just flew in from Hell and all that."

The pair watched her until she disappeared upstairs, her heels clacking across the second floor to the next staircase. Then, in unison, they looked down at Alaric's cupcake—chocolate base, vanilla frosting, a smattering of red sprinkles on top. Just as he went to unwrap it, Severus slapped it out of his hand.

"Don't eat that," he hissed, knowing his cousin too well to let Alaric go through with it. "Don't eat anything she bakes you unless you want to fall head over heels in love with her for eternity."

"Right. Yeah. Don't want that." Alaric wiped his fingers on his pajama bottoms, then scratched at the back of his neck, unable to meet Severus's eye. "So, what's the plan then?"

"Haven't a clue," Severus grumbled, stalking for the front door and slipping into a pair of shoes. "Think about it while I go find those building plans. We're getting her out of there tonight, whether we have a plan or not. Do you understand?"

Alaric sighed, arms at his side, the cupcake frosting-side down at his feet. "I understand that you'll do it even if I object."

"Damn right I will." Severus wasn't about to let Diriel butcher the only person who cared about him, the only one besides Alaric and Cordelia who seemed to *enjoy* him, the *real* him. In fact, if he had the opportunity to take that fucker out in the process, he wouldn't hesitate. Moira didn't deserve this—any of it. Severus was responsible for her lack of knowledge, her lack of *fear* around demons. He was the fool who had brought her to the Inferno in the first place; she had outed herself *defending* him.

He owed it to Moira to get her out, and once he did, he'd hold her to him, taste her, protect her, worship her as she ought to be worshipped—and never, ever let go again.

CHAPTER TEN

"Let's *go*, Cordelia." Severus glared at her from the front passenger seat of Alaric's new SUV. His cousin hoisted her middle finger at him on the hand that clutched Moira's bra, her eyes closed and her words flowing as she performed the location spell over the three-century-old building plans Severus had acquired for Mammon's abandoned castle.

It hadn't been easy to dig them up, but he'd managed, touching just about every human in the Farrow's Hollow city records department until he got what he wanted. They'd been locked away in a vault, along with plans to several other key demon structures—including a very accurate layout of the Inferno. Severus had taken that, too, and planned to hand it over to Verrier once they had recovered Moira.

"Just let her do her thing, Sev," Alaric muttered, ceaselessly drumming his fingers on the steering wheel as he stared out into the surrounding forest. Off the beaten path, they had put the vehicle—a gift from Alaric's father after he'd discovered the other one had lost a mirror—to the test, forcing it over rocky, rough woodland terrain to reach their rendezvous point just north of the castle. Out here, they were officially beyond city limits, which had been Cordelia's suggestion: many local witches were only human, imbibed with magic by a willing demon, and their reach was limited to Farrow's Hollow proper. No sense in triggering any alarms before they had confirmed Moira's location in the castle.

From there, Severus planned to just wing it—storm in, fuck up anyone who got in his way, and get her out. Diriel's whereabouts had already been confirmed: Dartanious had called about fifteen minutes ago to inform Alaric that the demon was trying to bully his way back into the Inferno. Thankfully, Verrier had been willing to settle the issue personally, though everyone knew he'd be in a foul mood after being pulled from his midnight meal at Rose's Corner for something so petty. Severus almost felt sorry for Diriel—*almost*.

The rustling of papers caught his attention again, and Severus watched as Cordelia's blood shot across one floor's layout and hopped over to the next. It scurried about, searching, searching, searching, until it finally sank into the last page of parchment. Cordelia tossed Moira's bra aside, along with the rest of the castle's building plans, then scrutinized the blood mark.

"She's two levels below," the witch said, pursing her lips as she tracked her finger across the page. "At the end of a hallway...in a circular room."

"Alive?"

"Her brassiere burned hot during the spell," Cordelia told him as she moved on to examine her bleeding hand. "She lives."

"Then let's get a move on," Severus growled before hurrying out, resisting the urge to slam the door behind him.

Alaric did the same, and the pair waited for Cordelia to take her sweet fucking time to join them, licking at the new wound on her palm as she sauntered through the underbrush, totally unfazed by the way the branches grabbed at her hair and the thorny bushes clawed at her dress. Severus rolled his eyes and grabbed her when she was close enough, dragging her along by her forearm until she delivered a well-aimed kick to his calf.

"Fuck," he hissed, releasing her with a glare. "*What*?!"

"I just thought you'd like to approach under a cloak of invisibility," his cousin remarked, a twinkle in her bright green eyes, the demon tucked back inside for now. "Or, if you want to ride up, cavalier and obvious as day, then I'm all for watching you get eviscerated from the sidelines—"

Severus closed his eyes in an effort to compose himself. It wouldn't do Moira any good to have him riled up and heated, his inner demon positively chomping at the bit to do some damage. He might be desperate to spring her from her jail cell, but he still had to be smart about it. "Just do it already. We don't have time for this."

"What—your attitude?"

"*Cordelia.*"

"You should have a sweetheart more often, cousin," she teased, tucking the rolled-up parchment into her skirt's pocket before sliding her still-bleeding hand into a silky black glove. "You're just too much *fun* like this."

His lips peeled back into a snarl, but before he could utter another threat, she grabbed his elbow and a sudden rush of cold washed over him. He shuddered, the brisk air burning with every breath.

"Guys?" Alaric's panicked gaze swept across Severus and Cordelia several times, looking but not seeing. He reached out with both hands. "This is my least favourite version of the plan. *Guys*?"

Cordelia watched him flounder about with pursed lips, clearly delighted, then snatched his hand as Severus rolled his eyes so hard they nearly popped out.

"Here, sweet boy," she cooed, threading her gloved fingers around his. Dressed in all black, from his leather coat down to his ridiculously clean lace-up boots, Alaric shivered more visibly than Severus did under the illusion.

"Cold."

"Very astute, Alaric," Severus said with a sigh, watching as his friend's breath fogged in front of him. "Invisibility usually is. Come along."

"Don't let go of my hand, darling," Cordelia instructed. "As soon as we three disengage, the illusion falls. So, hold nice and tight."

"Er, right."

"For fuck's sake," Severus grumbled, half dragging the two behind him through the forest. They had likely crossed into the city's limits by now, weaving their way around tree trunks, both fallen and upright, and avoiding animal burrows along the way. A faint spring mist had started, plunging through the overhead canopy and only making the chill of Cordelia's spell worse. Some ten minutes later, the castle loomed ahead through the forest, its crumbling outline reminiscent of the old-world architecture in Hell's capital city, Pandemonium.

They had opted to charge in through the front door—there was no other point of entry on the main level, according to the layout. Severus could only hope the building plans for the castle were accurate; he had beguiled more humans today than he'd done in quite some time, and by the end of it he'd had the whole department clamoring to get their hands on him, each one enchanted by his touch.

And Severus had taken every bit of human skin he could. He'd spent the day recharging his strength, and he'd been positively brimming with it when they had set out together a half hour ago. Cordelia might have been their element of surprise, a secret weapon, but Severus still wanted to be physically capable of overpowering his foes.

While the faint glow of light inside the castle suggested it was still in use for one reason or another, it had certainly seen better days. Nearly all the small windows had been shattered, bits of stained glass crunching underfoot as the invisible trio skulked around the perimeter of the building. Severus led the way, taking in the crumbling turrets and the overgrown ivy. Diriel might have claimed this place for his own, but it seemed unlikely he'd actually live in it.

Which only made Severus's rage thicken.

Because that meant he would be using it now for the express purpose of squirreling Moira away, doing fuck knows what to her in the meantime.

"Slow *down*," Cordelia scolded, stumbling into him when he stopped at the edge of the wall. "I'm wearing heels, for Lucifer's sake."

"Well, that was your stupid decision, wasn't it, cousin?" he sneered back, briefly glaring over his shoulder at her before peering around the corner. Sure enough, the front door was just where the layout had put it—and before it sat two chatting demons. Big lugs, sure, but he didn't detect anything particularly special about them.

The demon genetic lottery was a crapshoot, as Severus knew all too well, but most of the time it produced *them*: ordinary beasts of Hell who were strong, but hardly as influential as the rest.

He had never understood why *they* didn't make up the bottom of the demon hierarchy; there was nothing special about them beyond their physicality and their ability to inflict pain, which was a gift all demons claimed to possess. Still, they were the majority: unspecialized but cruel, they ranked higher than Severus strictly because their strength wasn't contingent on human life essence. Lucky bastards.

"We can take 'em," he whispered, then crouched low and shuffled around the corner. Cordelia and Alaric followed, but as soon as they were close enough to the leather-clad pair seated on the cracked front steps, one of them smoking, Alaric moved up beside Severus, which left Cordelia squished between them. Unfortunately, they *needed* to keep hold of her to maintain the spell, which meant Severus's right hand and Alaric's left needed to act as if they belonged to one body.

He waved to Alaric, then counted down with his fingers —three, two, one, *go*.

As Alaric kneed the smaller of the two brutes in the face, Severus wrapped his arm around the other demon's head, latched onto his ear, and *twisted* with all his might. The force snapped the unwitting creature's neck, his great big body sagging instantly. When he was through, Severus did the same to Alaric's demon, who was swiping at nothing with his enormous fists, face twisted in rage. Alaric had hidden behind Cordelia in the meantime, the witch suddenly plagued with a serious case of the giggles.

Severus huffed at them both, the demon inside *severely* displeased by how slow this was all going. "Can we try to be professional here?"

"Oh, lighten up, cousin," Cordelia teased, leading the pair up the stone steps to the front door. "There's always time for a bit of fun when you're committing murder."

"It's not murder when they'll heal." Severus went for the rusted doorknob, scowling. "So try to maintain just a *little* decorum, a breath of dignity—"

A piercing, skull-crushing alarm shrieked the second Severus forced the door open. Feeling as though someone was driving a drill into his temple, both in pain and in sound, he clamped his hands over his ears, staggering into the castle with a groan.

"Magic," Cordelia shouted over the racket, the only indication that it bothered her a slight wrinkle of her brow. "I'll disable it."

With the alarm triggered, Alaric came stumbling in after her, fingers shoved in his ears too. However, before either could get a word out, he forcefully wrenched Severus around—just in time for him to spy the onslaught of demons barreling toward them. Down the stairs from the second level. Out a door in the back of the entrance hall, likely charging up from the basement. All in all, about fifteen incoming black-eyed men, each donning the flashy accessories he often associated with Diriel's hang of partying halfwits.

Perfect.

Not entirely unexpected, but certainly not appreciated.

As he prepared himself for the first wave, a gunshot rang out just over his shoulder, and Severus staggered off to the side.

"Alaric!"

"Come on, it was a *great* head shot," his friend shouted over the din, grinning. "And you're *welcome*."

Given the fact that Alaric's demon refused to make itself known, they had all agreed to load him up with physical weaponry for tonight, whereas Severus would rely on strength alone. Luckily for him, Alaric was an excellent marksman, using the moonlight spilling in through the open door and the flash of each shot to pick off his attackers.

And the sooner he took them out, the better. Not only was this magical alarm system driving Severus up the fucking wall, but all of Diriel's thugs were roaring like this was *the* epic showdown of their lifetime. Was there not enough noise already? *Must* they contribute to it?

"Cordelia, for fuck's sake, *shut it up*!"

"I'm *working on it*," she bellowed back, her voice demonic and hands raised overhead, each pulsing with a soft red glow. "Just do your part, cousin!"

As a pair of brute demons charged him, Severus unlocked the cage—and let the beast free. Eyes completely black, he fought with every skill in his arsenal, using his speed and his nimble footing to his advantage. Ducking, weaving, dodging—he skirted a flurry of fists before knocking one of his attackers off-balance with a well-timed kick to the knee. As soon as the creature went down, he pounced, snapping his neck just as he'd done the first of Diriel's men. A broken neck was the surest way to keep a demon down, no matter their rank or ability.

Besides a bullet to the head, of course. The only way to recover from *that* was for someone to dig the bullet out before decomposition set in.

And since he wasn't the one with the gun, a broken neck was in store for the next demon who charged him, and the next, and the next, and the one after that. Shots rang out, but Severus was forced to divert back to the hybrid when they stopped—there were only eight rounds in Alaric's specially designed firearm. Out of ammunition, Alaric used the gun as a blunt instrument, even managing to crack one charging demon across the jaw before another slammed a fist into his face.

Severus tackled the third demon encroaching on Alaric to the ground, then hammered his head, face-first, against the cobblestone floor until blood spurted everywhere. It was only as the liquid soaked his knees that he realized Cordelia had managed to shut off the magical alarm. The high-pitched ringing in his ears hadn't dissipated any, and he stuck a finger in one, wiggling it about, all the while popping his jaw open and closed.

"Sev," Alaric grunted, a demon's thick hand wrapped around his throat, "a little h-help..."

Severus staggered to his feet, a little run-down and more than a little bloody himself, only to be knocked right back down by a *whoosh* of Cordelia's power. It swept across the entire space, white and grey shockwaves pulsing out from around her. While the impact left him winded and wheezing, all of Diriel's cronies vanished the moment it touched them.

"That should buy us some..." She sank to her knees, blood gushing from each nostril. "Some time."

"Cordelia!"

Much to Severus's surprise, Alaric charged to her side, catching her before she toppled over. His witchy cousin grinned up at the hybrid, the pair bathed in moonlight spilling in from the open front door, then patted his cheek.

"Don't fret, pet," she murmured. "Banishing incantations are always a little more taxing on Earth than they are in Hell. I'll be on my feet momentarily."

With both the pile of bodies *and* any remaining drones gone, Severus quickly took stock of his injuries. All his knuckles were split open, the skin still tender from his run-in with the angelic light a few days prior. Someone's ring had sliced a shallow gash across his cheek, and his body ached from the few hits that had landed—but he would survive. Just like Cordelia's spellcasting, hand-to-hand combat and the injuries it wrought always hit him harder outside of the underworld. Unlike Cordelia, Severus wouldn't feel it tomorrow. He'd be mostly healed, stuck with only the twinges of battle, whereas his cousin was scarred for life.

"Oh, darling, they broke that very regal nose of yours," Cordelia said, sounding stronger by the moment as she tsked up at Alaric. When Severus slowly glanced up, he found his friend beaming at her.

"Yeah. Injury twins." The banal comment was followed by nervous laughter, which Cordelia responded to like a wolf spying a stumbling deer amidst the fleeing herd.

"Not to worry. I still fancy you," she purred, her eyes flicking to full black. Alaric cleared his throat, then helped her to her feet, a hand on her waist to steady her.

"Alaric, did she bake you something while I was gone today?" Severus snapped, unable to find another reasonable explanation for...*that.* He waved his friend's stammering response away with a huff before standing once more and stalking across the circular foyer. "Where the fuck is the stairwell down?"

"To the left," Cordelia told him, and he heard the soft click of her heels on the stone as the pair followed him toward an iron door tucked away in the back left of the room.

When it wouldn't immediately open for him, Severus really threw his shoulder into it—only to have Alaric interject with a tentative: "I think it's a pull, not a push."

Frowning, Severus pulled—and sure enough, the damn thing opened without so much as a squeaky hinge.

While all he wanted was to throw himself down the dark, winding stairwell, Severus had Cordelia lead the way

—it was her blood on the map that would take them to Moira.

So he followed, as much as it killed him, gnashing his teeth and scowling when they happened upon the mazelike corridors of the castle's lower level. Dead ends aplenty, hallways that got narrower and narrower the farther one trod. Only a demon could have designed such a nightmare, and by the time they reached the second sublevel, the one Moira was supposed to be on, they had burned through an entire *hour* just mastering the maze. Severus's inner demon was all but intolerable at this point, his esophagus on fire and his head throbbing.

"Find the room," he growled, shoving Cordelia out of the second supremely claustrophobic stairwell they'd encountered tonight. "*Find* it!"

"If you push me one more time, cousin, I'll banish *you*," the witch snarled, fixing him with a withering look over her shoulder.

"We're running out of time!"

"Hey, look—"

"Well, better let me concentrate then," Cordelia snapped, speaking over Alaric as she planted her hands rather dramatically on her hips.

"Then fucking *concentrate*!"

"Don't get your knickers in a—"

"The door!" Alaric shouldered his way past both of them, jogging down the dimly lit dirt corridor ahead. Severus shoved by Cordelia again, ignoring her indignant curses—because Alaric was right. Dead ahead, the only thing on this level was a giant metal door. Torches flickered on either side, and Severus hastily helped Alaric with the half dozen locks, his fingers clumsy and his heart hammering.

When they finally had everything unbolted, Severus nudged Alaric out of the way and yanked the lead door open. The moment he stepped inside, the assault on his senses was instantaneous—and *strong*.

There was a palpable temperature difference between the outside hall and the interior of the room. While it took a few seconds for his eyes to adjust to the ceiling's pod lights, far brighter than the torches illuminating the corridor, when Severus *could* see, he wished he couldn't. His breath rapidly fogged in front of him, and he came to an abrupt halt, feeling like his legs just couldn't move anymore. Shock. It was utter *shock* at the sight before him.

For there was Moira, strung up, crucified on an invisible cross, her arms stretched wide by chains embedded in the walls. His inner demon fell silent as he drank her in, starting at the layers upon layers of pearl strands wrapped around her ankles, tight enough to keep her bound. Old blood smeared across her legs, having dried as it streaked down from a wound he couldn't yet see. Her nudity had his hands in tight fists, her ethereal skin aglow in the frigid underground cage.

Up, up, up his gaze traveled—stopping at her breasts. Someone had pierced them, with two sizeable gold rods plunged through her nipples, a delicate strand of braided gold hanging between them, connecting them. Time seemed to stop the longer he studied her.

Demons were accustomed to horror—but that didn't mean they felt nothing when it was those they cherished most at the end of the torturer's rod. Severus wanted to turn and run, to look away, blink hard, try the door again as if that might change things. But he couldn't. He had to see it all. He needed the image of her burned into the forefront of his mind—to fuel his rage, to power his vengeance.

Like Diriel's, her neck dripped with dozens of silver and gold necklaces, pearl accents throughout, crosses at the ends of some. Her head hung low—until Severus's gaze swept across the thick braided crown of hair around it. Slowly, Moira looked up, with noticeable difficulty, her lips blue, her eyelashes frozen.

Tears sliced through the frostbite on her cheeks the moment their eyes met.

A weeping angel—she'd turned her cage cold.

The sound of crashing behind forced him into action. Severus glanced back briefly to find Alaric smashing a mounted camera against the wall. Cordelia remained in the doorway, breath fogging in front of her in slow, even clouds.

His feet—feet he no longer felt—carried him to Moira, and he cupped her face with both hands. All he wanted to do was *touch* her, hold her, shield her from all the evils of his world, but he knew better than that. She winced at the feel of his hands on her icy cheeks—she wouldn't be able to handle the beast inside, what it yearned to do to her now that he had found her.

"Are you all right?" he whispered, then grimaced. What a stupid fucking question. "I'm so sorry, Moira. I—"

"'S my fault," she murmured, her voice hoarse—Diriel would have made her scream. It shouldn't surprise him, but Severus had to fight his natural response, his fingertips threatening to dig into her skin. Moira blinked up at him, then swallowed noticeably. "I... It's my f-fault."

He stiffened, then grasped her chin tight to get her attention, forcing their eyes to meet. "You listen to me. *None* of this is your fault, do you understand? *None* of it. *You* did nothing to deserve this."

"I left," she said, her words like a sigh, her eyelids heavy. "I—"

"It doesn't matter," Severus growled, resisting the urge to shake her, if only to make her understand. "Diriel did this, not you. This is not *punishment* for leaving the house. This is unwarranted savagery. *You* are blameless, and that's the end of it, do you understand?" He wiped the falling tears away, his gaze dropping to her blue, trembling lips, wishing he could kiss them back to life. "I'll kill him. I'll fucking *kill* him."

A slight rustling along the chain connected to Moira's wrist startled him out of his rage, and he realized he was just standing there, holding her face and glaring at her lips. Fucking useless. Alaric, meanwhile, was trying to wrench the chain out of the wall—trying and failing.

"Move, move aside," Severus ordered, wrapping both hands around the chain and *pulling* with all his might. It didn't pop out of place as easily as he would have liked, his entire body working and working and *working* to get enough weight behind him, but eventually it snapped. With one side free, Severus ran to the other, applying the same nearly unyielding pressure until it too broke free. Out of the corner of his eye, he spotted Moira go down. Thankfully Alaric was there to catch her, with Severus at her side seconds later, gently lowering her abused body to the ground.

"Here we are," he murmured, scanning her for any signs of fresh injury—and fuming at what he found. Two thick, still-healing lines sliced across her shoulder blades, and, even in his current state, straddling the line between crushing Moira against him and storming back to town to rip Diriel's spine out, he knew precisely why her demon captor had searched *there* of all places.

He'd wanted to find her wings.

The thought had crossed Severus's mind too after he'd

put all the pieces together and realized that Moira was an angel-human hybrid. Angels' wings were the pinnacle of magic—the best of the best, and they didn't lose their power when you plucked them off the source either. He hadn't been sure if a hybrid would possess such a powerful attribute—and he hadn't *cared*. Moira mattered to Severus. Just her. Not her abilities, and certainly not what he could do with them.

It had always been her, just as she was.

Shaking his head, he brought his attention back to where it belonged.

"Someone get these cuffs off," he snarled, spying Moira's arms limp at her sides as though unable to lift them. "*Cordelia.*"

"Take them out," Moira whispered roughly.

"I know, darling, I know, we're working on it—"

"No." Her watery eyes darted to his. "The piercings. Take them out. *Please.*"

Something glittery caught his eye, and as he brushed back a few loose wisps of her hair, Severus finally noticed all the new piercings along her ears, too. At least ten on the right side, all along the shell of her ear. Diamonds. Rings, studs—the works. He knew, however, that Moira wasn't referring to *those* piercings, not from the way her voice broke.

So, as Cordelia crouched on her left side and grabbed her cuffed hand, and Alaric used the knife hidden in his boot to tear through the strands of pearls around her feet, Severus saw to the nipple piercings. Solid gold. Delicate. They would be rather attractive on her—if she had actually wanted them. The expression on her face, the distress in her eyes, the fucking temperature of this room, literally frozen with angelic sorrow, all *screamed* otherwise.

Teeth gritted, Severus unscrewed the round end of one of the gold bars, working as gently as he could. He could feel her watching, the weight of her stare making him clumsier than he should have been, tugging the nipple more than he wanted. Moira exhaled sharply when he got the first bar out, the sound followed by one of her heavy cuffs falling to the ground. Without a word, the trio rotated around her, Alaric darting out of the way with the strings of pearls removed from her ankles, and Severus climbing over her to see to the left breast as Cordelia moved on to the right shackle.

And Moira sat in the middle of it all, shaking and crying in the most awful silence Severus had ever experienced. The sound of her next gasp wasn't much better, but at least he had two of her new piercings out, the ones that seemed to bother her the most. With her unshackled, it was time to get the fuck out of here.

"Cordelia, are we still clear? Any of his thugs back?" Severus asked as he shrugged off his knee-length black trench. He'd chosen one with a thick, wintry material earlier, totally out of season, because he had sensed he might need to wrap it around Moira later.

"I can cast another banishing spell before we go up," his cousin remarked, her teasing edge gone completely.

"Alaric, watch her back."

"Yup, on it," the hybrid said, shooting to his feet and hurrying after Cordelia. As their footfalls faded, Severus placed his thick coat around Moira's shoulders, and shifted about so he could hoist her up as he stood.

"Wait," she whispered, rooting through the polaroid pictures scattered around her. He frowned, only noticing them now. Most were facedown, but the few he could see told him he wouldn't want to see the rest—Moira, in various states of torture. Diriel's fucking face in a few.

Why would she want to keep any of these?

"Moira—"

"Okay," she muttered, snatching one polaroid and folding it in half before tucking both arms inside his coat, which practically drowned her it had so much excess fabric. "*Please* get me out of here."

She needn't ask twice. Severus stood and lifted her up in one fluid motion, with an arm under her knees and the other supporting her back. He gave her dungeon a final disgusted sweep—then stormed out.

And neither he nor Moira once looked back.

~

When Moira realized she had been standing under the steady spray of Severus's shower for the better part of an hour—just standing there, arms at her side, staring straight ahead at the expensive tile—she finally shut it off and stepped out. By then, most of the blood had been washed away, swirling down the drain. She hadn't done much by way of scrubbing, but the scalding-hot water had done the trick.

Once again, Moira found herself just standing there, staring ahead—at nothing, at everything. Slowly, she tilted her head down to study her body. A faint pink stained her legs where the blood had been left to sit and crust for the last three days. The cuff marks around her wrists remained a bright red, tinged with bruising. Her nipples, which had been in *agony* ever since Diriel stuck the first piercing through, no longer burned. Removing the gold bars had brought instant relief, and as she lifted a heavy hand to examine them in the steam-filled bathroom, she found that the holes were already starting to close over—barely. She checked her ears next, but all the holes on both remained, the skin swollen and painful. And why shouldn't they still be there? Severus had only just taken the diamonds out before she got in the shower.

Still dripping wet, she marched over to the counter, taking quick, short strides, but when her hips nudged against the marble, she stopped, frowning. How did she get here? A glance over her shoulder. She had just been *there*. With a deep breath, she closed her eyes.

She'd expected her head to swirl with thoughts—thoughts of anger, revenge, sorrow. But it was blank. Empty. Perhaps just exhausted. She swiped her hand over the mirror, clearing the condensation away, and then turned around to examine the marks on her back. They hurt the most, those long slashes over her shoulder blades. Pink and raw, they had only stopped ripping back open whenever she adjusted her position yesterday. Moira still felt it, the throb of pain, with every move she made. Diriel had wanted her wings. She swallowed hard and reached back, only just able to reach the start of each incision.

Moira still couldn't process that she would *have* wings.

Her gaze snagged on something glittery on the counter—all the diamond and gold studs, hoops, and bars that had been viciously poked through her ears. Diriel had wanted to make her beautiful—that had been his reason for all the piercings. Make her beautiful, make her a piece of art. If she'd just said *yes*, she wouldn't need to be beautiful. She would be his partner. An equal in this cruel game of black-market angel feathers that he would pluck from her, one by one, until she had reached the end of her usefulness.

Her jaw clenched. Her eyes narrowed. Fuck him.

And *fuck* the angel who'd handed her to him.

Leaving her shoulder wounds alone for now, she swiped all the diamonds and gold off the counter into one hand, then threw them in the toilet. She flushed three times to make sure they were all gone, gripping the fluffy towel Severus had left for her to her chest.

"Fuck you," she whispered as she watched the water spiral. "Fuck *both* of you."

When nothing glinted up at her, she finally started to dry her skin, taking extra care with her breasts, her back, and the area around her ears.

She was grateful Severus and the others had been able to get her out without her having to see her captor's face again. Moira wasn't sure how she would have responded—emotionally, sure, and probably with a lot of screaming. When Severus had all but kicked down the door, it had taken everything she had not to dissolve into a mess of heaving sobs and tears. She had done her best to fight it, to appear strong when her entire being yearned to break, to splinter into a thousand pieces so she could just stop *feeling*.

As she toweled down her hair, she thought back to that moment when Severus had first appeared, to the crippling sense of *relief* that had flooded through her. She had always known he would come for her, but it had been hard to keep the faith as the hours dragged on—harder still with every piercing Diriel added to her body.

But he had come for her. The black-eyed hero, there to save the idiot heroine who should have just listened to him in the first place. By his side, trusty Alaric, his face covered in blood and his nose noticeably broken. Hovering by the door, a woman straight out of a Victorian period drama, encompassing all the gothic architecture of Farrow's Hollow in her outfit and in her eyes. The woman had broken the shackles. The woman had banished the demons who had surged from the shadows of the woods as they raced back to the car.

Cordelia. Severus's cousin. As Moira wrapped the towel around her, she knew she owed this stranger her life, this magic-wielding demon who'd had no reason to help her beyond her ties to Severus.

She ought to despise them—*all* of them. Demons. Cruel, twisted, horrible creatures like the one who had tortured her for three days straight. She ought to loathe them.

But she couldn't.

Because Cordelia had fought for her.

Because, in Moira's moment of weakness, her body crumpling, Alaric had caught her.

And because Severus had come for her, freed her, *held* her the whole way home—just like she'd known he would.

Moira could never hate *them*. But she could hate Diriel. She could hate the demon who'd handled the camera, the ones who had come to watch, seated on the sidelines like Diriel's torment of her was world-class theatre. And she would—until she drew her very last breath.

Or, preferably, until Diriel drew his.

She would hate *him* more—her father, the angel who wanted her dead. She would despise him, but she would hunt him. Confront him. Out him and his sins.

Because. Fuck. Him.

With that in mind, she tiptoed across the slick bathroom floor and opened the door. Two shadowy figures stood in the doorway on the other side of Severus's dimly lit room, murmuring in hushed voices. Severus glanced back, revealing his cousin behind him, and as Moira stepped out, he said something else under his breath before the witch disappeared. Not literally. Or maybe she did—could witches do that? Dematerialize?

"She brewed you a sleeping draught," Severus told Moira as he shut the door softly. "It'll give you a dreamless sleep."

"That was thoughtful of her." Moira looked around the room, and when she didn't see her duffel bag, she grabbed a T-shirt hanging over the edge of Severus's laundry hamper and pulled it on. The cool material clung to her still-damp figure, and it smelled distinctly like him—not just cologne, but *him*.

"How are you feeling?"

"I don't know," she admitted before tossing the towel over the bathroom door, adjusting it so it hung straight. She felt—a lot. "I just... I don't know."

"Right. Come on then, into bed."

He hadn't once asked her for details. Not on the drive back to his place, not when he carried her upstairs and set her on the bathroom counter, not while he removed all her new earrings, and not after he got the shower water to the right temperature—scorching. He hadn't asked, and Moira hadn't wanted to tell, and they appeared to be leaving it at that for the time being.

As she crossed the room and climbed under the covers that he pulled back, she knew she should have been exhausted. Drained. Broken. But watching Severus place a cup of steaming green liquid on the bedside table, Moira couldn't decide where she fit on the spectrum. Was there even a normal response to what she had been through?

"Moira, why would you want to keep this?" Severus asked, his tone gentle as he lifted the polaroid she'd snatched before he whisked her out of that hellhole. He held it out, but kept the image facing him; Moira didn't need to see it to know what was on there. The final product. Diriel's crowning glory—her, bedazzled and bejeweled and bloody.

It was a rational question, but as she reached out toward Severus, Moira didn't feel all that rational. Because instead of grabbing the polaroid, she grabbed *him*, her hand fisting around the thin fabric of his button-down. She gripped it hard, twisting it, until finally she yanked him into bed beside her. Her lower lip quivered as he fell into place, seated next to her. Her throat burned and her eyes prickled as she climbed on top of him.

And as she wrapped her arms around his neck and buried her face against him, Moira sobbed. She stopped holding it in, stopped plugging the leaks. The floodgates opened, and the air around them cooled. Straddling him, Moira felt her tears streak down her face and onto his skin, just as the spring rain had fallen in streams down the window of the SUV on the drive back. Just as the thunder cracked above them now, lightning splitting the darkness, she wept and wept, unleashing the storm within on the only person she dared.

He weathered the storm in its entirety. Severus clasped the back of her head, his faced turned inward so she could feel his soft, even exhales against her skin. He let her shudder against him, all the while cautious in the way he touched her, his hands avoiding her back altogether. He said nothing when her nails sank into him, to the tortured rasp of each ragged breath.

While she had been strung up and exposed, pierced and mocked, Moira had thought she would never want to be touched again. Not by anyone. Ever. But from the moment Severus cupped her face, wretched guilt painted across his features, she knew she couldn't go on like that. She needed to be touched. She wanted to be held—and he was the one to do it. Diriel's touch sickened her, but Severus's saved her. Time and time again, in dire circumstances or not, Severus's caress breathed life back into her when Moira thought it was all over. The brush of his hands down her sides, the gentle whisper of his flesh over hers—it was her salvation.

When the storm finally quieted, she sat up slowly, her head thick and her eyes swollen. Sniffling, Moira wiped the tears from her cheeks, and then brushed the backs of her knuckles down his neck. A ghost of a smile touched her lips as she dried him off, fighting to make her breath settle, and she caught the way his gaze wandered to her mouth. He had held her, caressed her, but he hadn't kissed her—and Moira knew he'd wanted to. She could see it in his eyes, blacker by the moment, until one final blink and the humanity was gone.

It should have frightened her. It should have terrified her from the first time she saw it until now. Diriel had been nothing but black eyes and cruel smiles and sharp claws—but Severus was comfort. He was a safe haven within the darkness.

Biting the inside of her cheek, she brought her fingers to his lips, delicately resting them there for a moment. He leaned into her, but he didn't kiss her. He just stared into her eyes. Even if she couldn't see his pupils in this light, she could feel it, his gaze never letting hers go. Her ghost of a smile blossomed to something more tangible, something she felt in her cheeks. Fleeting. There and gone again. She trailed her fingers across Severus's lips, then down his throat, until she planted her hand firmly against his chest, his collarbone like an anchor while she leaned over and grabbed Cordelia's brew off the nightstand.

Scentless and thick. It was shamrock green and tasted

like nothing as it slid down her throat and warmed her belly, the first real meal she'd had in days. Diriel had permitted her to drink water with energy mix-ins—plus two bathroom breaks a day, which were to be taken still chained up. Yesterday, one of his peons had enjoyed his chicken nugget takeout in her cell—he'd offered her half, but only if she ate it out of his hand like a dog. And Moira had done it without a hint of shame, because that fried crap had quieted her howling stomach.

Cordelia's brew left her satiated—and instantly heavy. Every limb sagged, the effort to put the empty cup back more than she could manage. Severus did it for her while she sank down at his side, her head on his lap and an arm thrown around his waist.

"Give it to me," she murmured, reaching up, her fingers grasping until they wrapped around the polaroid. As she examined it, her lip trembling but her tears holding, Severus worked his hand into her wet hair, massaging the base of her scalp. It was quite soothing, and soon she found herself fighting the urge to sleep—to let the darkness take her.

"You want to know why I took it?" she asked, her voice sounding very far away, even to her own ears. "I want to see it. I want to remember it, what he did to me. Because without it, I'll forget. I'll forget the pain of the piercings. I'll forget the way my shoulders ached and burned... I'll block it out. I'll grieve and move on. But if I can look at it, I'll remember." She dragged in a shuddering breath, knowing with more certainty now that the *he* she referred to was plural. "I'll remember, so that when I finally have the chance to kill him, I'll do it. I won't back out, I won't show mercy, because I'll remember it. All of it. And I'll give him exactly what he deserves..."

Death. Moira would bless Diriel with death—by the

light of her touch, by the burn of her angelic fire. She would figure it out. She would master it. She would teach it to come when called, and then she would show him just how deeply he could be scarred by her, dozens of burns to match the first two she had given him.

And then death. An unremarkable death. No fanfare. No great show of it. Just—the end. Moira would be his end.

She would be the end for Diriel *and* her father.

Cowards.

But for now, the draught could take her, and she welcomed the peace of a dreamless sleep with open arms. Before she succumbed, her arm tightened around Severus, and she breathed him in. They would face the darkness together, until she had the strength to bathe them in light.

So, let the darkness come—and, for the first time, let it find her unafraid.

To be continued in The Hunt: Book Bundle #2, which will feature books #3 and #4 in the series. Look for it June 2018!

THANKS FOR READING!

Thank you so much for reading! You're awesome. Seriously. Go treat yo' self for being such a fabulous human being.

If you enjoyed THE HUNT and want to support the series, please consider leaving a review at the retailer of your choice, including Goodreads. Reviews help indie authors thrive. I also use reviews as a way to gauge what series to work on next. If paranormal romance is your thing, let me know!

Lots of love,

Liz

ABOUT THE AUTHOR

Liz is a Canadian author who grew up in the Middle East. She has a degree in Bioarchaeology from Western University, and when she isn't writing about her own snarky characters, she is reading about other people's snarky characters, babying her herb garden, loitering on social media, or taking care of her many animals.

Liz dabbles in both paranormal and contemporary erotic romance. Her paranormals are usually dark and angsty, and her contemporaries are stress-free smutfests, but you'll find both full of feels. Most of all, she loves writing realistic characters in fantastical settings.

More from Liz Meldon:

Paranormal Romance

The Hunt – a Demon Romance

Predator (#1)
Prey (#2)
Stalker (#3)
Killer (#4)
The Hunt: Book Bundle #1
The Hunt: Book Bundle #2
The Hunt: The Complete Edition
The Uprising: A Companion Novel

***Dark Days* – a Vampire/Wolf Shifter Romance**

Semester One

Semester Two

***Lovers and Liars: Immortal Wars* – a fantasy and paranormal romance series about the old world gods going to war**

Court of the Phantom Queen (2017) – Book #1 (fantasy romance, novella)

Apollo's Priestess (2017) – Book #2 (shifter paranormal romance, novella)

To the North (TBD) – Book #3 (fantasy romance, novella)

Contemporary Erotic Romance

All In Trilogy – Sugar Daddies, Billionaires, and Menages – oh my!

Finn (#1)

Cole (#2)

Skye (#3)

All In Trilogy: Book Bundle + Bonus Content

Unbowed – standalone erotic romances featuring kink escorts the alpha men who love them

Belle: Part 1

Belle: Part 2

Penny: Part 1 (2019)

Penny: Part 2 (2019)

Erotic Short Shorts – an Erotic Short Story Series

Happy Hour (2016)

Holiday Hell (2017)

www.ingramcontent.com/pod-product-compliance
Lightning Source LLC
Chambersburg PA
CBHW031121210626
46816CB00016B/1741
* 9 7 8 0 9 9 3 8 9 4 3 8 1 *